VISIONS
of Time

Lori Hines

LORI HINES

Advance Praise for *Visions of Time*

"*Visions of Time* is a must read. This is an excellent story for anyone interested in the metaphysical, historically significant landmarks, and indigenous culture. The author combines it all in an amazing, thought-provoking storyline."

—Roman Orona, Apache, Pueblo & Yaqui Native American performer, artist, and owner of iamHUMAN Media

"Lori Hines' vivid depictions of the desert landscape transport readers directly into Petrified Forest National Park where psychic investigator Ahulani Mahelona desperately searches for a missing child in this fascinating paranormal mystery."

—C. C. Harrison, Author of *Death By G-String,* a Colorado Humanities Book Award Mystery Winner

"*Visions of Time* by Lori Hines will immerse you in the world of a psychic investigator. You'll see the world through Ahulani Mahelona's eyes, Hines' primary character, with a deep appreciation of the earth. You'll be taken into her visions with detail I've never seen before. As she embarks on a missing child case, she keeps crossing paths with a handsome park ranger of Peruvian descent. Like her, David has psychic abilities and they quickly join forces. If you like being immersed into a story by rich detail, *Visions of Time* is the book for you."

—Barbara Raffin, Award-winning Author of the St. John Sibling Series

VISIONS
of Time

LORI HINES

Green Bay, WI

Publisher/Executive Editor: Brittiany Koren
Cover Art Designer: Ed Vincent/ENC Graphics
Print Interior Layout Designer: Katy Brunette
Ebook Interior Layout Designer: Maria Connor

Category: Supernatural Mystery
Description: Among the picturesque landscape of the Painted Desert in Arizona, a psychic investigator must solve a mystery.
Hardcover ISBN: 978-1-951375-44-7
Paperback ISBN: 978-1-951375-45-4
Ebook ISBN: 978-1-951375-46-1
LOC Catalogue Data: Applied for.

First Edition published by Written Dreams Publishing in April, 2021.

Green Bay, WI 54311

Dedicated to the Native Americans who lost their lives during the Covid-19 pandemic.

Chapter One

Too many visions. Not enough time.
Ahulani Mahelona, a professional psychic investigator, pressed her hands on either side of her head. As if this would clarify the rampage of images going through her mind. The wide expanse of Petrified Forest National Park in northeastern Arizona transformed to rugged high mountains and alluring green slopes of some unknown destination.

The colorful badland hills, flat-topped mesas, and sculptured buttes of the Blue Mesa Member of the Chinle Formation, which made up a large portion of the Painted Desert region, called to her in the late spring air. Tie-dyed, corrugated hills of light grays, blues, purples, and greens erupted among open valleys. Yet Ahulani could not let such beauty distract from her purpose.

Ahulani's worst fear since she started working as a professional investigator ten years ago was that there would be an important case she couldn't figure out, whether because the pieces didn't fit together, her messages were not clear, or if she doubted getting the correct messages from her guides or the Universe.

Her clients saw an experienced, confident psychic medium on the outside. Yet when Ahulani received that first phone call from the family or friend of a victim, she became nauseous, her stomach in knots until she started getting more involved and receiving messages from spirits.

The question constantly on her mind—would she be able to help? She always said a prayer to find the person alive. Unfortunately, many cases resulted in the search of a body. Sometimes, a spirit revealed at the start whether the victim was dead or alive. Other times, she was on her own. This latest case was one of those.

She had been hired by a Flagstaff family to figure out what had happened to their daughter, Hateya.

Hateya Thompson, a Native American archaeologist, had been working at prehistoric sites in Petrified Forest and hadn't returned home from a three-week dig. Since the archaeologist had been focused on her professional life and tended to stray from her family, they weren't immediately aware of her disappearance. Her mother had attempted to contact Hateya by phone, but all calls went to voice mail. Even though her daughter was busy, she had always returned her mother's calls within a few hours. A search ensured. Police, colleagues, friends, and park officials had failed to find Hateya, so the family decided to take a more unconventional method.

Ahulani stood across the road from the Blue Mesa overlook and pulled her long, dark hair forward. She gazed out at the 225-million-year-old logs scattered and embedded among pale white mudstone cliffs as she pulled a multi-colored barrette made of tiny beads out of her pocket.

She touched the hairpiece with her forefinger. Belonging to the missing archaeologist, the barrette had provided clues leading Ahulani to the remote, rugged terrain of the Painted Desert. Yet intermittent visions of massive stone walls, round structures, and llamas roaming gently sloping hills had attempted to overtake her current mission.

Ahulani knelt and laid her hand over the hardened earth. Her visions of a distant land so opposite of the place before her, collapsed.

She closed her eyes to welcome visuals pertaining to the missing woman's whereabouts. Ahulani held the barrette tighter, taking deep, relaxing breaths. Since she had driven into Petrified Forest, she had repeatedly experienced visions of bodies lying under the earth, though they were in darkness and unverifiable.

Sensing a presence behind her, Ahulani stood and slowly turned.

An old woman stood watching her. The woman was hunched over and held a wooden staff. She wore a long deerskin dress and moccasin boots. A brown leather medicine bag decorated in turquoise beadwork hung around her neck.

Ahulani's intuition told her the woman was a shaman spirit, a revered healer who had once lived here hundreds or thousands of years prior. *What tribe was she from?*

There was evidence of more than 13,000 years of human history and culture, including the prehistoric Mogollon, ancestral Pueblo, and Sinagua cultures in the area.

The ancient one's brown eyes pierced through Ahulani's soul.

Ahulani couldn't detect anything about the elder, who lifted her hand and pointed an arthritic finger in the direction of a rock panel about ten feet high.

Spirals, geometric crosses, and other indistinguishable shapes decorated the rock, as well as a foot-tall, stick-like human figure holding a staff to the sky. The petroglyphs had been mindfully carved by an archaic culture whose hands had labored and tilled the harsh land and soil into a fertile, livable landscape.

The elderly woman stepped closer to the rock and pointed at the rudimentary figure. *Could she be trying to tell Ahulani that this was an image of herself?*

Ahulani turned her head to the rock art image, then glanced back at the curious Native phantom in the high desert—the woman had vanished. A large hole had appeared underneath the panel of rock art.

Ahulani bent over and stared into the darkness, initiating a distinct vision. A tall woman, about 5'8" in height, worked under a full moon. The mystery woman had hair almost to her hips and a tattoo on her right arm. Ahulani couldn't get a clear view of the tattoo, but Hateya's family had told her about the tattoo of two orange dragonflies, face-to-face.

The woman was with a man, slightly taller than herself. Ahulani heard her call him Brent. He stood about six feet tall and appeared athletic with light brown hair and boyish good looks. They were digging up sections of dirt and dumping them onto a screen to sift out remnants of pottery.

Ahulani could see two other men in the background of her vision. They were using their hands, digging through smaller existing piles of dirt to try to find any other antiquated gifts from below ground.

A stocky, big-nosed guy was next to a shorter man who looked anorexic. The names 'Jerry' and 'Mac' came to Ahulani's mind while she watched them greedily sift through the earth, eyes wide open for precious fragments.

Brent gently placed some broken pottery pieces and smaller artifacts, one-by-one, into a small box. He carried it to a nearby tent, and Hateya followed him.

The young archaeologist lifted the flap of the tent, and glanced back at the two other men, busy in their search efforts. Then, she walked into the tent behind Brent.

Hateya sat on a cot and pulled something out from underneath it. Her eyes glinted with excitement, her hands shook as she unwrapped an object from its tomb of newspaper, removing a prehistoric pot. It was a perfect specimen of ancient artwork—a small pot of approximately four inches tall that was painted white and decorated in black geometric designs. A heartfelt prize for those fascinated by Native American history.

A stocky man ran into the tent and grabbed the ancient pot from Hateya. He threw her to the ground, punched her in the face, then beat her mercilessly with both fists.

Hateya attempted to repel the beatings, but it was met with a harsher hand.

Ahulani gasped as she heard the crunch of bone and witnessed blood spurting from the poor woman's face.

10

Startled by the violent vision, Ahulani fell backward. That didn't stop the persistent vision.

Brent tried to pull the stocky man off Hateya, but the thin man pulled a gun. He shot Brent twice in the chest.

Brent dropped to the ground, his eyes on Hateya the whole time. He reached out to her unconscious body before his eyes closed and his body went limp. This was much more than a business partnership; they had been lovers.

The skinny man tossed the gun next to Hateya's lifeless body. He grinned, then kicked her.

Ahulani realized Hateya and Brent had been involved in an artifact theft ring. Perhaps, Hateya had hidden the ceramic pot from the two violent men.

She'd heard of mediums who could feel the agony, suffering of the individual; Ahulani felt grateful she couldn't. She wouldn't be able to assist the family, or the victim, with such a burden.

Trying to recover from the sudden vision, Ahulani got down on her knees and stuck her head further into the unknown chamber.

Could this be where they were buried?

As her eyes adjusted, the afternoon sun helped to reveal a large, round room with a foot-high wall. Approximately ten feet wide by eight feet across, the room contained four holes that looked as if they could have held poles. Ahulani looked down upon a prehistoric pueblo. She recognized a stone fire pit and the wide deflector stone between the pit and the ventilator shaft. Ancient tribes had used such stones to push heat out through a smoke hole in the roof.

Ahulani backed her head out from the darkness. She reached back and took a small picture of Hateya from her jean pocket.

The photo was yanked from her hand by an unseen force and tossed into the hole, landing in the fire pit of the prehistoric pueblo. Ahulani barely had enough time to verify that the woman in the picture was the same woman in her horrifying vision.

11

Did the phantom medicine woman use Hateya's picture to confirm the location of Hateya's grave? Or was it a clue from Hateya herself?

Footsteps came from behind her.

She quickly turned and stared into the face of a park ranger. His name tag showed it as *David*. A few inches taller than Ahulani, the ranger was muscular in stature with long, wavy black hair pulled tight in a ponytail. He took her breath away—but only for a few seconds. She had no time for that sort of thing.

He looked at her quizzically, his eyes raised and mouth open. "Are you the psychic medium? I heard you'd be investigating, though I didn't know where exactly."

"Yes. A spirit guided me here." Ahulani glanced toward the opening. "I think Hateya Thompson, the archaeologist who disappeared, might be buried down there with another man named Brent. I saw a vision of them working together with two other men. They were all going through artifacts. I got the impression they were stealing from somewhere in this park."

"What spirit?" David looked at the panel of rock with the petroglyphs. "You mentioned a spirit guided you to this spot."

She expected him to ask more questions about Hateya or to look at her as if she were insane. Many people were open to the spiritual and paranormal, but so many more were not. "A medicine woman from the prehistoric era. I think she wore an animal skin dress and…"

"I know. I've seen her."

Ahulani didn't know what surprised her more—the horrifying encounter she had been witness to, or the fact that David had seen the healer as well. Did the elder normally show herself to others? Or did David have a special gift?

"I was at Puerco Ruin a couple of hours ago talking to some visitors," David said, "and she appeared in one of the pueblos. No one else seemed to notice. Right after I saw her, I got an overwhelming urge to come here to Blue Mesa."

David glanced at the ground around the rock panel. "Wait. Buried where? You mentioned the missing woman was 'buried down there.'"

Ahulani glanced to the burial place. "The opening is right..." Solid earth had replaced the dark aperture. Throwing her hands up, she stepped next to the once open spot. "It was here, and I saw a pit house. I believe the medicine woman threw Hateya's picture into the underground chamber."

"We weren't aware of any burial site here," David said.

She watched a groundhog scurry out into the wide-open expanse of high desert. "Perhaps whatever is down there is meant to stay a secret. I wanted to get closure for her family."

David smiled. "I'll contact local police and let my supervisor know about this place."

The previous visions of the mountainous green landscape hit full force, causing the beginning of a headache. Ahulani raised her hand to her temple.

David touched her arm. "Are you all right?"

"I...I'm fine. I keep getting these visuals of high mountain slopes, ruins, and llamas. This time, I heard the word 'Kuelap.'"

David stared at her in awe. "That's an ancient citadel in Peru on the northern slopes of the Andes. The original fortress covered 25,000 square miles. It was built by the Chachapoya civilization who flourished from 900 to 1400 A.D. Due to a sixty-foot-high wall surrounding the city, some think it's a defense fortress."

Ahulani tried to push her feelings back, struggling to retain a semblance of sanity. The more she learned about the handsome stranger in front of her, the more she *wanted* to know. She had never had the opportunity to travel to Peru, but she'd wanted to. Her mother had grown up in Arequipa, Peru.

Two turkey vultures circled overhead, watching the ground intently.

Ahulani stared past David, lest she reveal her emotions

by looking at him. "How do you know so much about the place?"

David shrugged. "I grew up in Lima, Peru and studied anthropology. I worked at Kuelap for three years." David's hand floated over the shamanic figure with raised hands and staff. The ranger seemed lost in translation— somewhere between the past and present.

He looked at Ahulani, offering her an innocent half grin. "That's why the old woman led me to you. I have a feeling that Kuelap has something to do with your next investigation."

She didn't want to admit it, but something told Ahulani that wasn't the only reason she and David had met.

Chapter Two

A light breeze blew into Ahulani's office window. She stood up, stretched, then stared into the lush green forest surrounding her cabin near Oak Creek Canyon in Arizona. The stream glinted in the sunlight and bubbled over smooth river rocks before cascading a foot down into a small pond.

The serenity, lush foliage, and crimson red formations had drawn her to Sedona and Oak Creek three years ago—after her divorce. She had met Will while living on the island of Molokai, and she'd thought she had found her fairy tale. He'd been visiting from New York and found her walking along the white sands of Papohaku Beach.

Ahulani had waded in the cool water and stared out into the glassy aquamarine ocean. Will had startled her by jogging right by her—she felt a breeze when he passed by within a foot of her.

She had quickly turned her head to see who would dare to invade her space and recalled the frustration at the harsh interruption of tranquility.

Will had stopped running. "I am so sorry. Didn't mean to scare you."

When she looked at his face, she couldn't recall why she had been mad.

That's when he smiled. It had changed her life.

Tall, with dark brown hair to his shoulders and naturally tan due to his Seneca Indian heritage, Will drew the attention of many women.

They were married in Molokai and had moved to

Tucson, Arizona due to their love of the desert, and had spent many hours hiking and mountain biking. The first four years of their marriage had been nearly perfect. It seemed Will would have done anything for her.

She had never forgotten the day she'd seen Will and the *other woman* together at a restaurant close to their home. She had stopped in the Mexican café to get dinner for her and Will—and saw her husband holding hands with a blonde woman who looked to be at least ten years younger.

The first thing Ahulani remembered thinking— *She's the exact opposite of me. Have you tired of my looks? What have I done? I thought we were so happy.*

Will had seen Ahulani walk in. He looked up at her with eyes void of emotion then back at this new love interest.

Ahulani hadn't known what was more shocking—the fact that he'd been cheating or that he hadn't looked surprised. Her eyes welling with tears, she quickly ran out of the restaurant and returned home.

Looking back, she realized he had wanted to get caught, flaunting his prize so close to home. Will had returned home long enough to pack his bags. She tried to talk to him. He ignored her and walked out the door without a word.

Ahulani had a couple of friends who'd tried to help her through the lonely days, but the 2,800 square foot home felt too big. Too empty.

A month later, she decided to do a weekend getaway to Sedona for hiking, relaxation, and a spa treatment. During her retreat, visions of a cozy cabin in the woods continuously popped in and out of her thoughts—a place with a stream hugging the side of the home.

Three weeks later, she had come across a quaint cabin while walking through the forest of Oak Creek. It had a front porch extending the length of the home and a trickling stream along the side.

It was the home she had been seeing in her visions.

Time stood still as a doe stepped delicately across the stream in front of the cabin.

That one moment almost made up for the grief she had endured, and she had smiled for the first time since Will left. The deer had stopped and stood within five feet, watching her. It glanced back at the 'For Sale' sign and continued into the forest.

Ahulani had immediately contacted the realtor and scheduled an appointment to see it that day. Surprisingly, there had only been one other offer. The couple had pulled themselves out of the deal with no explanation. She moved from Tucson to Oak Creek Canyon two weeks later.

Now, she glanced down at David's business card on her desk. He had written his home phone and cell number on the card to keep in touch regarding Hateya's case. The calendar on her desk showed the date to be April 15. April 17 was the day she and Will had been married in Molokai.

Ahulani had found it strange that David was from the very place of her visions, and that both of them had ties to Peru. But perhaps David *was* her mission.

She'd have to contact the park service to find out if the bodies of Hateya and Brent had been among the remains of the pit house.

When David had appeared after her vision, the hole had vanished—perhaps Hateya's way of saying that things should be left as they are—undiscovered and protected. She had cried for the lovely Native woman that night after Hateya appeared in her dream, thanking Ahulani for finding her and gaining a certain sense of closure for her family. She informed Ahulani that neither her nor Brent wanted their bodies to be discovered. They were happy at rest among the starkly beautiful landscape and the prehistoric people they both cherished.

Before Ahulani left the Painted Desert, she had placed a cairn marker stacked with a few spectacular chunks of petrified wood, aged with manganese, copper, and iron from water and mud, giving the long-lost tree a new appearance after turning it to stone. A memorial to a strong woman who lost her way long enough to pay with her life. When Ahulani had placed the last piece of petrified wood on the shrine, Hateya's mother had texted Ahulani, saying she had seen her daughter's smiling spirit and she knew her daughter was truly at peace.

Her spirit guides had told her Hateya had a great future as a leader of her own community and as an archaeologist. That had all changed when Hateya had made the fateful decision to steal from the land. Perhaps staying buried among the remnants of the past was her way of giving back.

Ahulani walked out of the office. She removed a hooded sweat jacket off a hook by the front door, slipped it on, and went for a walk along the stream.

A half mile into the hike she sensed she wasn't alone. She turned her head to see the medicine woman from Painted Desert, barefoot in the stream, watching native brown trout.

The elderly phantom looked up at Ahulani and stared at her sternly. Spirits occasionally followed Ahulani home—spirits that needed help crossing over. This particular ghost seemed to have a different mission.

Ahulani continued to walk slowly along the stream, observing the enigmatic spirit.

A disturbance in the brush ahead startled her. A huge elk stared at the healer. After a few minutes, it stepped into a thicket and vanished. Seconds later, the medicine women abandoned her place in the stream, becoming a series of wispy tendrils that floated away in the sunlight.

Dark clouds passed over the sun. Ahulani shivered and pulled her jacket tighter. She glanced around. There were no other hikers, yet her clairsentience picked up on other specters from beyond. The trees spoke softly in the delicate morning breeze, yet the sounds of the forest weren't the only whispers.

Ahulani did a 360-degree turn, taking in the vibrant, sun-drenched forest. "I know you're here."

It became completely still. *They* were listening. She focused on the strong energy of a male ghost who stood a few feet away. Though she couldn't see him yet, his energy enclosed him.

Ahulani had always been able to see the auras of ghosts, and this male entity had interesting hues. She picked up on three out of seven auric layers. The color closest to his form was bright lemon yellow, which signified a struggle to maintain power and control.

She took a step toward the figure.

His body started to take form. Five-foot-eight with massive shoulders, he had wavy black hair to his neck, and legs almost as thick as the trunk of the tree he stood next to.

The aura colors became more brilliant, including violet in the center. The most sensitive color, violet represented intuition and psychic power of attunement, as well as visionary, magical qualities. The outermost color was a soft black, capturing and consuming light. In some of her clients, this had indicated long-term unforgiveness that had led to health problems—in one instance, colon cancer.

Though she sensed him as a modern spirit who'd passed away in the 1980s, a brilliant headdress of colorful feathers appeared above him. A jaguar stood next to him. It looked from Ahulani to him and then back at her. The figure didn't acknowledge the cat's presence.

"You have a past life as a high priest," she said.

He had brought his magic and powers from his Aztec, or perhaps Mayan personae, to his most recent lifetime. Ahulani could tell from his unusual aura that this man had fought hard to maintain control over who he was and what he represented.

"You knew what you were, and you had special powers to rival those of the greatest magician. You didn't want such responsibility. You didn't want to be *too* different. You only wanted to keep your power over others— friends, family, strangers. It was never enough."

The powerful spirit didn't nod or speak to acknowledge her statements. He stared at her. The jaguar faded away, but the black spots remained, hanging in the air for a few seconds, as if to emphasize the darkest color of his aura and his soul.

She took another step toward him. He looked to be no more than forty-five. He had died young and angry. He was blocking the reason for his death, and his identity.

Is that how you lived your life, by preventing others from knowing who you really are?

Others were around, watching. Were they awaiting their turn?

Ahulani could feel her spirit guides around her. Two Apache guides had a tendency to stick close. She had recurring dreams of a past life with one of them, in the Sangre de Cristo Mountains in northern New Mexico. She had been his wife but had been murdered by white men.

If the male phantom before her had been a threat, her guides would have warned her. The spirit with the past life as a high priest glanced at something behind Ahulani.

She turned her head to see what distracted him but couldn't see anything. When she glanced back, the male ghost had vanished.

Footsteps crunched through brush, leaves, and twigs. People were headed in her direction on the trail. Were they the living? The gaps in the trees revealed someone wearing a black sweatshirt and jeans heading in her direction.

As they came closer, she could see a younger man with long dark hair in a braid. He walked with a woman. The couple approached within five feet and stopped.

Her mouth dropped and her heart ceased its rhythmic beat for a few seconds.

How can this be?

David, the park ranger from Petrified Forest, stared back at her. The woman he was with looked at both of them curiously.

Part of Ahulani hoped that she wasn't his girlfriend. Another part of her didn't want to care.

He came up to her and hugged her. "Ahulani, it's great to see you. What are you doing here?"

She pulled away and glanced at the girl he was with, who didn't seem fazed by their meeting. She looked Native American—tall with straight black hair that fell below her waist. Ahulani pointed in the direction of her cabin. "I live a mile from here."

David's companion smiled at Ahulani. "That's so weird. I live a quarter mile in the same direction, closer to the cliff." She glanced at David. "My brother is here visiting me from Holbrook."

Ahulani breathed a sigh of relief. *Her brother.*

"This is Shelly," David said.

Ahulani stepped forward and shook her hand.

"David's been telling me about your encounter," Shelly said. "It was bizarre enough the first time, considering all that you have in common. But to run across each other again so soon."

David seemed to focus on something in the stream.

She didn't have to look. Ahulani suspected the old woman was still watching. "I saw the medicine woman earlier. Can you see her?"

David looked at Ahulani. "Yes. I've also seen her guarding that panel of rock above where you saw the pit house."

He took another step toward her and she could see two brown spots, darker than his eyes, one on either side of his pupil. "The weird thing is visitors, park law enforcement— no one can access that area—it's like there's some sort of invisible barrier."

"That makes sense." Ahulani glanced at something behind David's sister. A light mist twisted its way around the trunk of a Cottonwood tree. "I'm sure it's not only a place of rest for Hateya and Brent but for those who used to live in that village."

David nodded, then glanced in the direction of the stream again. "Absolutely. There are many undiscovered sites all over the world. Not all are meant to be found."

The curious mist wound its way down the length of the tree before being sucked into the earth, littered with leaves. Ahulani recalled the photo of Hateya being snatched from her grasp, then dropped into the remnants of the long-lost pueblo. She struggled to look away, knowing some secrets were meant to stay buried.

Chapter Three

David Huaman stood in the backyard of his sister Shelly's home. He craned his neck into the sun, absorbing the afternoon rays while a soft breeze refreshed his skin. Chapparal, ponderosa, juniper, and cottonwood surrounded the single-story, A-frame home with massive windows facing the tall canyon wall. A pocket of cypress trees nearby created a haven for meditation. Two mule deer cautiously approached a handful of sliced apples near the bird fountain. They watched him closely while they ate.

He recalled the mystical, wondrous notes of the pan flute that had danced through his mind when he'd first seen Ahulani. As a Peruvian pan flute and wooden flute player, David had a tendency to interpret everything in sound, including the Petrified Forest and Painted Desert. When he wandered the roads in Painted Desert or walked among the teepee formations, mesas, and time-weathered landscapes, he heard long, steady notes combined with shorter, more uplifting tones.

Seeing Ahulani had brought a soft, wavering pattern that eventually rose in pitch—like an eagle floating on the currents only to be lifted into the azure sky. Unlike the great bird, David hoped the beautiful psychic investigator didn't disappear from his life. He'd never felt ready for a relationship, until he'd seen her.

He had given her his phone number hoping she would follow up with him about the mystery near Holbrook, yet his intuition told him she wouldn't. Ahulani didn't know of David's unique abilities. No one did, except his sister and her husband Larry.

David sensed things about Ahulani—things *she* probably wasn't aware of. Knowing more about others than they did about themselves was not always a good thing. Her story unfolded as her dark green eyes locked onto his and then glanced away. When he met certain people, their lives were no longer their own. He sometimes received telepathic messages about those he felt a connection with. Ahulani was not ready. She had trusted, loved deeply, and been rejected. And though everyone had stories of lost love and lost hope, David sensed that she had given up more than a possible relationship. By pushing away memories of a past love, she had also rejected memories of her youth.

The quietude, the birdsong, the gently flowing creek, his sister...it all disappeared when he saw her again. Simultaneously, a surreal scene appeared distinctly in his mind.

David was alone in a deep, dark, thick forest; Ahulani was inside a stark white room with blank walls that floated among the trees. She looked at him through a window yet didn't see him. The borders were too great between them.

He and Shelly asked Ahulani to come back to Shelly's house for lunch, but she made an excuse. "I...I have to make some follow-up calls to clients."

He felt crushed.

There were things he could see about Ahulani's past, but he couldn't tell for sure if he would be in her future.

He heard the sliding glass door open behind him. Shelly came up and touched his shoulder. "Don't worry so much. The way you and Ahulani have been brought together is fate. I believe the ancient elder thought you to be the perfect pair, and she seems rather determined to make it happen."

Ahulani knew the medicine woman had shown herself to him, but he hadn't said how often. The elder seemed to follow him around the park. No other rangers or staff claimed to have seen her. David liked being the only one. Had the woman known of Ahulani before she'd arrived at the park? For that matter, had the spirit known about David before he'd started working there? Could the ancient one have led him *to* the park?

David turned to face his sister. "Maybe Ahulani's not attracted to me."

His sister took his face in her hands, her brown eyes reflecting back the moment in time when he and Ahulani had seen each other in the forest.

Within his sister's eyes, he saw Ahulani blush, glance away, and play with strands of her long dark hair. "What do you think? How did I react every time I saw Larry?" Shelly asked.

David watched a shadow slice through the crimson cliff behind the house. He had been there the moment his sister had met her Cherokee husband at a pow-wow in New Mexico. He'd known they would be married a few months later. She and her husband both hung on to their traditional native ways, including dance, culture, and language—Shelly with her Peruvian/Jicarilla Apache heritage and Larry with his Cherokee background.

David frequently traveled with them to Indian markets and pow-wows, and though he'd met many stunning women, he'd never met someone who made him feel the way Ahulani had.

Frustration and heartache threatened to overcome him. She was so close and yet so far away. He would be leaving Oak Creek Canyon on Tuesday—only two days away. And he would be leaving Holbrook in three weeks to go to Central America to explore the Mayan ruins.

When they first met, Ahulani mentioned having a vision of the Kuelap fortress in Peru where David had participated in a dig five years prior. Would she travel to Peru for a future investigation? He felt the massive Kuelap fortress had a part to play. It was one of the reasons fate had brought him and Ahulani together.

A small trail led from Shelly's house to the canyon wall,

which reflected the wear and tear over time—between ten thousand and one million years ago. Large faults had developed in the earth's underlying rock layers as they were being pushed up during the Colorado Plateau's formation. One of the larger of these faults had formed the north-south Oak Creek Canyon.

David wondered why Ahulani had picked Oak Creek Canyon as her home. Could she have been attracted to such a respite for the same reason as Shelly, who happened to have lived a past life as an ancient Lemurian from 14,000 years ago?

Supposedly, the race had gone underground when the Great Flood came that caused the destruction of Atlantis. It was said the Lemurians emerged from different points around the world, including Sedona. The legend stated that when the flood receded, about half of those who were underground had emerged. Half remained below because they believed it was not safe. Those who'd come above ground saw that conflict was already beginning on the surface once again, so they'd retreated and kept to themselves. Some believed that this explained the division between Western society and the native people.

Perhaps Ahulani had been a member of the Lemurian race and felt drawn to the area to reconnect with a past life culture. Or maybe the land of vortexes, red rock, and mysticism caught her in its web during an attempt to escape reality.

David grabbed his pan flute from the patio table and walked the path to the canyon. Once there, he sat cross-legged on the ground, closed his eyes, and played the tune he had heard when he'd first seen Ahulani.

The old woman was near. He could see her in his mind, watching. When he finished playing, David opened his eyes, and the elder from the Petrified Forest stood in front of him.

As he got up, he realized he had never been that close to her. She stood a little straighter and didn't lean on the staff as much. Her face had less wrinkles, her gray hair had started to turn black. She looked about ten years younger, but it was the same woman.

The elder had never followed David outside the park. Yet since he had met Ahulani, they were both seeing the prehistoric figure in Oak Creek Canyon.

"Can you tell me your name? Why have you come here?"

She didn't answer, merely stared at him and gave him a sly smile. He could not pick up on any information about her, though the word *Mogollon* came to mind. He also sensed a desperate attempt on her part to get Ahulani and him together. But Ahulani wasn't ready.

"David!" Larry called from the house, and the elder vanished before David's eyes.

David hiked down the path. He, Shelly, and Larry had planned on going for brunch.

When he arrived, the mule deer had moved on. Larry and Shelly stood at the sliding glass door, staring at something just outside of the house. A trail of smooth stones, tumbled by the water, led away from the yard and around the side of Larry and Shelly's home.

Could the spirit of the medicine woman have done this?

With David in the lead, the three of them followed the trail past the front of the house. David saw a stunning yet bizarre woman walking barefoot in the creek who leaned over repeatedly to pick up stones—a translucent, elf-like wraith. She was tall with flowing, straight blonde hair past her mid-back, and pointed ears. When she bent over to wash off a rock, the V neck on her white dress revealed a peek of her cleavage.

Most stones were placed gently in the water. A few larger ones took their new home within her graceful fingers. They were delicately stacked by the side of the stream.

"She's amazing," Larry said.

David nearly forgot that Shelly and her husband were there. "Yeah." David was mesmerized by the sight. He didn't want to take his eyes off her. It wasn't romantic, like

26

with Ahulani. No, this was much different—a mystery to be solved. *Where had she come from?*

Shelly stood next to David.

David reached out and touched his sister's shoulder. "Have you seen her before?"

Shelly shook her head. "No, never."

David cautiously approached the stream.

The woman sat down on a big rock in the center of the stream and began to play a wooden flute. The birds stopped singing. The forest became still. A cardinal flew from the top of a tree and landed on a branch next to her.

She's an amazing flute player.

He listened to her play for a few minutes before slowly approaching again.

The woman stood straight, turned her head toward him, and smiled. On top of the pile of stones was a miniature heart stone that had striations of dark red, pink, and what looked like white quartz. It was the most beautiful rock he had ever seen.

He picked it up and turned it in his hand. As David did so, the lithe beauty vanished. The remainder of stones that had been so elegantly extracted from the stream were also gone.

"Treasure her...forever." The blonde woman's voice was like a song on the wind.

Chapter Four

Ahulani sat at the top of Bell Rock with the city of Sedona sprawled out before her, along with a distant view of Oak Creek Canyon. Mesas, buttes, and formations erupted among a wide array of plant life, including agave, yucca, various types of juniper, and creosote bush.

One of the many red rock formations in the area, Bell Rock helped her get in touch with her intuitive side because of the dynamic vortex of energy associated with it. If she had trouble focusing, getting in touch with her creative side, or helping solve the mysteries of life, Ahulani would come to this dark red sandstone formation. The Schnebly Hill sandstone was layered in flat-bedded horizontal layers, interspersed with multiple thin white layers of limestone.

Yet, she didn't come to Bell Rock for the geology. As a vortex, or a site of spiraling spiritual energy, Ahulani visited Bell Rock to meditate and heal. Many people came from all over the world to experience the many vortexes of Sedona, which they believed to have energy flow existing on multiple dimensions.

Ahulani had come to Bell Rock to figure out the vivid and disturbing dreams she'd had the night before. She'd seen David with a tall blonde woman, walking together in a forest.

To Ahulani, the place had felt familiar. She'd thought they were in Oak Creek Canyon. Dreams were frequently forms of psychic visions, but she hoped this one featuring David and the woman was wrong. They weren't holding hands or being intimate, but David looked at her in awe. Even amidst the surreal world of her sleep subconscious, Ahulani remembered feeling heartbroken. When she'd awoken, she'd felt a trickle of moisture on the side of her face.

David's sister, Shelly, had asked Ahulani to come over for lunch. David's brown eyes had seemed to plead for her to accept. She couldn't. Though her heart had wanted to say yes, her mind had told her it would be a mistake. Time was a thief to relationships. One day, you were both madly in love. The next, you were merely strangers, a stepping-stone to someone younger, prettier.

Hikers—some alone, some in groups—walked the myriad of trails below. Ahulani glanced up to see something forming in the sky besides the distant storm clouds. It was the face of a little boy, and her inner voice told her he was seven years old. He had shaggy brown hair and brown eyes filled with terror.

She stood slowly and stared at the spectacle above Sedona. A young couple sat together nearby holding hands, but they didn't notice her or the curious cloud.

A heavenly message meant for her, maybe? She had never received a vision in this manner.

The child's face continued to appear while dark clouds built up around him.

The couple looked at the sky, at each other, then got up and walked back down Bell Rock.

Perhaps, the sanctity of the area had initiated this vision among the heavens. Or was there something about the boy himself?

A few minutes later, his face faded.

Ahulani's phone rang, breaking the spiritual moment. She glanced at the display to see a private number and hit the accept key. "This is Ahulani, psychic investigator."

Static threatened to overtake the voice of the caller. She could only hear bits and pieces.

"Hi...name is Tabitha Miller and...calling for a friend..." The woman spoke hurriedly.

Ahulani could hear others in the background.

A fork of lightning split the sky, and Ahulani climbed back down Bell Rock. She had nearly been struck in Hawaii while walking along the ocean's shore and didn't want to take another chance.

"I can barely hear you. Where are you calling from?" she asked.

The woman spoke louder. "Peru."

Ahulani leapt off the last rock and landed on the trail heading to the parking lot.

"My friend's name is James Torres." The static disappeared.

"I'm from the States and am visiting him and his wife in Northern Peru, the town of Chiclayo. We went to see the Kuelap Citadel and..."

This is it. The visions from Petrified Forest.

Silence came on the other end as another fork of lightning lit up the sky from east to west.

Ahulani ran toward her car as the drops of rain became heavier, stinging her skin. "Is everything okay?" In the background, she could hear a woman crying hysterically and the voice of a man attempting to comfort her.

The boy. It's about the boy in the clouds.

"Their seven-year-old son, Eric, disappeared while wandering through the ruins. We don't know how it could have happened. We were the only ones there."

The caller's voice started to crack with emotion, and Ahulani's heart went out to the victim's family. In her mind, she called upon Archangel Michael to provide hope.

Arriving at her vehicle, Ahulani unlocked it with her remote and slid into the driver's side, closing the door. "When did this happen? Have you contacted the local authorities?"

"This morning. James and his wife don't want me to call the police."

Ahulani prayed she could help, but law enforcement would probably have to be involved.

"I am sorry to hear of such a frightening event!

Of course, I'll do what I can to help." Anxiety, fear, and doubt collided, threatened to overcome her—the same initial insecurities that began each unique case. Ahulani gripped her phone, her chest tightened a bit, and she felt her stomach stir.

She took a deep breath. *This child needs your help. Focus on Eric.*

She recalled a case in Hawaii of a five-year-old boy who had wandered from home, climbed through a hole in the fence and fallen off a steep cliff. It had only taken her a few hours to find him after seeing the location where he died in her mind. She hoped this missing boy didn't suffer a similar fate, especially considering the steep hills she had seen in her visions.

Getting control of her emotions, Ahulani asked, "How did you hear about me? I don't handle too many cases out of the country."

"I don't remember. It's strange, because I found your business card in my purse a few days before this happened. Something told me to keep it."

Ahulani had never been to Peru, but she had traveled to many states, either through vacation or for investigations. It was possible she had met the woman in person.

"Send me some pictures of their son. I use psychometry, or direct association with physical objects, to help me pick up information. Also, please send me your contact information and that of his parents."

"On its way," Tabitha said. "I took some pictures of Eric last night and this morning."

Tabitha released a heavy sigh. "I can have his parents send some as well."

Raindrops continued to hit the car with a tinny sound. Ahulani started the ignition and turned on the heat.

Her phone notified her with incoming texts. She glanced at the photos from Tabitha. The images she saw of the child verified the identity of the face in the clouds. In the photos, Eric roamed happily among what appeared to be the remains of round stone towers.

She was about to ask Tabitha about the possibility of the child wandering off when a distinct vision informed her otherwise. The little boy stood inside a circular stone wall. She saw him wave, presumably to his parents or Tabitha, though they weren't in the vision. The child then walked the inside perimeter of the ruin before he disappeared into thin air.

"Did I see that right?" Ahulani whispered the question to her spirit guides.

In response, she saw the exact same vision again. Could that represent the moment he vanished or the *way* he vanished?

"You're seeing something, aren't you?" Tabitha asked.

Ahulani watched as an older couple ran through the Bell Rock parking lot, hands over their heads, shielding themselves from the rain. It made her recall the description that David provided about the pre-Incan site occupied by the Chachapoyas culture.

Missing persons cases could be easily solved—but not always. Sometimes, the children or adults were found alive. The supernatural investigations were the hardest due to a lack of evidence. Intuition told her this was going to be her toughest case yet. Could the boy have been abducted? If so, why would his kidnapper be blocked from the vision?

Ahulani started detecting two aura colors—a dark, muddied red that could represent anger, and a dark, murky pink that usually meant a dishonest nature. She could be picking up on Eric's abductor.

At the other end of the call, Tabitha blew her nose. "Listen, James said he'd pay for you to come to Peru. Maybe if you spent time at the fortress, you would be able to find out more."

Putting the call on speaker, Ahulani pulled out of the parking lot as the rain began to lighten up. "I really appreciate it and I'll keep that gracious offer in mind. I'm going to see what I can do from here initially since it will take time to get my papers for travel arrangements. I will be in touch first thing in the morning. My sincerest wishes for Eric and his family!"

"Thank you. Call anytime. We won't be sleeping." Tabitha ended the call.

Thunder rolled across the heavens and rain continued to pelt her car. She slowed down, barely able to see the winding road in front of her.

Could the child still be among the ruins, lost and alone?

One of her Apache guides shook his head no.

According to her vision, it was as if Eric had been transported, but where? And by who?

A loud clap of thunder made her jump in her seat. Could the sky above be trying to warn her of the danger Eric was in?

A couple of years ago, Ahulani had figured out that she could use crystals and gems from the region or country where a victim vanished to help solve a case. In this instance, Andean pink opal, huebnerite, leopardskin jasper, blue sodalite, and icicle calcite were all from Peru or South America.

She hit her hand against the steering wheel. "Of course! I can't believe I almost forgot about Lemurian jade."

The most powerful of all South American stones, Lemurian jade was only mined in Peru. It contained jade, quartz, iron, pyrite, and other minerals. It usually assisted anyone with a difficult past life or to heal abuse of any kind. It opened the heart and instilled a sense of gratitude. Ahulani occasionally used it to deepen the connection with the Earth Mother.

A half hour later, Ahulani arrived home, drove across the wooden bridge to her property, and pulled into the gravel driveway. She threw open her car door, got out, and quickly closed the driver's side door. She ran to her front door and struggled to put the key in the lock due to the pouring rain.

Finally managing to unlock the door, she walked into her Hawaiian cabin in the woods. A five-foot primitive Tiki mask hung in the corner and a large painting of

Rainbow Falls on the big island of Hawaii hung above the couch—a single waterfall drew her back to her homeland as it cascaded into a cove surrounded by lush foliage. An eight-inch Maori Tiki stood sentinel in the center of the long table behind the couch with Tiki torch candle holders on either side. A bookshelf held stories pertaining to Hawaiian, Mayan, Aztec, and Southwestern cultures, interspersed with Tiki statues, amethyst geodes of various sizes, Hawaiian instruments, and replicas of ancient weapons.

Ahulani went to her bookshelf and picked out the Peruvian gemstones from her collection in a wooden bowl. When she turned, she nearly dropped the stones.

The medicine woman stared at her from the middle of the living room—a clear quartz arrowhead was on the floor next to her. The elder from the Painted Desert was hunch-backed and her cane shook as she continued to stand. The medicine pouch hanging around her neck nearly burst from its hidden contents. Her hair was grayer, and the sparkle had vanished from her eyes.

She's dying again.

Chapter Five

Empathy and compassion were the driving forces for Ahulani's career choice, but they could also be deterrents to locating the victim alive—or finding the body. Especially when it came to children.

Though she had strong gifts of sight, sound, and intuition, spirit did not make it easy. Her guides did not tell her what had happened, why it had happened, or where she could find the clues. It was her responsibility to use her God-given abilities handed to her at the age of ten. Being a psychic, a medium, or both, did not mean you had all the answers. It meant relying on guidance from the spirit world to help those in need.

Ahulani sat cross-legged on the floor in the center of a circle of gemstones she had made around her. She was familiar with many types of crystal grids, including the triangle and five-pointed star, but since Eric had vanished inside an ancient circular stone house, she thought that shape might provide the right energy.

The circle included Andean pink opal, huebnerite, leopardskin jasper, blue sodalite, and icicle calcite with clear selenite wands connecting each gemstone. The center of the grid contained the picture Tabitha had sent her of Eric—the last photo they had taken of him that Ahulani had printed. The Lemurian Jade was on top of the photo. In her hand, she held the arrowhead left by a powerful, ancient apparition.

"I call upon my spirit guides, angels, and Archangel Metatron, Patron Angel of Children, to assist me in finding Eric Torres, who went missing in Northern Peru among the ruins of Kuelap."

Ahulani had learned to combine her visions with remote viewing so that she could become one with her destination. This ability meant she could see and experience other locations through focus and concentration. If it worked, it would be as if she were roaming among the prehistoric fortress.

"Light and love surround me and keep me safe from harm as I perform remote viewing." Ahulani closed her eyes and imagined a clear, protective bubble around herself to avoid picking up any negative energy at the ruins. "Take me to Kuelap Citadel in Peru, to the spot where Eric Torres went missing."

She had engrained the picture of Eric in her mind. It took a few moments, but after concentrating heavily on the child, Ahulani traveled to an ancient village built along uneven highland terrain on the slopes of the Andes. A narrow entrance through a massive wall made of huge limestone blocks led her to the remnants of round stone houses. Green grass saturated from recent rain, and llamas roamed among the Chachapoyan buildings. A re-creation of one of the homes stood alone among the rest. It was built of the same limestone and had a cone-shaped thatched roof but for a split second, Ahulani thought she saw a person inside the home—possibly an entity drawn to familiar energy.

As she started to sense the Pre-Incan phantoms among the ruins, her vision took her to azure seas teaming with life. The direction of the waves led her into the most beautiful cave she had ever seen.

Could such a place be real?

She entered an elaborate network of tunnels, smoothly twisted columns, and hollows with marbled striations and mesmerizing patterns in colors of gray, blue, white, and yellow. The water in the cave reflected the hues and designs, creating a dizzying, subterranean splendor. With such serenity, she nearly forgot about Eric.

Where is this place? And why am I seeing it among the visions of Kuelap?

Despite her curiosity, Ahulani did not obtain an answer. She wondered if the marble cave could be somewhere in South America. Did it have anything to do with the missing child?

Her vision brought her further into the cave and into darkness. She was not alone. Ahulani heard nothing, but something or *someone* waited.

Panic overcame her, and she tried to back out of the hidden recess and into the marbled light. She was trapped.

A ball of light zipped around her twice before diving into the water. An eternity seemed to pass.

Seconds later, two light anomalies rose up and danced around the chamber, skirting from one side of the cave to the other. The larger one, a little bigger than her fist, stopped in front of her.

These things are intelligent.

Normally associated with spirits, intuition told her these orbs were different. The brilliant sphere slowly circled her. She couldn't detect any eyes, yet she was being watched—closely. She wanted to run, but couldn't move.

Come on, Lani. This is just a vision. You can control this. You can escape.

The orb shot through her spiritual form. She screamed. It felt like her insides were melting.

Ahulani opened her eyes to the comfort and familiarity of her living room, still in pain. She dropped the Lemurian jade. A burning sensation caused her to double over. She lifted her shirt and saw a baseball-sized red blotch. Within seconds, the mark vanished.

The doorbell rang, pulling her further into reality.

Figuring a passerby had heard her yell, she took a deep breath and extended a shaky hand to open the door. She had no idea what excuse to use. *"So sorry to scare you, I was in an unknown cave with killer orbs."*

The person in front of her was no neighbor. An unusually tall man, almost seven feet tall, stood on the threshold. His eyes were the same magnificent marbled colors of the caves, and his hair was long, black, and slicked back. The stranger broke his gaze and glanced to her stomach.

"Can I help you?"

He turned and walked away without a word. The world became still—the birds, the breeze—and she could no longer hear the stream. His footsteps didn't seem to hit the earth. When he walked by the trees, the leaves fell *through* the ground.

Could he represent a human form of the dangerous orb?

"Who are you?" she asked.

He turned to look at her.

She felt enclosed by the darkness again, and the burning sensation returned—worse than before. She yelled in agony and dropped to her knees.

"Ahulani!" A woman yelled her name.

Her intestines felt like it was being twisted.

"Let's get her inside the house," a male voice said.

Two people lifted her under her arms and carried her to the couch.

Why is this happening to me?

She sat down and the pain began to subside. "Where is he?"

Ahulani looked up to see Shelly and a Native American man with long, wavy hair and an athletic stature.

"Who?" Shelly asked.

"A tall man with dark hair. He came to my house a minute ago."

Shelly and the Native man glanced at each other, and then at Ahulani.

Shelly took Ahulani's hand in hers. "We didn't see anyone, but you look better."

Ahulani gave her a weak smile. "I'm feeling much better." She didn't want to reveal all that had occurred. They would probably think her insane. Perhaps she was.

The Native man placed his hand gently on Ahulani's back. "I'm Larry, Shelly's husband. Shelly mentioned that she and David ran across you while out walking."

"Yes. I try to walk every day, but it's strange I've never seen either of you," Ahulani said. She wondered if Shelly could be upset with her for rejecting her lunch offer.

She thought about David. Could he be with the woman she saw in her dream last night?

Larry smiled, then winked. "We travel quite a bit. When we are here, we usually explore trails in Sedona or Flagstaff."

"Would you like us to take you to the hospital?" Shelly asked.

David appeared at her door. "Hospital? What happened?" He rushed inside and knelt in front of Ahulani. "I came looking for Shelly and Larry and heard them in here. I had no idea this was your place."

Ahulani nodded. "I'm fine now. Had a little stomach trouble."

David took her hands in his. "Well, you look great."

His unexpected touch took her breath away. For a split second, she wanted to throw her arms around him and take in his comfort.

Will had never looked at her the same way as David. Thinking back, her ex-husband had approached her with cockiness, not confidence. Will had known he would be able to get Ahulani—like he knew he'd be able to get any other woman. She supposed she had been a victim of sorts, of her own insecurities.

Shelly and Larry looked at the circle of gemstones on her floor.

David followed their gaze.

"Those are beautiful," David said. "What were you doing?"

Shelly and David knew she was a psychic investigator, but would they understand one of her methods of research?

Ahulani diverted her attention to the trees in her backyard, lest she be drawn too deep into David's eyes. "The stones originate from South America and Peru. I was using them to determine what happened to a little boy who went missing there."

"How horrible," Shelly said. "This sort of work must be really hard. I mean, you probably get awful visions."

David glanced at Shelly and Larry, then at Ahulani.

"I know you're not normally supposed to reveal details about cases, but did the kid disappear at Kuelap, like your vision at Painted Desert suggested?"

Ahulani nodded her head. "I could see the ruins where Eric vanished, but I also saw a stunning cave by the sea. I have no idea where it is located, but it looked like striated marble. Not sure if the cave is a piece of the puzzle." She stood slowly, moving gingerly from the couch.

David held her arm.

She waited a few seconds before reaching down to collect the gemstones. She held the pink oval tightly in her hand and looked at her new friends. "I hope he's okay. It can be stressful thinking of what the victims can be going through and not knowing if I will be able to help."

David helped her pick up the remainder of the stones. He held out his palms for her to take them.

Ahulani blushed as she took the stones from his hand, glancing into his eyes for only a second. Then, she placed the stones in the bowl on the bookshelf. "Or if help will come too late."

Shelly stood quickly. "The Marble Caves."

Ahulani took a step toward her. "You know about the caves?"

"Yes, of course. David and I are from South America. It could be the caves in Patagonia, Chile—on the border of Chile and Argentina. Only they aren't in the sea, but in General Carrera Lake."

She couldn't believe her luck, having met people who were familiar with Peru and her visions. Or did fate bring them all together to help a missing child?

David took his phone from his back pocket and appeared to be searching for something. A minute later, he handed Ahulani the phone. "Are those the caves you saw? Carved into the Patagonian Andes, they are located on a peninsula of solid marble. They're formed by about 6,000 years of waves washing up against calcium carbonate. The smooth, swirling blues of the cavern walls are a reflection of the lake's waters."

"Breathtaking." Ahulani wondered what the orbs had to do with the magnificent marble caves. Were they spirits or something supernatural? Who was the bizarre man that came to her door, and did he deliberately cause her to collapse?

David glanced at Shelly, then Larry. "Shelly and I have been there many times, and she took Larry to Peru and the caves for their honeymoon."

Larry leaned forward on the couch, flipping his long hair behind him. "Are you planning on visiting Kuelap to find out more about the boy?"

"I'm not sure. Eric's father offered to pay for a trip there, but I wanted to try and get clues remotely first. It could save time." Ahulani looked from David to Larry and Shelly. "And Eric's life."

She handed David his phone.

"Listen." David slid the phone in his back pocket. "I was planning on visiting Central America in three weeks. If you want, I can forego my planned trip and take you to Kuelap. I've already saved the money."

Larry and Shelly glanced at each other.

"I don't know," Ahulani said. "I would hate to make you change your plans. If I do go, it would have to be as soon as possible."

"That's not a problem."

Ahulani had always wanted to go to Peru, but this trip would not be for pleasure. Would she be able to focus with David around? What would the client say? She realized it would be safer traveling with a man. Not to mention, he was familiar with the area.

Shelly placed her hand on David's arm. "Wait, you're supposed to be with the park service for the next few weeks."

David shrugged. "I'll tell them it's an emergency. Plus, I know another guy who would be willing to take over for me."

Ahulani watched a hummingbird hover near a feeder in her back yard. "David, you could be in danger. I don't know who, or what, we're dealing with."

David smiled genuinely at her. "I'm willing to take the risk. After all, we're talking about an innocent child. I want to help."

Fate had brought David to her at the opportune time, obviously for a purpose. Should she give him a chance—was she ready to take that risk?

Larry stood and stared at the area of the rug where the circle of stones had been. "David, isn't that the rock you took from the side of the stream?"

Ahulani glanced over to see a heart-shaped stone in the same spot she had been sitting for the ritual. It was gorgeous with magenta, pink, and white stripes circling it.

David bent over and picked it up hesitantly. He turned it slowly in his hand. He gave it to Ahulani, looking at her in wonder. "I don't believe it. The woman by the stream—I believe she gifted this to me from her pile of stones, but I couldn't find it this morning."

"Ahulani was meant to have that," Shelly said. "How the heck did it get here?"

Ahulani's head reeled from the complicated series of events—the case of the missing child, the chance meeting with David and his family, the sightings of the medicine woman, and the precious arrowhead. And now, David's river stone in place of her gemstones.

Perhaps her collection of crystals *weren't* the answer. This case wasn't going to be that simple. Like the child in the clouds and his family, she would be tested.

The trip to the Painted Desert, meeting David, the arrowhead, and the stone heart—was the medicine woman preparing Ahulani for the fight of her career? Or would an innocent life be lost, caught between the past and the present?

"I'm not sure how it got here," Ahulani said. "We were all standing next to that spot."

"She's been here." David stepped toward Ahulani. "The woman from the stream. Somehow, she placed this here without any of us seeing it. I believe the medicine woman has a rather powerful connection, not only to the Petrified

Forest and Painted Desert, but to all Mother Nature."

Ahulani traced her finger over the smooth stone, mysteriously placed where her other crystals had been. Did it represent feelings and a future between her and David? Or, the love between Eric and his family?

A tool shaped by Mother Nature—could it be more powerful than any gem or crystal?

Chapter Six

Ahulani stood in a cave grotto at Palatki Ruins State Park in Sedona, Arizona. It was Wednesday, and she was the only visitor in this section of the park that featured over 1,000 petroglyphs and pictographs. She preferred the solitude among this hidden prehistoric site of the ancient Sinagua past. It gave her a chance to connect with the spirits who'd lived and died so long ago.

Ahulani had attempted to use the circle of Peruvian stones again in the morning, but for some reason, they had provided a visual of Palatki. She had visited in the hopes that reminders of the ancient past would initiate visions of Eric.

She hovered her hand over a white petroglyph of a geometric shape and closed her eyes.

This is the most challenging case of my career. What if I can't handle this, and can't find Eric? Perhaps, I don't have the abilities to bring him back from wherever he is. Would it make a difference if I went to Peru? I might be able to pick up on the child, but do I have the abilities to return him home?

Were her intuition and psychic talents waning? The petroglyphs and pictographs lining the rock walls included a black ladder, white four-legged animals, human figures, and wavy snake-like images.

She hadn't heard anyone approach, yet she felt someone's hot breath on her neck.

Ahulani turned to see a man over six feet tall whose face had been bashed in. Good looks were hidden among roughly cut, short dark hair and a scar on his face that extended from below his right eye to his mouth. He wore animal skins and fur-lined moccasins. He smiled—something she wouldn't have expected, considering his harsh demeanor.

She had a clear vision of him hunting, pursuing deer down a stream.

The vision switched to a deer being roasted over a fire in the grotto she stood in. She could almost smell the smoke and taste the savory, cooked meat. The spectral figure in front of her sat next to a woman with long dark hair, and they were sharing a portion of the meat. Neither took their eyes off each other while they chewed.

Ahulani stared at him. He looked at the ground. The word *murder* echoed in her mind.

There were no other visions to show her who the killer was or what had occurred. Could it be the phantom before her? As if picking up on her thought, a tear rolled down the scar on his face, then he vanished into thin air.

Within seconds, footsteps came up the walkway to the grotto. She turned to see a Native American man wearing jeans, a white shirt, and a black vest. He wore his hair in two braids.

She sensed something special about the handsome, dark-haired stranger.

"Good morning," said the man with the broad nose and shoulders.

Ahulani smiled. She could still sense the Sinaguan spirit's presence. "Good morning."

"I'm Joe, Joe Luna."

For a split second, her third eye revealed an unusual looking child with large eyes—larger than any she had seen on a human. Milky white skin clashed with the dark raven hair yet added to her beauty. This bizarre vision had some sort of association to Joe. Could it be his daughter?

"Nice to meet you. My name is Ahulani."

Joe shook her hand and took a step toward Ahulani. He stared at her as if she looked familiar to him.

"It appears you have your own unique abilities," Joe said. "There is a powerful spirit here from the time of the Sinagua who has revealed himself to you."

Ahulani didn't know how Joe knew this—unless he could feel the man's presence. Or had the male spirit told Joe about the encounter? Her intuition told her she had nothing to fear with this newcomer. He had a powerful, yet gentle presence.

She glanced toward the back of the grotto where the entity had stood. "You have the sight also? He gave me a vision of himself with a woman."

He nodded. "I do. Did you think about why you were drawn here?" Joe asked. "Your guides brought you here. That spirit recognized you."

"Well, yes. He knows I can identify him and help him move on."

Joe took another step forward until he was only inches from her face. "He was murdered by a man who wanted you for himself. I saw the same spirit you did as I approached the grotto, and in my dream last night. Particular past lives are brought forth for us to learn. This one is to help you cope with loss, though the man who stole you from your true love," Joe glanced in the direction where the Sinaguan man had appeared, "is also associated with you in *this* life, but as a much different person."

Will? Could he be talking about Will? After all, he did steal my heart and my soul.

Joe put his hand on Ahulani's shoulder. "I said he *is* associated in this life, not *was*."

Ahulani stared at the Native man in shock. Joe seemed to know what she was thinking. Had he come to the Palatki Ruins to give her this message?

She heard the words *"Medicine Man"* as a whisper on the wind.

"I don't know who you are talking about. I'm not married, nor dating anyone."

Joe turned away from her and started gazing at the petroglyphs. He stopped in front of a panel of a hunting scene with black animal figures drawn with charcoal. Without looking at her, he said, "There is someone waiting. The agony from loss in this life and your past life are colliding."

Ahulani knew about past lives. She had been able to detect those of her clients. Could a tragedy from a past life really have such an impact in this life? Will had been the one to abandon her so callously. Could David be the person who stole her from the prehistoric Sinagua man so long ago?

She could no longer sense her spirit lover from the ancient past. Ahulani and Joe wandered through the grotto, observing the rock art.

Ahulani thought of David and his offer to come with her to Peru. Though it would make her feel comfortable to have him as a travel companion, she didn't know how they would get along. Could she trust him?

She jumped when her phone rang, disturbing the silence. "This is Ahulani."

"They're gone." She recognized Tabitha's voice.

A shiver went down Ahulani's spine. Not a shiver. More like a quake.

"James, Linda, and I headed up to Kuelap. They attempted to figure out what happened to Eric on their own. They went missing while at the ruins."

Ahulani watched Joe roam into the forest and walk the path to the ruins. "The same spot where Eric went missing?" she asked.

Tabitha let out a gasp that changed into a heart-wrenching sob. "Not sure. The last I saw them they were standing in a circular house foundation. I believe it was the same one, but I can't recall. There are 400 of those houses here."

Ahulani let out a sigh of frustration. She did a 360-degree turn before leaning over to steady herself.

"Let me try remote viewing. I am in a quiet place and might be able to pick up something about the family."

An inner male voice spoke to her, a spirit guide.

"They are all safe. For now."

"Tabitha, where are you?" she asked.

"I'm at a hotel in Chachapoyas, a couple hours from the ruins. I need to return home. My daughter is sick with the flu."

"I'm sorry—I hope she gets better soon."

"I feel horrible about having to leave Peru. I am abandoning my friends when I should be here working with the police. I did contact them and told them that something happened at the site—that the family disappeared. They wanted to detain me. That's when I found out my daughter had gotten so sick."

Ahulani could hear children's laughter in the grotto but there were no tourists around. It felt as if a small hand had placed itself on her upper thigh. "This is not a typical missing persons' case. We have no idea where they are or what can be done to help them. I can touch base with law enforcement, and my friend David is from Peru. Maybe he knows someone who can help."

Ahulani was surprised she had used the word 'friend.' She barely knew David.

She didn't know if Eric and his parents could wait for her to get to Peru. She only had enough funds to remain in the country for little over a week. Could they still be at Kuelap in an unseen portal? Had they been teleported to another dimension? Something supernatural had occurred—not once, but twice.

"Okay, let me know what you find out. I need to go," Tabitha said and sniffled.

A whole family had vanished in Tabitha's presence. Now, Tabitha insisted she had to return to her daughter.

Could Tabitha be responsible for all three disappearances? Ahulani had seen a distinct vision of Eric vanishing within the remnants of a round structure during her first call with Tabitha. It looked like he had been alone. Had Ahulani been wrong? What if Tabitha were the one doing the deceiving? If so, she could win an Academy Award.

"I'll be heading home to Connecticut tonight, but I will keep in touch and let you know if I hear anything from Eric's parents."

Ahulani watched as a shadow moved from the cave and into the woods. "I'll send light and love your way, and please have a safe trip." She disconnected the call, went to the back of the grotto, and sat down cross-legged. Her Sinaguan lover was still close by.

"I ask of my angels, guides, and spirits associated with this tranquil location to make sure that this place is safe and remains quiet for my remote viewing session to Peru. If you know where Eric and his parents are, please show me."

She closed her eyes, focused on the remains of the citadel, and in her mind, she cloaked herself to remain unseen by visitors. She had done this a myriad of times while meditating at national parks and sacred locations, and it had never failed to work. Before she focused, she remembered one instance when she had scared an elderly man as she removed herself from the invisible state. He had told his wife Ahulani had "come out of nowhere."

Rather than the ruins of Kuelap, Ahulani's mind took her to the marble caves.

A tall, lithe woman with wavy dark red hair sat in a boat with two other people. The boat gradually moved over the unearthly blue waters of Lake Carrera into the caverns carved by crashing waves.

The woman and the other two tourists in the boat were mesmerized by the light show from the reflection of the azure water on the marble walls. They stared quietly at the hobbit holes, graceful limestone columns, and a 360-degree view offering sensuous curves of stunning rock. Their excited voices echoed off the cavern walls, but only for a few seconds.

Ahulani didn't want to go in after the boat. Not wanting to risk harm again, she focused on the entrance to the cave, but the tourists never came out.

Flashes of light emanated from inside the darkness.

"You must go in," a female spirit guide whispered.

Ahulani extended her invisibility talent from the grotto to her remote viewing location to avoid further attack by the unknown.

Then, she cautiously entered, floating above the water. The atmosphere felt heavier than the first time she'd entered.

Ahulani tried to take a deep breath but went into a coughing fit. Archangel Michael's wings surrounded her, and she stopped.

"Thank you," she whispered.

He remained close, along with her other angels and guides. She was steered toward the back of the cave. Enough light came in from the entrance that Ahulani could see a wide passage—wide enough for a boat to pass through.

An angel entered the passage, then turned and waited for her.

"I get it. You want me to follow." She could rarely see her angels and guides so clearly, except when doing remote viewing. Ahulani figured it was because of her focused metaphysical state, her vulnerability. Or maybe both.

Haunting voices echoed throughout the mysterious passage. The sound bounced off the walls and resonated around her, giving her chills.

She hesitated, glancing back into the main cavern where comforting light resonated from the entrance. The unknown murkiness ahead made her uneasy.

Is the disturbing, dark-haired man who showed up at my house lurking here? Could he have something to do with the disappearances?

A large mass coalesced in the darkness, taking up the width of the tunnel. Ahulani couldn't move, transfixed by the object. It became more solid and headed in her direction. It seemed to have a life of its own.

She was pulled away from the side passage, back through the Marble Cave, and out of the entrance.

"Ahulani?"

She opened her eyes to see Joe kneeling in front of her. "Are you okay?" he asked.

"Yes. I'm fine." She didn't know if she should tell him what she was doing, though she had a feeling he would understand.

"I thought you'd gone to the ruins," Ahulani said.

Joe extended his hand to her. She took it and let him help her stand.

"I made it to the site, but a force prevented me from stepping into the ruin. I felt as if I needed to return here."

She wondered if any tourists had visited the grotto while she was in her remote viewing state.

"I was meditating." She didn't feel like discussing the case. The universe seemed determined to throw obstacles in her way. Yet her intuition told her the man in front of her had been placed in her path for a reason.

Joe watched something in the distance. "Is that all it was?" He looked back at Ahulani. "Meditation, that is."

Hesitating, Ahulani didn't answer right away. "I think I'll walk over to the ruins. You're welcome to wander over there with me."

Would the prehistoric walls at this site inspire a connection with the ancient remains in Peru? Why am I being drawn to the Marble Caves?

Joe guided her out of the grotto. "Of course."

Just as they left the grotto, a large group of tourists came up the path.

Joe moved in front of Ahulani and walked a few feet ahead. As he crossed the path with large boulders on either side, he stopped to pick up a river stone. He held it tightly in his hand and closed his eyes.

While he focused on the energy of the rock, Ahulani saw him transform in her mind into an otherworldly being with no facial features, two arms and legs, and short wings extending from his back. She smiled. She was seeing a past life form, which not unlike Joe himself, represented peace, healing, and love.

After about thirty seconds, Joe opened his eyes and showed the stone to her.

She took the river stone and turned it in her palm. It had the appearance of an abstract painting with swirls of dark brown, tan, and red. A turquoise-colored spot was in the center. It was nearly as stunning as the heart-shaped rock that showed up in her living room the day before.

"Amazing," she said. "I've seen similar river rocks, but usually the coloring is only on one side."

She handed it back to Joe, and they walked in silence to the ruins. She didn't see or sense her Sinaguan lover from a past life. Maybe he was gone. Ahulani thought of David. He had mentioned he would be working at Petrified Forest this week, or at least until she decided if she would need him to go with her to Peru.

Joe and Ahulani approached the Palatki Ruin. She walked past him and the multi-storied mud and brick rooms built against the canyon wall. Then, Ahulani entered a pueblo through an ancient doorway and placed her backpack on the ground.

Palatki Ruin and its surroundings transformed into a mountain top location with llamas, a grand river far below, and remnants of an archaic Peruvian village.

Could Eric and his parents have entered an inter-dimensional portal among the ghosts of the past? Could she be in jeopardy—even in a remote viewing state?

Chapter Seven

The palatial ponderosas towered protectively above the prehistoric village known as Elden Pueblo in Flagstaff, once inhabited by the Northern Sinagua people. David wondered how many visitors drove by the shady, historic respite without being aware of its ancestral existence and perhaps, that was a good thing.

David breathed in deeply of the trees' intoxicating scent mixed with that of a nearby campfire. The 65-room village contained trash mounds, smaller pueblos, a kiva, large community room, and numerous pit houses. He imagined a thriving village and wondered how the Northern Sinagua managed to live together in small pueblos, to cook, hunt, learn, and grow together as a tightknit community.

The Northern Sinagua had resided in what was now Flagstaff including the nearby areas of Walnut Canyon National Monument and Wupatki National Monument. Yet the range of the Sinagua didn't end in Northern Arizona. The Southern Sinagua had called the Verde Valley of Central Arizona their home—Montezuma's Castle, Montezuma's Well, and Tuzigoot National Monument. David had visited each place, which had generated their own special tune on his pan flute.

He thought back to the day when the gracious, elf-like woman had led him, Shelly, and Larry to the stream where the woman had collected stones.

She had said, "Treasure her forever."

The stone David picked from the top of her collection had mysteriously ended up in Ahulani's living room. How?

David had placed the stunning stone on the nightstand in his bedroom. It seemed an impossibility. Who was the tall, blonde nymph? Could the alluring stone collector be trying to get him and Ahulani together? Did she have a tie to the medicine woman from the Painted Desert?

Though he knew Ahulani wasn't open to a relationship, he couldn't stop thinking about her. He had told her he would be willing to travel to Peru to show her around and take her where she needed to go, including the Kuelap Citadel.

Yet, he had the impression she didn't want him around. Considering they didn't know each other all that well, he could understand, but he still wanted to help. What had happened to the missing child? David had never heard of supernatural activity happening at the ruins high above the Amazon.

Ahulani had mentioned having a vision at the Marble Caves, but what did that have to do with the ruins on the slope of the Andes?

David stared at a series of partial room blocks along the pathway. A woman began to appear in the center of one of the rooms, overgrown with tall grass, weeds, and flowers that had been inhabited around 1070 A.D.

"It's you again," David said.

The medicine woman watched him. She appeared even younger than she had a few days before at Oak Creek Canyon. Perhaps in her fifties now, she stood about 5'7" with dark brown hair cut above the shoulders. She wore a deerskin dress lined in multi-colored beadwork.

He approached her cautiously. "Do you have a message for me? I have seen you many times, including near my sister's house. Is there something I can do to help you?"

She shook her head and turned her back to him, wandering among the small room blocks. She ran her hand along the walls, then knelt and picked up some white and yellow wildflowers, placing them into a neat bundle.

When the medicine woman turned back to face David, she had reverse aged yet another ten years.

54

Does she know what's happening to her?

The woman—the apparition who resided in the Holbrook area hundreds of years ago—walked toward David and handed him the flowers.

He hesitantly accepted the earthly bundle, looked into her dark grey eyes, and thought he saw a hint of the much older medicine woman.

She smiled at him and quickly faded away. Had she given him the flowers as proof of her visit?

The sky had become cloudy and the air cold and windy. David placed the flowers on the wall of the ruins and slipped on his jean jacket. When he went to pick them up again, he noticed small purple flowers in the bunch.

The temperature had dropped at least ten degrees in minutes, and the dark clouds continued to lumber in over the ancient village. A few hikers who were without long pants or jackets ran past David and Elden Pueblo toward the parking lot.

David attempted to wait out the cooler weather so that he could explore the pueblo, but a light mist began that turned into a downpour.

He struggled to remove his keys from his jacket as heavy rain soaked his clothes. He raced to his vehicle, unlocked it with his remote, threw his backpack in, and quickly slid into the drivers' side.

He decided to wait in the car to see if the rain would stop soon.

His pan flute lay half out of the backpack.

That's strange. I had the flute zipped inside the front compartment.

Grabbing it, he closed his eyes, began to play, and envisioned himself among the Amazonas. His music started out slow, deep, to reflect the region and the Utcubamba River Valley. He followed the notes as they meandered among the curves of the river and jungle and increased in pitch as he imagined walking up the Northern slope of the Andes. The notes became higher as he gradually worked his way higher into the clouds.

The scene became more real, like a vivid dream.

David's pan flute frequently took him on spiritual journeys near and far. Maybe his flute would take him to the Kuelap Citadel if he set the intent. The ruins of Kuelap had saved his life in a way, helping him grow as a person and showing him his purpose. Perhaps he could use his experiences there to help save Eric.

Walking through the narrow entrance of the Kuelap Citadel, the pan flute seemed to play of its own accord, rising in a feverous pitch. The mountain top ruins were vacant of visitors, save for the llamas grazing among the ancient round structures. At least, it *looked* empty.

Something waited for him—something he couldn't see. It thought it had remained hidden, but the thickness of the air and the goosebumps on David's skin belied the truth.

The pan flute ceased playing. David tried to continue, but no sound would come out. It was as if the instrument knew a dangerous secret.

David wanted to run but couldn't move. He remained frozen in the foundation of a round stone house. Footsteps circled the area around him, yet he couldn't see anyone or *anything*.

A petite woman stood with her back to him in the distance. She turned.

Ahulani's eyes opened wide with shock.

"David! What are you doing here?"

"I was, I mean, I am at Elden Pueblo in Flagstaff. It started raining so I ran to my car. I decided to play my flute to see if I could help find Eric here at Kuelap."

David ran up to her. He tried to place his hand on her arm, but it went right through her.

Ahulani attempted to touch David on the shoulder but had the same results.

"I can see you so clearly, even though your visitation is spiritual," Ahulani said. "I walked through a portal at Palatki Ruins in Sedona, so my physical form *is* here."

David looked around nervously. "Listen, my pan flute stopped playing. *Something* is here. Something doesn't feel right. We should leave."

Ahulani directed her attention toward an area David couldn't see.

"I can't," she said. "I saw an ancient Chachapoyan, but he took off. I have a feeling he and the other spirits who lived in this village are aware of these supernatural occurrences." She looked at David. "I sense others have disappeared besides Eric. I found out his parents have vanished also, in their attempt to search for him."

"Oh, Ahulani. I am so sorry." He wanted to reach out to her. but it wouldn't do any good. He couldn't touch her—physically or emotionally. Perhaps, that's the reason for his dramatic vision in Oak Creek Canyon when he saw her again.

David didn't know what to think. Kuelap had been his safe haven during his tenure in Peru. He didn't have kids, but it had to be unimaginable to lose a child. How did Ahulani feel, not knowing where to begin her search?

Ahulani looked beyond him again, toward something or someone behind him.

He couldn't see anything—human or paranormal. Yet his intuition screamed peril. He wanted to grab her and take her back with him to Arizona. Unfortunately, it wasn't possible.

Or was it?

Ahulani turned her face to his. "David, maybe you should go. I don't know what we're dealing with here."

"I am not about to leave you alone." David thought back to the medicine woman's flowers. Had that initiated the thunderstorm leading him to his car?

"I was guided here for a reason, Ahulani. We'll both stay. Not to mention, this place used to be my home, so I might be able to find the place where Eric and his parents vanished."

"I think I did already," Ahulani said.

"Really?" he asked.

Ahulani indicated for him to follow her. She led him to one of many round stone houses once inhabited by a culture referred to as *Warriors of the Clouds.*

They stood next to the structure, observing it.

She pointed to an unusual shape in the dirt.

Before he could stop her, Ahulani had stepped over the remnants of the block wall and into the dilapidated home.

"What are you doing?" David leapt over the wall and tried to pull her out but remembered he couldn't connect with her physically.

"It's okay, David," she said.

David cautiously stepped over the wall and stood next to Ahulani.

She put her hand in front of David, preventing him from stepping on something drawn in the dirt.

He saw the shape of a large bear imprinted among the dirt and grass. Ahulani outlined the animal figure with her finger. "This could represent a bear fetish. I've heard it relates to solitude—reluctancy to step out of the cave and into the sunshine after a long period of hibernation."

David hovered his hand on the bear. "I'm sure these people had their own version of a shaman or medicine person. Maybe someone of that caliber lived here."

Ahulani looked up at him. He continued to scan the surrounding ruins for danger.

"This drawing wasn't here when my archaeology team researched Kuelap five years ago. I recall this particular stone building because of a raised bump on part of the wall." David pointed to a section of stone on the inside of the home that looked like a face coming through the rock. "No other homes in this part of the village have that feature. Maybe this thing, human or otherwise, is targeting those with special abilities. Or perhaps, it could refer to solitude since not many know about this place compared to, say, Machu Picchu."

She held her hands over the animal figure. "There is an energy associated with this, but I wonder what this fetish has to do with Eric, his parents, or any others who have disappeared."

David walked slowly around the mystical shape. "We can't be sure this is related to the missing people."

Ahulani picked up a large rock. "Stand back." She motioned him to the side of the round house and dropped it onto the bear.

As soon as it hit the ground, the rock vanished.

"*Shit.*" David couldn't believe the four-letter word that had erupted from his mouth. It was the first curse word he had used in years.

Ahulani stared at him.

"Sorry," he said.

"It's all right, I understand. Anyone, or anything, that happens to interact with this bear could be a victim. Eric and his parents might have stepped on it without knowing it. That's why I tried to chase that ghost down when you arrived, hoping he could provide some clues."

Ahulani glanced around at the nearby ruins. "I wonder how long the bear has been here. Obviously, less than five years since you didn't see it before."

"At least that long," David said.

She stepped out of the ancient house. "I know there are spirits, watching, listening. I beg you to help us please. There are at least three living people missing. I want to find these innocent victims and make sure they are safe."

Ahulani did a 360-degree turn as if to see any entities but threw up her hands in the air a minute later. "It's my turn to say a curse word."

David smiled.

Ahulani began to fade from view. She tried to talk to him, but David couldn't hear her. He pointed to her body. "I think you're going home."

She noticed her form fading and looked at him in desperation. Within a few seconds, she was gone.

An overwhelming sense of panic threatened to overtake him.

Had she returned home? Or was she another vanishing victim?

Chapter Eight

A hulani felt lost, disoriented. She couldn't recall where she had been or where she was now. She glanced around and realized she stood inside a reddish clay structure. She looked up at the remains of what used to be a second story wall. Brilliant rays of light reflected off the piles of prehistoric boulders surrounding the once magnificent dwelling. The trees alongside offered much needed shade.

She saw a blue backpack lying on the ground and picked it up. Her backpack. She breathed a sigh of relief, knowing she was home.

I can't believe I walked through a portal. Her whole body trembled.

She wondered how David had gotten to Kuelap. Could he still be there?

She glanced at her watch—2:45 P.M. She had looked at the time right before she teleported—if that's what one could call it—and her watch had read 12:15 P.M.

A variety of birds were chirping and singing loudly as she knelt and squeezed through a small, rectangular brick doorway, most likely built by the shorter Sinagua. Ahulani didn't see Joe around. Maybe he had left the park. She had hoped to find out more about him.

The shaking had subsided, but she still felt off kilter. She leaned against the canyon wall to steady herself.

"There you are!"

Ahulani jumped.

Joe approached her, giving her a once-over with his intense gaze.

He glanced at the doorway where she had emerged from. "What happened? One minute you were in that room and the next, gone. At first, I thought you had decided to leave, but your backpack was still here."

Joe walked up to her and placed his hand on her shoulders. "You're shaking. Are you okay?" He gently tilted Ahulani's head to the side to look at her neck. "Where did *this* red spot come from?"

"What?" Ahulani felt her neck. It was warm to the touch and a little sore.

Joe looked at her quizzically. "It's in the shape of a bear."

Her legs buckled and she collapsed forward to the ground on her knees.

Joe knelt beside her. "Do you think you can make it to the Visitor Center? There are some benches, or we can talk in my truck." He helped Ahulani stand.

She was beginning to feel more grounded. "It's not that far. I should be fine."

By the time they passed the visitor center fifteen minutes later, the trembling had stopped, but her neck was still sore. Joe helped her to a wooden bench.

Ahulani glanced at Joe. "I am doing much better. Thanks."

Joe sat next to her and watched her closely. "What happened to you back there? You can tell me the truth."

Ahulani let out a big sigh. "I walked into that pueblo and found myself in another country. Before I knew it, I was at Kuelap Citadel in Peru where there are ruins built by a pre-Columbian culture. A family from Peru vanished at the site—first, their little boy, Eric, and when the parents returned to figure out what happened, they went missing as well."

Joe smiled at a passing park ranger who walked by from inside the Visitor Center. Then, he turned to her, the smile still on his face. "For some reason, I feel the need to call you Lani."

Ahulani returned his smile and nodded. "My parents

used to call me Lani. It's much easier, I suppose." She hadn't heard the nickname in years. Will had called her that, too.

"So, tell me more about what happened?" Joe asked.

"It wasn't my intent to go to Kuelap. I stepped into a portal and ended up there. My friend David was visiting the Elden Pueblo site in Flagstaff at the same time I was here. He appeared at Kuelap within minutes of me, only he arrived through astral travel."

Ahulani closed her eyes, lifted her head, and enjoyed the cool breeze on her face. "There is a round stone house, or rather the remains of it, where Eric and his parents vanished. Within that ancient home is the outline of a bear fetish imprinted in the dirt and grass. David swears it wasn't there when he and some archaeology interns were there to work five years ago. And it looks fairly recent."

Joe gently turned her head so he could see the red spot on her neck. "Hmm…that is interesting. How does your neck feel now?"

"It's fine."

"The spot is gone," Joe said. "There is no more redness."

"I wish I had seen it. Joe, you're not shocked by what I just told you? Because I am still freaked out. I consider myself a spiritualist and have abilities, but nothing like that has ever happened to me. I mean, I'm aware of portals and other dimensions…"

Joe put his hand on hers to still them. "I have a friend named Jacenda who has the ability to travel between Indian ruins, but I don't think this is a normal thing for you. You and David were meant to meet there for a reason." Joe waved at a lone male hiker passing by. "I wonder if David had the same mark as you."

"David told me his body didn't travel to the Andes. He was in his car playing his pan flute, sort of like soul travel. I doubt he has a mark."

"There are no real answers when it comes to the unknown," Joe said. "As a former FBI agent *and* medicine man, I've seen it all."

62

Ahulani nodded her head. "I knew there was something different about you, even *before* you picked up on the Sinaguan spirit in the grotto. One of my spirit guides mentioned you were a medicine man."

"You aren't the only reason I ended up here today," Joe said. "I had a dream about you after I decided to visit ruins in the area. I was at Honanki Ruins down the road before I drove here."

Ahulani grinned. "Well, I am happy you did."

Joe tightened his grip on Ahulani's hand. "So am I."

Ahulani stood. "I'll be fine. I plan on heading home now."

"Do you want me to follow you?" Joe asked.

"Oh, no. I live here in Sedona—Oak Creek, actually. You should visit sometime." She reached into her pocket and gave him her business card.

Joe stood and placed his arm around Ahulani. "Absolutely. Sedona is such a peaceful place. You're lucky to live there. You're also welcome to visit us. I have a place in west Phoenix, but I'm usually in Flagstaff."

She wondered why Joe spent more time in Flagstaff. Maybe he had a significant other.

Joe got up, took her backpack from her, and walked with Ahulani to her car. He handed her the backpack, and she removed her keys from her bag and unlocked her vehicle.

"Are you sure you're all right?" Joe asked.

"Positive. Apparently, the shakiness and weakness were side effects from the travel. I'm fine."

Joe gave her a long, fierce hug. Warmth radiated down the center of her body through her chakras, the energetic entry gates to her auras. It ran from her crown chakra at the top of her head to her third eye in the middle of her forehead to her throat and heart chakra. Then, the sensation quickly went through her solar plexus and root chakra at the bottom of her spinal cord.

He released her, and she pulled away, watching him. She suddenly felt renewed and ready to face whatever waited for her ahead.

Joe opened Ahulani's car door for her, then placed her backpack behind her seat.

She slid into the driver's seat. "Thanks for your help today."

"My pleasure, Lani. Be careful driving home."

He closed her car door and waved. His truck was parked next to hers, and she watched him get in. He started the engine and waved again as he pulled out of the parking lot.

When she turned her head back, the tall, dark-haired mystery man who had appeared at her home sat in the passenger seat. His head was bent down to avoid hitting the roof.

Ahulani panicked. Joe had left and no one else was around. "What are *you* doing here?"

"I came to see you." His voice was so deep, it sent shivers down her spine.

She felt tempted to throw open the car door and run, but she wanted answers. "Why are you following me? You came to my home and minutes later, I ended up in unbearable agony."

"You assume I was responsible," he said.

"Of course. I had just been to the Marble Caves in Chile by remote viewing. A large orb approached me, went through me, and I had the same sensation. Then, I return home and you arrived at my door minutes later without a word. As soon as you left, I had the same horrible pain."

The man shook his head in disgust.

She tried to pick up on his aura but couldn't. She didn't see or sense any angels or guides associated with the stranger, which meant he might not be human. She took an inward breath to calm herself.

His eyes, with swirls of grey, arctic blue, and white, watched her for a while—without blinking.

"I am trying to figure out why people are disappearing from Kuelap. I suspect you have something to do with it."

His gaze never faltered. "Not quite. The two worlds you have visited are connected."

64

"Worlds? You mean Kuelap and the Marble Caves?"

He didn't reply or verify her words.

How can this guy not blink? Her intuition provided no indication as to whether she could trust him, if he was human at all. She didn't know what to believe. He had just verified for her a suspicion she had that Kuelap Citadel and Marble Caves were somehow related. It could be a clue. Were the missing people ending up at Marble Caves? During remote viewing, she had witnessed a boat full of tourists go into the caves and not come out.

Ahulani watched as a cardinal perched on a branch a few feet above the hood of her car. "Have the visitors who disappeared from Kuelap also been to the caves?"

He sat there quietly.

She threw up her hands. "Why am I talking to *you* about this?"

He focused his attention on the cardinal. The bird jumped off the branch and landed on the hood of her car. It walked up to the windshield and peeked in at him. The man cocked his head, and the bird did the same. He leaned toward it and the cardinal thrust its head forward. He glanced at Ahulani and the dazzling bird flew away.

A car drove into the parking lot and parked on the other side of her car, catching her attention. When she looked back at the passenger seat, the enigmatic man was gone. She shook her head. So much had happened in the past few days, yet she still had so few answers.

Her phone rang, startling her. She didn't recognize the number and was tempted to send the call to voice mail, but intuition told her to take it.

Heavy static interrupted a distant male voice. "David? Is that you?" she asked.

Bursts of static exploded in her ear. "Hello," she yelled. "I can't hear you!"

The static ceased for a few seconds. "It's James. James Torres." Eric's father! Ahulani couldn't believe it. "Where are you? Tabitha said you and your wife had disappeared at Kuelap."

"We did. We were in the same stone ruins as Eric when he vanished. I have no idea where we are or what's happening. We…"

Another burst of static interrupted James.

Did the mysterious man in her car have something to do with this uncanny phone call?

Ahulani shouted into the phone. A passerby leaving his car to go to the Visitor Center stared at her as if she were insane. Perhaps she was.

"Is Eric with you?" she yelled.

"No."

She hoped Eric and his parents could be rescued.

James continued to talk through the static, but she could barely hear several words. After a few seconds, the noise subsided. She caught the middle of a sentence.

"Dark and light…" A quick burst of static. "…isn't right. Looks sort of like home, but it's not." Yet another burst of noise.

"James, are you there?" Ahulani gripped the dashboard. "I am trying to find you!"

She attempted to get a visual of their location as he talked, but her mind was blank.

"Like home? James, do you mean Peru?"

"Yes. We are seeing Kuelap fortress in a cloud of white light high above our own hometown of Chiclayo. Only, there is no one else in here in Chiclayo, as if it's been abandoned, like Kuelap. Something is really wrong, Ahulani but…"

Her phone went dead. She stared at it in exasperation. Her immediate reaction was to call him back, but when she tried a busy signal sounded at the other end.

"Darn," Ahulani said.

James had mentioned Kuelap as being "high above." The ruins had been built on the slope of the Andes Mountains, but why would James and his wife be able to see the fortress from Chiclayo? What was responsible for such chaos? Could Eric be lost in the same place—so close, yet so far from his parents? It'd been days. Was he still alive?

Kuelap seemed to be connected to portals in other areas; for Ahulani, it was the Marble Caves. For James and his wife, it was Chiclayo.

Overwhelmed and exhausted from the morning's events, Ahulani pulled out of the parking lot and drove down the dirt road. How could she help people who were no longer on the earthly plane?

***

As she drove home, Ahulani recognized the voice of a Mayan male spirit guide. He spoke one word in her ear—*Moldavite*. A powerful stone with many uses, moldavite was used for spiritual awakening, transformation, and evolutionary growth. The forest green stone facilitated clear and direct connection between one's consciousness and the Universal Source.

The gemstone, supposedly created by a meteorite that crashed 14 million years ago in Czechoslovakia, could help star children and other sensitives connect with ascended masters and cosmic messengers.

As a star child herself, Ahulani frequently observed the heavens, wondering where she had originated from among the vastness of the many planets and universes. Her spirit guides had told her that she had many past lives among the galaxies—once as part of a species who were made of the stars. So, getting a visit from the enigmatic man wasn't totally surprising for her. Her most vivid dreams involved being on a spaceship in a large, open area. Though it was a blur, she remembered seeing short beings watching her from the back of a room. A round window above her had revealed a triangular craft—from the looks of it, the size of a baseball field—amid the darkness of space. Only hours before she'd had the dream, she had meditated with Moldavite.

She had also awoken on a number of occasions to about a dozen tranquil smiling faces watching her *through* her ceiling. The genteel beings had blended in perfectly with the color of the walls and floated above her—somehow as a part of the house. Ahulani had felt calm as she observed their movements.

Could Moldavite be the answer to help Eric and his parents? It might help her connect with the alternate dimension they were trapped in but releasing them from their prisons would be another matter.

"I am going to need help." She thought of David.

No, not David. Joe was brought to her to help with the case. "I know why we met, but why didn't I get *his* contact info?" She didn't know how soon he would contact her.

Situations, opportunities, or people could come into your life as if destiny itself dropped them into your lap, yet the Universe sometimes wanted you to work toward the end goal.

She turned onto Forest Road 525, heading toward 89A.

Her Mayan guide spoke again. "Joe was brought to you for many reasons."

Minutes later, she saw Joe's truck off the side of the road. He was removing a cooler from the back of his vehicle.

Relief filled Ahulani and she smiled at seeing him. Had Joe pulled off onto the shoulder of the road to wait for her? Did he know she would need him?

Ahulani pulled in behind him. She got out of her car and approached Joe, who pulled a few bottles of water out of the cooler. "Hi," she said. "Long time no see."

Ahulani didn't know where to begin to explain the situation. Joe knew about the case in Peru, but she felt uncomfortable asking for his contact information. He'd only told her that he lived in Phoenix and Flagstaff, not a specific street.

Joe gave her a bottle of water and then grabbed sandwiches from the cooler. "You look like you could use some refreshment. I should have offered you something before I left." He held up two sandwiches—one marked 'egg salad' and the other 'BLT.'

She realized she hadn't had much except a granola bar,

and the smell of bacon made her mouth water. She took the BLT and removed it from the plastic bag.

Joe unwrapped his sandwich from its plastic baggie and took a bite.

The sun hid behind the clouds, creating a cool breeze. Joe opened the passenger door for Ahulani. "We can continue our picnic in here."

She slid in the front seat of his truck and saw a chunk of Moldavite in the center of the dashboard.

Joe noticed her staring at the otherworldly gem and handed it to her. "Beautiful, isn't it?"

She placed the sandwich on the dash. A section of the stone was missing. The remainder of the rock was in a rough U shape. Ahulani's Moldavite had a rounded end about the same size as the chunk missing from Joe's. Intuition nearly pushed her out of Joe's vehicle. She didn't understand why, but she had to go to her car.

"I will be right back." Ahulani placed Joe's Moldavite on the seat, jumped out of the truck, and ran to her car door to look in her backpack. The front pocket of her bag bulged. She unzipped it and saw her Moldavite.

I don't remember packing this. Weird...

She went to his truck, sat on the edge of the seat, and then placed the two stones together.

Joe's usual demeanor changed from concentrated, purposeful intensity to utter shock. He stared at the two sections of Moldavite with disbelief.

Joe was a powerful, highly intuitive individual, yet the Universe had kept a secret from him regarding their real purpose for meeting.

Chapter Nine

David didn't understand why he was still stuck at Kuelap Citadel. Located in the northeastern Peruvian region of Amazonas, the fortress had thrived from about 1000 A.D. to 1450. He imagined the stone homes as they were in the magnificence of the Chachapoyan era— once covered by cone-shaped, grass-thatched roofs and decorated with triangular architectural friezes circling the bottom of the structure.

A llama roamed among the prehistoric remains, occasionally glancing at David.

"I don't suppose *you* could tell me how people are disappearing?" David asked.

The gentle beast stared at David. Or rather, it watched something behind him. Then, the llama ran in the opposite direction, and David slowly turned to face the unknown.

A dark mass waited between two stone houses. Nearly human-shaped but without arms, the thing seemed to be observing David. It bulged and grew in height until any human similarity was nonexistent.

He took a few steps backward, unsure if it would attack him. He'd never encountered anything like it before during his research years ago at Kuelap, nor anywhere else. Could the frightening entity be associated with David's soul journey?

The blob shape-shifted again into a human figure and vanished.

In its place, David saw a wavering light effect about twenty feet off the ground. Almost the size of a theater screen, it began to show an image. David gazed up at the bizarre movie.

70

Brilliant azure waters hovered above the ruins. The swoosh of mildly choppy waters could be heard, and he felt a slight breeze ruffle his hair.

The scene shifted to unique rock formations. David felt drawn into the realistic, vivid landscape of sapphire, turquoise, and seafoam green. The sound of footsteps came from behind him.

He turned to look—nothing. When he glanced back at the light, the re-creation of Marble Caves had disappeared.

It was as if he were traveling backward through a tunnel at breakneck speed, away from the clouds, away from the ancient fortress. Seconds, no, minutes later, he couldn't be sure, he was back inside his car, flute in hand. He'd traveled to other locations spiritually by playing his pan flute, but never had it seemed so real. The other experiences had been mere deep meditations.

The rain in Flagstaff had stopped, and the sun was shining through the pines. David's phone stuck out of his backpack, and he saw the time.

"It can't be," he whispered. The display read 3:40 P.M. He recalled looking at his watch before he ran to his car at 12:45 P.M. Over two hours lost.

David noticed two calls had come in. The first was his sister who had called while he was wandering Elden Pueblo. The second number was all nines. *Odd.*

He listened to the message from Shelly. Something about upcoming pow-wows that she and Larry would be competing in. Ten seconds of silence filled the next message.

The strange call that came in from the repeating nine number happened when he was at Kuelap. Could it be a warning? Had Ahulani received a similar call? Though worried, David didn't have her number to call and check on her.

He decided to head to Shelly's house in Oak Creek, and then visit Ahulani.

He drove out of the parking lot and headed down 89A to Highway I-17. The feeling inside his car became charged.

His breath fogged the windshield, and it became very cold.

Did something come back with me?

The seat next to him looked empty, yet a sense of dread overcame David.

Imagining himself protected by light and love, David spoke to the visitor. "I am asking you to leave. You are not welcome."

He turned on the heat and it became colder. He considered whether it was safe to get on the freeway with the potential danger in his vehicle. The on-ramp to I-40 was only a quarter mile away, but he didn't know what was happening. David didn't want to risk his life, or anyone else's, by becoming distracted at seventy miles per hour.

The black mass he had seen at Kuelap did not serve a good purpose, and it could have followed him from the Andes. He pulled off into a gas station, got out of the car, and went into the mini mart to use the restroom.

A few minutes later, he returned to his vehicle and opened the door. The atmosphere in the car seemed normal.

David said a prayer, slid into the driver's seat, and started the engine. He turned onto the ramp to the freeway and quickly sped up to seventy miles per hour.

He glanced at the passenger seat and grimaced. A dark entity formed.

David cranked up the heat to account for the dropping temperature. "I do not fear you, and I will not let you harm me."

The mysterious form seemed to twist its body, as if to look at him. There was no eyes, nose, or mouth, but when his car performed a 360 turn on its own accord and faced oncoming traffic, David closed his eyes and made one last desperate prayer.

Can this be happening again?

Chapter Ten

Ahulani gazed at the connected Moldavite stones in disbelief. "This can't be," she whispered. She looked at Joe. "What are the odds?"

They fit perfectly. The two had been one—hundreds, perhaps thousands of years prior. She'd never know. Did the Universe have plans on reuniting the precious gemstones? And on bringing her and Joe together? Coincidence was one thing—this was pure fate.

When the two stones had merged, a disturbing vision made her drop them on her lap.

With her eyes still open, she saw David driving his car, getting onto the freeway; she saw the sign for I-40. He'd told her he was spending time at Elden Pueblo and she figured he was heading to his sister's place. She watched as David glanced at something in the passenger seat before his car spun out of control. The look of terror on his face nearly made her heart stop.

Joe grabbed her hand. "What's wrong?"

She closed her eyes in the hopes of seeing what happened more clearly, but the vision was gone.

Ahulani stared at Joe, emotion filling her voice. "He brought something back from Kuelap."

Joe reached over and took the stones from her, placing them between them on the seat. "Are you talking about your male friend who you saw in Peru?"

Ahulani nodded, a lump forming in her throat, and went to open the car door. "I have to go. I saw his car going the wrong way on I-40."

Joe placed his hand on her arm. "Wait, Lani. Did you see him crash?"

"No, it could be a future event. David was at Elden Pueblo."

"Your car will be safe here. I can contact the police to find out what's happened. We can head to that section of I-40, where the exit for Elden Pueblo is."

"You don't have to do this. It's not that far," Ahulani said. "I can go alone."

Joe started his vehicle. "Of course not. I want to help." He glanced back through the rearview window to check for traffic and pulled onto the road. "There are a number of reasons we were supposed to meet, and this is one of them."

Ahulani watched Joe. His hands were firmly on either side of the steering wheel, his face curious and concerned at the same time.

"Joe, you know something. What is it?"

No response. He watched the road intently. She wondered if she should contact Shelly, but Ahulani didn't have her number. She felt guilty about David's possible tragedy. If he hadn't found her at Kuelap, he might not be in danger. She prayed he was safe.

Every second felt like an hour. Joe wound his way through the dirt road leading back to 89A. It would take a while to get to the interstate once they were on 89.

"I'll call the police in Flagstaff." Joe pushed a few buttons on his dashboard screen, then came a dial tone.

"My name is Joe Luna with the FBI, and I am calling about a possible accident reported on I-40 near 89A, near the exit for Elden Pueblo and Sunset Crater Wupatki. A young man named David was heading south toward Phoenix."

Ahulani waited anxiously while Joe listened for an answer.

Joe sighed impatiently. "I will wait. I have a young lady here who knows this person, and she's very concerned."

A few minutes later, he glanced at Ahulani. "There are no reports of any accidents in that area."

74

A bright orange and black Gila monster lie on a slanted boulder by the side of the road. The foot-long lizard watched Joe's truck as it passed, its dark-colored lips and head cocked to the side, as if curious and intuitive to Ahulani's thoughts.

She felt relieved, yet anxious.

Joe placed his hand on hers. "I'll drive onto Interstate 40 heading toward Albuquerque. Maybe there's a way to prevent the crash, if that's what's going to happen. Your visit to Kuelap might have you a little on edge, which probably caused the vision."

Ahulani watched the road ahead. "I hope so." She had been fearful of letting David get too close. Now she might never be able to get to know him. The red rock vistas passed by at about sixty miles per hour—faster than the speed limit for the forest road.

Ahulani's vision had revealed a brief glimpse of David glancing over nervously at something in his passenger seat. Had that something attempted to kill him?

"How close are you and David?" Joe asked.

"I met him on an investigation at Petrified Forest last week. He works as a park ranger there."

Joe turned left onto 89A and sped through town.

Ahulani closed her eyes and breathed in deeply. She picked up the two chunks of Moldavite, feeling their smooth surfaces in her hand. She envisioned David when she had first met him at Petrified Forest—in his ranger uniform and curious to her purpose at the park. She hoped thinking back in time to their meeting would prevent such a nasty crash.

"Lani, Lani! Look!"

Her eyes flew open. Time had sped by and Joe had arrived on Interstate 40. He had already turned around and was heading back toward Phoenix.

She saw a semi-truck pulled off the side of the road. The cab was a large black sleeper with a striking pink and purple stripe on the side; it looked to be a privately-owned truck. There were three cars and a small truck parked on the same side of the road as the semi. About seven or eight people surrounded another vehicle in front of the semi.

Joe braked his vehicle. Ahulani opened the passenger door before Joe's truck came to a complete stop.

He attempted to grab her, but he was too slow. Emergency vehicles wined and groaned somewhere among the pine forests of Flagstaff, drawing near.

She raced toward the car in front of the semi and could hear Joe's footsteps coming up fast behind her.

The crowd of people turned to look as she approached.

"Ahulani, what are you doing here?"

David stood in front of his car.

A couple stood next to him; a tall cowboy with long dark hair, who appeared to be Native American, had his hand on David's shoulder and his other hand on a petite blonde woman's shoulder. The woman's face was splotchy, her eyes moist and red.

Ahulani's focus went from David—healthy and unharmed—to his car. The only recognizable thing was the light tan color. The vehicle itself was totaled. She placed her hand on the driver's door and looked inside. There was barely enough room for her to see through to the other side of the car.

Joe put his arm around Ahulani's shoulder and squeezed.

Ahulani wanted to say something but didn't know where to start.

Dropping his arm off of Ahulani, Joe gestured to David to come toward them. "Are you okay?" Joe asked. "I think you should sit until help arrives."

"No, I am fine, thanks. I called my sister to come get me," David said.

Ahulani could see David's body was trembling. He looked okay but she suspected he needed to get to the hospital to check for injuries.

David glanced at Joe, then at Ahulani and back to Joe.

"Ahulani and I met this morning," Joe said.

"I...I had a vision on the way home from Palatki Ruins," Ahulani said. She couldn't take her eyes off his vehicle.

"I was concerned..."

Joe looked at the couple for explanation. "What happened?"

The man hugged the blonde woman. "My wife and I were heading into Flagstaff for a bite to eat." The cowboy looked at David. "This young man's car suddenly did a 360 right in front of us. My wife was driving and couldn't stop. Not sure if he was on the phone or was distracted. Anyway, he was climbing out of the vehicle before we could get to him."

"I did call the police," the blonde woman glanced to the freeway. "I thought they would be here by now."

David shook his head slowly back and forth. He didn't take his eyes off Ahulani. "I wasn't on the phone."

His delayed response to the cowboy's comment meant he could be in shock, whether from the accident itself or the fact that Ahulani was there, she didn't know. Perhaps, both.

A few people from the crowd walked away.

One short, rotund woman with tattoos up and down one arm glanced at David. "Not sure what the hell happened, but you have some sort of purpose on this planet." She walked to a small blue truck, opened the door, got in quickly, then drove onto the freeway.

The other onlookers scattered soon after.

Joe put his hands on David's arms. "Listen, you've been through something pretty major. I think you need to go to the hospital. If you don't want an ambulance, I will take you. You can call your sister and let her know to meet us there."

"I don't believe it." The blonde woman stared in disbelief at her phone. "I took pictures for the police." She looked up at David. "This is how you made it through unscathed."

Ahulani knew what she would see before the woman showed them the image. A human figure bathed in golden light floated above the car, graceful angel wings folded to her chest. Another was in front of David's car with wings outstretched. A white light took up the whole back seat.

"Is there any damage to your semi-truck?" Joe asked the man, then glanced back at David and Ahulani.

"Minor, don't worry about it. He said he had insurance and so do we. I'm grateful he wasn't seriously injured." The cowboy looked in David's direction. "Or worse. That's not something my wife or I would want to live with." He glanced at Ahulani and smiled. "Nor would your friend be able to."

Ahulani glanced up in surprise at his comment: *Nor would your friend be able to.*

The cowboy wrote quickly on a piece of paper and handed it to Joe. "I provided my insurance info, but I will give it to you, just in case. And here is my business card."

The man and his wife headed back to their truck.

"Let's get David to the hospital. It's not that far," Joe said.

Ahulani and Joe were walking to Joe's truck with David when they heard a yell.

A large white truck pulled off Interstate 40 as the semi entered the highway traffic. Ahulani recognized Larry at the wheel and Shelly in the driver's seat.

Larry and Shelly jumped out of Larry's truck and ran over to David. David fainted in Larry's arms.

Shelly shouted to Joe and Ahulani. "Follow us to the hospital." Shelly glanced at David's totaled car before getting into the truck's passenger seat.

Shelly swayed as if she, too, would collapse. She grabbed onto the door and managed to climb in.

Joe and Ahulani jumped in Joe's truck. Joe pulled onto the freeway, then took the first exit. They were at the Flagstaff Medical Center within ten minutes.

Joe parked near the entrance to the hospital and Ahulani barely waited for him to pull into a parking spot. She ran inside, hoping to see David. She turned around to see Larry racing into the hospital with David in his arms and Shelly behind. Somehow, Joe had passed them on the way there.

Larry was out of breath and frantic. "My brother-in-law's been in a bad accident. He needs to get checked out."

Within minutes, a gurney came through double doors. David was gently placed on the rolling bed, then a nurse took him into the ER portion of the hospital. The last Ahulani saw of David was his long hair hanging off the gurney. Shelly and Larry followed him inside.

Joe put his arm around her. "At least he walked away. That young man survived something pretty horrific."

She heard a flute playing and realized it was the ring tone to Joe's phone.

"I'll be right back," he said. Joe went through the automatic doors of the lobby. Ahulani could see him talking outside as she sat in a waiting room chair.

A few minutes later, Joe came back into the hospital. He knelt in front of her. "My lovely lady called," he said. "I need to get home, but I'm glad I could help."

"What? Are you married?" Ahulani asked.

"No, not yet. But we have a child that is sick."

Ahulani was surprised. Joe had focused so much on her problems that she hadn't spent much time finding out about him. She'd enjoyed being around him and hoped she would see him again.

He took her hand in his and squeezed it. "I will take you back to your car. I think the family needs some alone time."

She smiled. "Yes, I suppose you're right." She stood up. "I can take a cab back to my car."

"Absolutely not. That would cost a fortune, and though I have no doubt you do well for yourself, I won't have you spending that time with a stranger. I'd be honored."

Ahulani was relieved. His presence felt familiar, comforting. She wanted to spend as much time with him as possible. She stopped by the main desk to let them know she was leaving, in case Shelly and Larry tried to find her.

As she walked with Joe to his truck, she wondered what

might have followed David home from Kuelap. Perhaps David had merely been distracted for a second—just enough to send him careening out of control. What if it had been *her* fault?

Joe pulled away from the hospital's parking lot. "Don't feel bad about the accident." He looked over at her. "You were both at separate ruins in Arizona and I believe that created a common thread. What happened on I-40 might not have had anything to do with your chance meeting in Peru."

"You always seem to know what I'm thinking. How is that?" Ahulani asked.

"Well, this one wasn't difficult to figure out. I'd be feeling guilty about it, too."

Ahulani leaned her head against the seat and closed her eyes. She felt as if she could sleep for days—between her day excursion to Palatki, her spiritual journey to Peru, and the mounting pressure of the Torres case. Not to mention David's terrifying accident. She felt spiritually, emotionally, and physically drained.

She knew she needed to focus on Eric and his parents, yet it was all she could do to stay awake. Somewhere in between reality and dream world, she heard a muffled voice.

"Lani, wake up. We're at your car," Joe said.

Ahulani opened her eyes. Joe had parked behind her car.

"Oh, sorry." She yawned and opened the passenger door. "I guess I nodded off."

"Are you alright to drive? I can take you back to our place, but with Mintaka being sick…"

"No, go. Once I get behind the wheel, I'll be fine. It's not that far."

Joe gave her a card with his name and contact info. "Call me. Things will be fine." He leaned in closer. "For you and for David."

"Thanks, Joe. For everything." She got out of his truck and used her key fob to open her car door.

"Lani, wait!" Joe got out of his truck and handed her the two sections of Moldavite. "Something tells me these will be better off with you."

He gave her a hug, then whispered in her ear. "We'll meet again, I'm sure."

He got back in his truck and waited for her to leave.

She slid into the driver's seat and placed the stones in the center of the dashboard. Once she drove onto the road, he pulled out behind her.

She glanced over to see one of her guides, an Iroquois man from the Northeast United States, in the passenger seat. The well-muscled, six-foot-tall man was unclothed, save for a breechcloth at his waist and animal skin boots that went to his knees. A knife, still in its sheath, hung around his neck and he had streaks of black painted on his chest. Ahulani knew him to be a guide because he had shown himself in her dreams a number of times, though he had never spoken to her.

The Iroquois warrior looked as real to her as Joe had— the 1700s came to mind when he appeared. "You won't need to travel to Kuelap to help the Torres family, but…" His sentence trailed off. The warrior hovered his hand over the Moldavite stones. "You and Joe are both healers and you worked together in a past life. Joe will help you and David."

"He already has," she said, and glanced from the spirit to the road.

The warrior shook his head. "He will help with your case." He placed the Moldavite stones gently back in the center compartment, then vanished into thin air.

Chapter Eleven

Nukpani hid behind a large boulder during the middle of the night. He watched the woman and her mate as they huddled together, sleeping, inside the grotto. The woman didn't know, but Nukpani had been observing her for weeks. He saw her when his tribe had passed through the area of the red rocks, and had decided to stay—waiting for an opportunity.

This woman thought she knew of her true love, but she would change her mind.

The couple stirred when a coyote's lone, haunting howl echoed among the high desert canyons and buttes.

Nukpani had planned on waiting another week to try to get her alone but he didn't want to wait any longer.

He inched out slowly to pick up a round stone a few feet from his hiding place. He grabbed the fist-sized rock and crept on his knees to the side where the man lay and who never saw his fate coming. Nukpani smashed the rock against his head hard.

The woman, who had been sleeping, awakened and saw Nukpani. As she realized what had happened to her lover, she sat up and screamed.

He shoved a piece of deerskin into her mouth, threw a blanket over her head, and half-pulled, half-dragged her from the cave and into the nearby trees.

"I will not harm you," he said.

She glanced toward the cave where her dead lover lay. Nukpani hadn't planned on killing anyone, but he was anxious to get back to his tribe.

He had only killed one other time, months before he joined his current tribe—a woman. She had forced it upon herself by attempting escape. He had told her he would take care of her forever, but she hadn't cared. She should have been grateful.

Instead, she had cried all the time and begged him to let her go back to her tribe. They had only been together three days and nights until he'd snapped her neck while she slept. She had refused to lie down next to him. She hadn't trusted him, and he would not tolerate such behavior. She had been much younger, but this time Nukpani had chosen a woman closer to his own age.

Tears covered his new partner's face, and she was shaking. Her sorrow only made her more beautiful. He didn't care what her name was now—she would change it to "Keegsquaw." All men before him didn't matter. He considered her his virgin, and she would have a new life with him.

Nukpani threw the blanket over Keegsquaw's shoulders and removed the deer skin from her mouth. He hoped she wouldn't try to run. His lack of preparation meant he had nothing to tie her arms with.

"You will come with me," he said. "We must find my people."

Nukpani wasn't sure how the others would accept Keegsquaw. If they knew he had killed before, he would be shunned. He wondered if he and Keegsquaw should try to make it alone. There were some in the tribe who didn't trust him, and it wouldn't take long for them to figure out what he had done.

He heard yelling from the direction of the grotto and turned to see a short man walk into the cave where Keegsquaw and her lover had been sleeping.

A loud yell erupted from the cave and the man came running out.

Keegsquaw started screaming, but Nukpani slapped her hard to quiet her. He grabbed her arm and dragged her further into the forest.

She kept looking back as she was forced to run.

Male and female voices and shouts mingled, footsteps came closer. Keegsquaw kept stopping and tried to escape his grasp.

Angry shouts followed, and he knew he couldn't get away with her in tow. He let go of her arm and ran as fast as he could.

Rapid footsteps encroached from both sides. A man jumped him from the side, tackled him to the ground, and punched him in the face.

"I found her," a man yelled.

"You killed my brother and took Honovi," the man who held him said. "You will be very lucky if we don't feed you to the coyotes."

Two strong men lifted Nukpani off the ground and dragged him past the woman he had hoped would be his. He had killed one of their family members, and he knew he wouldn't make it out alive.

The men threw him into the small cave where he had murdered Honovi's lover. Guards watched the entrance while a group of men talked outside, discussing his fate.

Hysterical sobs came from somewhere nearby, probably Keeqsquaw in her grief for the man he had killed.

Nukpani had never cared when he murdered the first young woman who was supposed to be his wife. And he didn't care about this man. He stood and paced the length of the cave. One of the men posted outside watched him carefully.

Eventually he sat and drifted off to sleep, staring at a white 'X' painted on the cave wall. After a fitful slumber, Nukpani awoke to the sound of drums in the early morning. One man remained as his guard—the short burly fellow who had found the body of Honovi's lover.

He observed Nukpani with rage and disgust. Yet amid the anger, a smile began to erupt. The man knew Nukpani's fate.

The drums stopped. Immediately after, the burly man and the murdered man's brother came in and dragged him out of the cave into the sun. Nukpani squinted from the brilliant rays that flooded the forest with light.

They held him as an elder approached—a slightly hunched man carrying a hand-carved staff with an eagle's head at the top.

The medicine man ripped Nukpani's shirt off with a force he wouldn't have expected. He dipped his fingers into a white chalky substance and painted marks on Nukpani's stomach. He glanced down to see a zigzag symbol on his skin. The elder was in the midst of creating a dark grey rain cloud above the lightning.

Within minutes, the medicine man had finished his scene.

Though he could see no men playing drums, the sound started again, only more pronounced, as he was dragged along a stream.

The two men let him go. "Go now!" the shorter one shouted, and he pointed toward the trees.

Nukpani turned and ran into the forest. They hadn't murdered him, but he had been set up.

He had walked for a few miles when dark clouds began to overcome the sun's glory. Nukpani frantically tried to rub the paint off. It wouldn't smudge.

He plunged into the stream, wiping at his body and rolling in the water.

Finally, he sat up and looked down at his chest. The symbols were brighter. Trees started to sway and whisper in response to a cool breeze. The clouds had joined to form one massive dark sky. Nukpani wrapped his arms around his body to elicit some type of warmth, though it did nothing to help.

They wanted him to suffer.

A loud cracking sound warned him of potential danger above as a gust of wind blew through the forest and threatened to drop branches from the trees. He tried to run amidst the tempest. That's when the rain started— heavy drops that felt like river pebbles.

Explosive thunder lumbered through the atmosphere while a bolt of lightning hit a nearby pine, splitting it in half. The electricity from the strike filled the air and sent tiny shockwaves through his body.

Glancing around in desperation, Nukpani could see no place to hide from Mother Nature's wrath. Or rather, the wrath of man.

The rain soaked his body, and the drops stung his skin. He couldn't stop shaking. The frigid air made it harder to breathe.

A deafening crack split the air as lightning hit another tree. A branch fell in front of him. A bald eagle dove by, then flew up and landed on the largest branch of the tree next to him.

He had never seen an eagle fly that low, unless it was diving for prey.

Nukpani remembered the medicine man's staff.

The large raptor watched Nukpani until a single bolt of lightning penetrated his body—exactly where the symbol had been placed on his stomach.

As he dropped to the ground, the eagle flew off in the direction of the village. Nukpani's last breath came as the drums intensified to a beat that drowned out a thunderous boom—that of the storm—and that of his heart.

David sat up in bed and glanced around, his heart pounding, pulse racing. He was in his room, in his sister's home. Shelly slept in a chair next to him. He barely recalled Larry driving him home from the medical center.

He didn't understand how he knew, but the man in his dream, the killer—Nukpani—had been himself. The woman he abducted, Ahulani.

"Ahulani," he whispered. "I murdered her boyfriend."

Shelly awoke. She leaned forward and placed her hand on David's shoulder. "What's wrong?" she asked.

"That was the most vivid dream I ever had. I was outside the grotto at Palatki Ruins. A couple slept inside, and I was there to take the woman. She was beautiful and had a similar appearance to Ahulani. Only a couple inches taller, darker skin."

He leaned back in bed. "I murdered her husband, boyfriend, not sure. I kidnapped her and dragged her into the forest. But they found me—her people."

Shelly took his hand in hers. "You've been through a lot. Could have been a nightmare due to the trauma of your accident."

David shook his head. "No. Maybe our bizarre meeting at the Kuelap Ruins heightened our connection. I mean, she did show up soon after the crash."

"People do find each other from past lives," Larry said from the doorway. "Shelly and I were told that we had been lovers in a past life. Until I was killed fighting in a battle. I don't recall where this took place, but apparently, I had made a pact to find her again."

Shelly smiled, then took Larry's hand in hers.

"This was horrific." David tossed the blanket aside and threw his legs over the side of the bed. "A medicine man painted a storm symbol on my chest."

He hugged himself, then rubbed his arms. "I was bare chested, freezing. The rain, wind, and lightning all around. I couldn't escape."

Larry sat on the bed next to him, then put his hand on David's back.

David stared at an image of a bald eagle in flight over Stoneman Lake near Flagstaff. He had taken it six months ago. It was one of the best photos he had ever taken. "It watched me die."

Larry followed David's gaze.

David stood up and walked over to the image of the raptor. He had managed to capture an image of the eagle as it looked down in his direction, eyes piercing the landscape below. "A bald eagle. It sat on the limb of a nearby tree and observed as a bolt of lightning struck me down."

David turned to face Larry and Shelly. "I deserved it, though. I murdered Ahulani's lover in a past life, so that I could have her for myself. I think we were meant to be together in this life so that I could make it up to her."

Chapter Twelve

A hulani placed the Moldavite stones on her bookshelf next to the other crystals, then went into her bedroom. It was only 5:00 P.M., but she needed sleep. Too tired to change clothes, she laid down on the bed and closed her eyes.

An explosive cacophony of animal noises surrounded the river she floated on. The chorus became so loud, she had to place her hands over her ears. A monkey leapt from one tree to another and disappeared into the top of the tree closest to the water.

"Amazon," one of her guides whispered.

The pandemonium ceased. Quiet solitude surrounded her. The thick foliage on either side of the river hid a secret. The river narrowed quickly, and Ahulani's boat floated closer to shore, then landed.

She stared into the tropical forest, feeling drawn to the impenetrable growth. She stood up, grabbed onto the side of the boat, then stepped out onto dry land.

She followed a narrow trail along the river and into the forest. A fog rose above the muddy river and penetrated the jungle, becoming mist around her shoulders.

The fog culminated into a tiny, slow-moving tornado and just as quickly dissolved to reveal a perfect open circle in the forest.

The sun had turned the round patch of grass into a brilliant green. As she approached the circle, Ahulani heard a man yelling.

At first, she couldn't understand the words, then the name "Eric" echoed over and over throughout the endless array of trees.

Another voice called for his father. A child?

The man's voice grew more desperate. "Where are you?"

The boy's frantic shouts stopped.

Misty shadows crossed in front of Ahulani and ran into the clearing—some human and some animal. They avoided the direct rays of the sun and ran in circles around the circumference. A spiral staircase made of tree limbs and vines materialized in the circle. Ahulani stared up at it but couldn't see where the bizarre jungle creation ended.

Drawn toward its twisted steps, she climbed for an eternity, unable to see on either side of the staircase. Dizzy from the spiral motion, she pushed on. She had to see where it led. Her life depended on it. Or someone else's?

After what seemed like hours, Ahulani arrived at a platform at the top with huge overhanging branches. She could see how the river wound its way through the jungle. An adult monkey grabbed onto a vine by the tree house platform with its prehensile tail. Cacophony started up again.

The voice of a little boy erupted among the animal noises.

"Dad, it's me!"

The child sounded close. Though the Amazon jungle seemed to be a prison, Ahulani's intuition told her Eric was somewhere else. Far below was the ancient village of Kuelap.

Yet, when she turned to the opposite side of the platform, Ahulani could see the prehistoric city thriving with activity. Llamas, cows, chickens, and other livestock roamed the walled city, along with the villagers.

Could Eric be lost amidst the hustle and bustle of the prehistoric past? Had her guides brought her here to see where Eric and his parents had been lost?

She had the ability, as other intuitives did, to help move the deceased on to a higher plane while dreaming. Was she being guided to find Eric and his parents among the mysteries of her dreams? Worlds, portals, and dimensions were colliding. Could they already be dead?

She imagined Kuelap, focused on the house with the

bear fetish, with all her hope of traveling there to find the Torres family.

She glanced around her, wondering if any of her guides would appear.

"Come on, you brought me to this frickin' jungle. Help me find them!"

Before her eyes, the Pre-Columbian city transformed from the thriving town center with cone-shaped dwellings to a lost city of collapsed structures, roaming llamas, and phantom memories.

Ahulani spotted her boat by the narrow river channel. Nearby, a black jaguar lay by a massive tree next to the water.

Is there another purpose to this dream?

As the thought crossed her mind, everything faded into the trees, vines, and sunlight.

Ahulani awoke and looked at the alarm clock on her bedside table—7:15 A.M. She had slept for over twelve hours.

She got out of bed, stretched, and undressed out of the previous day's clothes. Stepping into the shower, she thought over her plans for the day. She wanted to visit Shelly to see how David was doing.

After a fast, hot shower, Ahulani put on jeans and a light sweater. She pulled her hair into a ponytail and grabbed her house keys. During the quarter mile walk to his sister's home, she felt eyes watching her.

"Who's there?" she whispered.

She turned to see the medicine woman standing behind her.

"Not again," Ahulani said.

The healer from Petrified Forest looked as if she could barely stand. The cane shook with her weight and her body trembled uncontrollably.

Ahulani moved toward her, but the elderly woman vanished almost as quickly as she had appeared.

Ahulani threw her hands up. The woman's repeated appearances brought more questions—whether about the Torres family or the mystery of the Native woman who had been murdered among the ruins in Blue Mesa, she couldn't be sure.

She jogged the rest of the way there and waited a moment to catch her breath before she knocked on Shelly's door. Pots and pans clanged, and she could hear Larry and Shelly talking inside.

A few seconds later, Larry opened the door.

"Hey, there! We wondered what had happened to you and Joe," Larry said, and stepped aside to let her in.

Ahulani wiped her feet on the doormat decorated with sunflowers. An expansive kitchen with island was to the right. The kitchen opened to a large living room with a cultural theme of pow-wow, Native American art, and scenic pictures of Sedona, Oak Creek Canyon, and other spectacular locations. A giant picture above the couch displayed the Grande Falls on the Navajo Nation in the Painted Desert. Fed by snowmelt and rain from the White Mountains, it was a site to behold. Whoever had taken the picture had managed to capture a rainbow above the falls.

"Joe received a phone call from his girlfriend," she said. "Their daughter was sick, so he had to head home. I figured you'd want time alone with David."

"Did someone say my name?" he asked.

Not far from the entrance, David sat in the living room on the sofa but tried to get up when he saw Ahulani.

She approached and put her hand up to prevent him from standing. "I thought you might still be in the hospital, at least overnight."

"Thanks for coming. He was insistent on recuperating here," Shelly said from the kitchen doorway. "The doctor gave the okay." She gave Ahulani a hug, then went into the kitchen. "Getting ready to fix breakfast. You should stay."

Larry gestured to a spot on the couch for her to sit. "No doubt he'll get more rest here." He went into the kitchen with Shelly.

Ahulani sat on the sofa, leaving a space next to David. Normally in a ponytail, his hair was loose and damp.

She must have been staring at him, because she felt his eyes on her.

She blushed. "How are you feeling?"

"Sore, but no issues," David said, smiling at her. "I had all sorts of tests done yesterday and everything is fine."

"Talk about a miracle," Larry said. "I can't believe he walked away from that wreck."

She shook her head. "Me, either."

Taking her eyes off David for a moment, she looked at the Native American paintings and regalia that adorned the walls. One was a massive picture of a group of Native warriors riding on horses. The table in front of the couch was the replica of a large pow-wow drum.

She wanted to ask what had distracted David on the freeway, but she already knew. "Are you taking time off from work?"

David nodded his head. "I'll have to borrow Shelly's car or Larry's truck when I am ready to return. I'm still waiting on the insurance claim."

Ahulani smelled waffle or pancake batter—a breakfast treat she hadn't had in years.

"We're fixing a big breakfast to celebrate David's miracle." Shelly removed a carton of eggs from the refrigerator and placed them next to the stove. "Homemade waffles, eggs, bacon, and sourdough toast."

Her stomach growled, impatient for sustenance. She'd left home without even eating a granola bar.

"Sounds amazing, Shelly. Though, I really should get home and see what I can do about the Torres family."

Ahulani planned on using the Moldavite to see if she could get answers about Eric or his parents. According to her Iroquois guide, the stones would be helpful for remote travel.

David leaned forward on the sofa. "Who is Joe?"

From the kitchen doorway, Shelly and Larry glanced at each other, then at Ahulani, then returned to their duties in the kitchen. "He seems nice," Shelly said.

"We met yesterday, at Palatki Ruins. He's a medicine man."

David looked away and stroked a section of his long hair.

"I think he can help me with this case," Ahulani said. She thought back to their initial meeting at the cave grotto. Joe had also picked up on the Sinaguan spirit, and about her relationship with David.

David leaned back into the cushions. He looked at Ahulani and smiled. "I was surprised to see you at the site of the wreck. I mean, I know you're gifted, but I didn't think you'd pick up on something like that."

"Yeah, I saw a vision of your car out of control while I held some Moldavite."

"Funny." David got up slowly and stood, looking out the patio doors. "I had a dream about some green stones. You had one and Joe had the other. Then, I saw both stones coming together."

Ahulani was surprised that David had picked up on the reuniting of two high energy gemstones, especially after such a traumatic event.

"Well, Joe gifted me with his after we left the ruins. I remembered I had mine in the car, so I went to get it. When I looked at both stones together, I knew they would be a perfect fit. My guides told me Joe and I were meant to meet to help find Eric and his parents."

Ahulani glanced to where Shelly and Larry still stood in the kitchen, to David. He continued to stare out at the back yard.

"I heard they are powerful healing stones," Larry said. "It has a high frequency, a stone of greatness formed from meteor impacts."

"Yes, that's right." Ahulani smiled. She was impressed about Larry's knowledge of Moldavite.

Tongs met pan, and the bacon began to sizzle as Larry fried it.

"Correct me if I'm wrong, but aren't those stones found only in Czechoslovakia?" Larry asked.

Shelly glanced at him and grinned, taking the tongs. "Yes."

A shadowy figure rose out of the floor behind David, like a flower sprouting from the hard wood surface.

Ahulani saw two eyes, darker than its misty body, stare at her. She stood up slowly and it backed away. She hoped it would vanish before frightening the family.

"Moldavite is named for the area in which it is found, near the Moldau River. Most scientists agree its formation coincides with the crash of a large meteorite nearly fifteen million years ago," she explained.

She heard something drop to the ground and turned her head. Larry stared at the figure with disdain.

David quickly spun around. As he did so, the shadow entered David's body with a force that knocked his head and body against the glass doors, then to the ground.

Ahulani ran toward David.

He moaned in pain. Then, he opened his eyes. As he did so, Ahulani saw they were as black and void as the universe.

"It's back, and it's going to kill me," he said.

She looked up at Larry and Shelly standing behind her. "We need Joe."

Chapter Thirteen

David felt a hand on his forehead, followed by a mild warmth. The intensity increased as two hands progressed to David's feet. He opened his eyes. Shelly and Larry were on one side of his bed, and Ahulani and Joe on the other. The medicine woman stood in the corner of the room by the window. A golden aura surrounded her, and she smiled warmly as the hands worked their magic. She looked younger than at Elden Pueblo and as beautiful as ever.

Joe's hands hovered above David's legs.

"Just relax. I am performing energy work," he said.

David breathed in deeply of an earthy, overpowering scent—sage. The last thing he remembered was the force of something slamming into his body.

"Where is it?" David asked.

Joe and Ahulani looked at each other.

"It's still inside me. I can feel it." David didn't want to look at Ahulani. What had he said and done while being overtaken by the entity?

"David." Shelly placed her hand on his arm. "I told Ahulani and Joe about your experiences years ago, with that malevolent entity. We think your energy during the visitation with your pan flute might have reconnected you to that damn thing. Or maybe, you picked up something new."

David held Shelly's hand in his. "I felt it next to me, in the car. After the crash, I hoped, prayed that it would be gone when it realized that I had a strong force to protect me."

"Has this entity taken you over before?" Joe took two chunks of Moldavite and placed them on David's chest.

"Not that I remember. It was more like a poltergeist, making things disappear, causing chaos with the family. I saw it in the seat next to me when the car went out of control on I-40."

The medicine woman remained in the corner. Her eyes were closed, as if meditating.

David looked at Larry, then Ahulani. "Do you see her in the corner?"

Larry followed David's gaze. "Who?"

"It's her," Ahulani said. "The elderly spirit from the Painted Forest. But she doesn't look so good."

"She's beautiful, like an angel." David couldn't take his eyes off her. He glanced from the medicine woman to Ahulani. "So do you."

Flustered, Ahulani turned her face in the other direction. "Thanks."

"You and Ahulani are seeing her quite differently. Not sure if that's her intent or because of your outlook on life right now," Joe said.

David asked Joe, "Do you see her?"

"No, but I sense her energy. She was a force to be reckoned with in her day. She's rather enamored with you and Ahulani."

A knife twisted inside him causing David to sit up and scream in pain.

Shelly let go of his hand and placed her arm around David's shoulders. "What's happening to him?"

"The entity is fighting like hell to stay inside him," Joe said. "Ahulani, get the sage stick and run it over David's body."

Joe stared at Shelly and Larry. "I need you both to help David lay still. Hold him down if you have to."

David couldn't think. He wanted the excruciating pain to stop. "I can't."

Larry gently guided David's head onto a pillow while Shelly held his shoulder and arm down.

Ahulani went to the other side of the bed and placed the smoking sage stick at his head. She moved it slowly over the length of his body.

The pain made it hard to stay still. David attempted to sit up but was held in place.

Joe closed his eyes and began to speak in hushed tones.

A minute later, the agony went from a ten to a five. As Joe continued to pray and heal, David could see an eagle above the man's head. Maybe it was his animal totem.

The entity inside of David fought hard against the positive energy directed at David. He could feel more positive energy being directed to him from Ahulani and the medicine woman.

The pain level went above a ten. David threw his head back and screamed. His intestines felt like they were being ripped apart.

"No," David yelled. "You can't have me."

Ahulani placed her hand over David's heart. The pain level dropped to a three.

"Keep fighting, David," Larry said. "Joe's a phenomenal healer. I've heard stories of what this guy can do."

Ahulani looked at Larry, but it was clear her focus was on David. She left her hand above David's heart, while she continued to cast sage over his upper body.

His strength waned, but David continued to fight it internally. He watched Ahulani and felt pure love—a love he hoped would fight this being. He could tell Ahulani had been hurt before, and he would give her time.

The medicine woman opened her eyes and approached his bed. She stood next to Ahulani. "You're safe," the medicine woman said. "You are too strong. Being inside your body will kill this beast. Your power animal is working hard for you."

What power animal?

David saw a large black bear standing at the end of the bed on its hind legs.

Bear. I've seen a bear recently. Where?

He couldn't remember.

The evil specter held firm. Every muscle tightened in David's body. For a few seconds, it felt like he would implode. David tried to scream in pain but couldn't.

"Keep thinking of her," the healer said and glanced at Ahulani. "You will have a happy life together."

David watched Ahulani as she continued to hold her hand above his body.

He had never wanted anyone so much.

Ahulani approached the top of his bed. She stroked the top of his head while he held tightly to his stomach. If he could have moved, David would have grabbed her hand.

That single action stirred something in him. He wanted to get better so he could spend the rest of his life with her.

He heard Shelly talking, but the words were garbled.

David imagined his bear consuming the entity, tearing it apart. The horrible phantom beat up on him from the inside. Could it be trying to escape from the merciless brutality of the bear?

He glanced up at the medicine woman again, pain distorting his face.

"It is almost done," she whispered. "Joe and your power animal have destroyed the entity."

Finally, David felt at peace. Anxious faces surrounded him.

Exhausted, his body relaxed. He could barely keep his eyes open.

"How are you feeling?" Joe asked.

"Much better," David whispered.

As he closed his eyes to fall asleep, an angel floated above him. "Ahulani has sent Archangel Michael to you."

The words of the medicine woman lingered in the air as she vanished.

Ahulani looked to David, then she leaned down and kissed him on the lips.

Am I dreaming?

Chapter Fourteen

Ahulani looked through her sliding glass doors. It was early morning, and three hummingbirds flittered around her feeder while a deer bounded through the back yard.

She'd awoken to a new reality the day after David suffered at the hands of the entity. Her soul was dying. She had been denying relationships, denying love, and denying her true persona. It showed in her perception of the ancient spirit.

It made sense David was seeing the medicine woman in a positive light. David was a happy person who appreciated life, his family, music, and everything around him. Ahulani had been more focused on herself and her pursuits. Her ex-husband had only been *part* of the reason for her psychological transition. Internet technology, including the use of online dating sites made it easier for him to cheat. It seemed the majority of relationships were temporary. People didn't want to commit. Emotional baggage was a heavy burden, and for most, it was a lifelong friend. She had repeatedly seen firsthand the damage done by not only childhood trauma, but past life trauma.

The night before the entity took over David, she had dreamt of Eric in the Amazon jungle and heard his father yelling for him. She hadn't been able to determine where they were or how she would be able to help.

The hummingbirds took off. Movement through the brush caught her attention. Something big and black moved through the trees.

I can't be seeing this.

A black jaguar approached the back of her house stealthily. The animals resided in South and Central America, particularly the Amazon basin. It walked up to within a foot of her glass doors and sat down, watching her. The jaguar, with its dark eyes, sleek look, and cryptic air reminded her of the dark-haired mystery man.

"Let me in." The words came in a barely audible whisper. *How could she be hearing this thing talk?*

The voice of her Mayan spirit guide spoke to her. "You will be safe."

Ahulani opened the sliding doors.

The creature stepped into the house and circled her living room. She followed it as it walked down the hallway leading to the bedrooms. The beast explored each room, came back down the hallway, and sat in the center of her living room completely still, watching her.

Am I dreaming?

She heard the word *shapeshifter* whispered from one of her female guides. "You are the man that visited me here last week, the one that was in my car at Palatki."

The jaguar transformed into the striking enigmatic man within seconds. He smiled at her jaw-dropping reaction and then turned back into the jaguar.

It took Ahulani a minute to regain her composure. She sat down on the couch. "What is your name? Why are you here?"

It spoke in the same voice as that of the man, but without opening its mouth. "Bahlam. I am a jaguar god—a supernatural being of the underworld who protected the Mayan people. I know of the power of the bear."

"About the fetish in the stone house at Kuelap?" Ahulani asked. She wanted to laugh out loud. She was talking to a big cat, a carnivore that sat calmly inside her home.

"Yes. As you and David discovered, it is recent, or rather the deceitful magic implanted on it is recent. The fetish has been there for centuries."

"You know who is responsible for the disappearances?

There are other victims, aren't there?"

The jaguar god looked down at the floor. "No one knows who placed the magic in the ruins. And yes, there have been others—though the last one was a tourist, a young lady who was alone and happened upon the house. Her guides tried to warn her. A couple of the ancient Chachapoyan spirits tried warning her also, but she could not see them."

Ahulani used to struggle with the difficulties of having the deceased come to her day or night. She would wonder why she had been chosen to relay messages from the deceased. It made her unique and susceptible to childhood torture. Now she felt bad for those who couldn't.

"That's horrible. Can any of these people be saved?"

"There is still hope." The black creature walked closer. "But not for long."

Ahulani stared at a few gemstones on the table by her couch. Celestite, prehnite, angelite, and apophylite—all used for spirit and angel communication. "I had a dream about Eric in the Amazon."

Bahlam laid down on the floor in front of Ahulani. "Eric has a fascination with animals and cultures in Central and South America. The boy is highly intelligent and is an old soul. He has had many past lives, mostly in South America. The maturity of this child is unheard of at such a young age. He is destined to be a great leader."

Ahulani rubbed her temples. "So, this mystical bear fetish…it sends people to those places they have ties to?"

"Past life ties, yes. That can include other worlds or places that look similar to where they resided in their past lives."

Ahulani shuddered to think of the locations the victims were being exposed to. Were some of these places livable? What were the conditions? How long had the travelers been gone and were they still alive?

"What about Eric's parents?" she asked. "Did they have a past life together in Chiclayo? James stated he and his wife are in a place that looks like where they live now, but there was no one else around. Plus, Kuelap was floating above them."

The large cat licked its front paws. "They have a great love for the town of Chiclayo, and they have had a past life together in Kuelap. That is what drew them both to the area. James and his wife are highly-regarded professors. Amazing individuals. They could be in between dimensions, caught in their past life, or perhaps both."

Ahulani took the angelite and held it tight in her palm. She loved the soft blue color of the stone. "Interdimensional travel could explain why they are seeing two different places at once." She looked at the jaguar. "I could hear Eric and his father yelling for each other. Is Eric in the Amazon, lost and alone?"

"Eric is separated from his parents, yes. The jungle you saw in your vision is not truly what is there."

Ahulani turned the angelite over in her fingers. "That seems odd. I'm not sure why I would be able to hear Eric's father calling for him if they are in different places."

"You could have heard a residual imprint from right after his parents vanished from the hilltop fortress. For a brief few seconds, his parents were able to see Eric and tried to reach him."

Bahlam got up, circled around the living room, then looked at a bowl of gemstones on her bookshelf. "David can help. Thanks to the evil entity, he has realized who his power animal is. His abilities can help them all get back to their original whereabouts."

While she had saged David, Ahulani had seen a bear at the end of his bed. She'd seen it again above his head before he fell asleep. "His spirit animal. Why didn't I think of that?"

The jaguar didn't respond.

"If you are a god, can't *you* help?" she asked, her eyes seeking his.

"That's why I am here, why I drew you into the Marble Caves to help you remember one of your past lives, call upon your strengths. You and David must work together to save the victims. I may be a god, but I am a representation of your past. How will you learn or grow if I lay out a path, inform you of the steps? The Universe hasn't provided access to all the answers on this situation—even for me. Do you expect your spirit guides or angels to hold your hand?"

"Of course not." Ahulani threw up her hands. "What happens if we can't figure this out?"

"I *know* you will be able to solve this, Ahulani. You are a savior."

Bahlam turned toward the table in front of the couch. His dark eyes inspected the clear quartz arrowhead the medicine woman had left in Ahulani's house.

"That was sort of a gift," Ahulani said.

Bahlam turned to face her. "That is more than a present. It is a powerful tool for crossing into other dimensions. There are only three in the world."

Ahulani picked up the arrowhead.

"Look closer at the tip."

Ahulani peered at the inside of the clear quartz object. A 3-D spiral had been etched into it. She wondered how an artist could have created such a piece.

A flash of light burst through from the inside of the arrowhead. "Where did you get that?" Bahlam asked.

A strange energy began to emit from the arrowhead. "From an ancient healer in the Petrified Forest. She has been visiting David and me."

"Healers are the holders, though they normally aren't ghosts, and arrowheads aren't passed on to anyone."

Bahlam transformed into a man so quickly, the animal and human forms blurred.

How had the medicine woman obtained such an object? If it assisted in crossing between dimensions, then maybe she could use to help Eric, his parents, and the others.

"She gave it to you because she knew who you once were. That arrowhead was made by omnipotent people who integrated magic into it—magic to help. Many tools can be used for both good and bad." Bahlam took the arrowhead from Ahulani. He stared into the clear quartz as if extracting its secrets. "This can only be used to protect."

"What happens if someone with negative intent tries to use the arrowhead?"

"Ahh...but that's part of the magic. It can see into their soul and will not work." The jaguar grinned a toothy smile.

"Knowing what I do now, why did you cause me such pain when I first saw you here?" she asked.

"I didn't harm you. The orb was created by you through memories and burdens—of this life and others. It was carried forward when you awoke from your travels. You and I have been very close in a past life, which I believe you detected in your dream. You were a strong healer once—during your past life with me. You relied on my animal prowess to help you."

She glanced at her phone. "Eric's father called again. I can't imagine how that's possible, especially if they really are in another dimension."

She pressed the *call* button on her phone. It rang once, then went dead.

Bahlam took the device from her. "They wouldn't be able to connect with anyone by telephone from where they are. I'm not sure."

"Perhaps, it was the arrowhead that allowed him to connect with me," Ahulani said. "Especially if it enables communication between dimensions."

"It's possible."

"I am not sure I could get to these places where Eric and his parents are. How can you travel to a place that doesn't exist on the earthly plane? I can't drive or take a plane. How will I be able to get all of the victims back home?"

Bahlam paced slowly around the living room, opening and closing the plantation shutters repeatedly with his paws. "You traveled to Kuelap without trying. Interdimensional travel is easier than humans realize.

It's a matter of tapping into places of energy, such as portals, ley lines, or vortexes. The energy of Palatki probably helped, but you've always had the ability to travel in such a manner. There are dimensions visible on Earth, but the majority of humans don't have the perception."

Her phone buzzed, and Ahulani noticed a text message from Joe.

Mintaka wanted me to tell you she is watching over Eric.

She texted Joe back.

Who is Mintaka?

A star child who used to live on Earth. She has returned home—to her true self.

Ahulani glanced up at the spot she had last seen the massive jaguar, but he was gone.

"Bahlam?" She quickly went through her house, but he had left.

She heard the voice of a male spirit guide. "Don't worry. You will see him again."

Chapter Fifteen

Ahulani sat on a fallen sycamore tree by the stream near her home. The clear, bubbling water polished river rocks, creating abstract art in colors of red, brown, tan, and more. The gentle trickling stream, whispering leaves, and birdsong were energizing and helped open her mind and spirit.

David was doing well—a miracle, considering his car had been mangled by a semi days before and he had been invaded by an evil shadow entity.

The mystery investigation was by far the most complicated of her career. She not only had to find three lost victims, but she needed to figure out how to prevent the same thing from happening to other visitors at Kuelap. Ahulani had attempted to contact the police in Chachapoyas, but no one would take or return her calls. Ahulani wasn't surprised. She was a psychic investigator and her viewpoint was but a joke. She'd contacted a few tour guides local to the region—they both mentioned that Kuelap was still taking tourists. Attempted warnings from Ahulani to avoid entry to that particular ancient structure went unheeded, so she performed a ritual with the South American stones. She connected with some of the local phantoms and asked if they could help prevent visitors from entering the ruin with the bear fetish. Her goal was to get any tourists to completely pass it by. She hoped her energy and that of the indigenous spirits would prevent any further disasters until the case was solved.

She closed her eyes and absorbed her surroundings.

Bahlam's visit had been shocking, but she was grateful the jaguar god was on her side. She had known about some of her past lives, including those of a healer in Lemuria and a Mayan high priestess, but had never dreamt or heard from her spirit guides of a past life in Patagonia, Chile.

Not that it was surprising. Most people had many past lives, yet never realized how many of their own spirit guides were associated with them through those past lives.

Ahulani heard the sound of a cell phone ringing from somewhere. The ringtone sounded like her own, though she had forgotten to bring her phone with her.

It rang a third time, and she looked down at the ground beside her. Her phone lay on a tiny pile of leaves. Staring at it in amazement, she picked it up on the fourth ring.

"This is Ahulani," she said, answering the call.

"I am so glad I got through to you," Tabitha said.

She wished she had good news for the friend of the Torres family. "Is everything all right? Is your daughter feeling better?"

"Joy is still sick, but it's not the cold or flu. We're not sure what is making her ill."

A dark cloud passed over the sun, cooling the air and making her shiver. Something had told her from the second Tabitha mentioned the illness that it wasn't typical. "I'm sorry. What's going on?"

"I'm not sure. She has been having dreams of Eric and his parents."

Ahulani realized Joy could have psychic abilities. Or perhaps she was sensitive to her mother's worry over the Torres family.

The somber cloud held the sun captive. "Does she remember the dreams?" Ahulani asked.

"Yes. She describes them for me. They are vivid and disturbing."

Ahulani stood and walked alongside the stream. "Did she see Eric in a jungle by chance?"

"No, but she heard the family all yelling for each other. Joy has never met them, only seen pictures. She said she saw James briefly amid some sort of mist. He looked terrified, and she could feel her heart racing during the dream. I thought I was going to have to take her to the hospital because her pulse was so high."

"Your daughter must have been picking up on James's fear. Our pulses can race faster during times of fear."

"Joy couldn't tell where she was, but she heard a piercing scream right before she woke up."

Ahulani needed to call Joe. Maybe he would be able to help her interpret Joy's dream. Intuition told her the ancient medicine woman was helping her also by leaving the arrowhead with her. What would Bahlam's part be? Thinking of jaguar god, she shared what she could with Tabitha.

"Your friends aren't the only victims. A portal was placed into that stone house where they disappeared, and I believe there are other victims."

"That's horrible, Ahulani. I haven't been able to sleep knowing they could be in real danger."

Ahulani pursed her lips together. *I hope I can get them home safe.*

"I will begin performing long distance energy healing on Joy. There's obviously some sort of connection to the Torres family. Your stress could be causing more of a spiritual connection with your daughter. Be aware of it."

Additional thunderheads joined to form a more ominous cloud above her. The temperature dropped, and she thought she felt a drop of rain. She headed toward her house. "Please call any time, Tabitha—day or night—if there are problems or if your daughter obtains some sort of evidence through her dreams."

"I will. Thanks for your help."

Ahulani disconnected the call with Tabitha. She called Joe immediately but got his voicemail.

Leaving a message, she said, "Joe, this is Ahulani. I am very worried about Eric and his parents. Their friend's daughter is having disturbing dreams about them, and it sounds like they are in serious danger. Can you help?"

Her voice broke and it was all she could do to not break down in tears. "This whole thing is way beyond my abilities, Joe. Please call me."

One of her male spirit guides spoke to her clearly. "Patience. You will be getting the help you need." She thought that was the end of the message. "To help yourself. This is *not* beyond your abilities."

Ahulani didn't feel as confident.

Ten minutes later, she was home. She went through her back patio, opened the sliding glass doors, and entered the house. As soon as she'd set her phone down, the doorbell rang. She walked through to the living room, past the kitchen, and to the front door. She peeked through a side window to see Joe. He wasn't alone.

Ahulani opened the door and saw David. This wasn't the David she'd met at Petrified Forest. Since the accident, David wore his hair down, which could be a reflection of a more casual, grateful attitude. There was something else, too—a strength, confidence she hadn't detected before today. When she looked at him, she could see a bear standing on its hind legs.

"What the heck are you both doing here? David, you should be at home, in bed taking it easy."

David took her hands in his. When he did, she was back in Hawaii, walking on the beach. This time, it wasn't Will she'd encountered.

She and David smiled at each other. He opened her palm and placed a shell inside, then closed her hand. Whether it meant a new beginning or something in the future, she couldn't be sure. For the first time in a long time, she hoped it meant a promise of love. Realizing Joe was still standing there, she remembered her manners. "Please come in."

"Thanks," David said. "Between you, Joe, and the medicine woman, I feel fantastic. I know..." David glanced at Joe. "*We* know how urgent this case is."

Joe placed his hand on David's shoulder. "I told David he should chill out for a while, but he insisted on coming."

Ahulani gave David a hug. She whispered in his ear. "You don't have to do this."

David put his arms around her waist and kissed her on the cheek.

Trembling, she pointed to her couch. "Have a seat."

Joe and David sat near each other on the couch. Ahulani sat across from them on a loveseat.

"Everyone's been so focused on me lately," David said. "We need to help the victims of Kuelap. I can't even imagine if something happened to Shelly or..."

David stopped talking and looked down at the carpet, embarrassed. She knew he meant her.

Ahulani twisted a lock of her hair, then placed it behind her ear, ready to update them. "I left a message a few minutes ago for you, Joe. Tabitha's daughter is having nightmares about Eric and his parents. It sounds like they are suffering. Plus, I had a dream about Eric being lost in the Amazon jungle."

She picked up the arrowhead from the coffee table. "I was told this could help by enabling inter-dimensional travel. The medicine woman left it for me last week."

Joe took it from her and turned it over in his hand. He held it vertically and stared at the tip for a while. Could he detect its supposed powers? "This could be the key to preventing any more disappearances. You and David discovered *how* it's all occurring, but perhaps this arrowhead can help *stop* what's happening."

"Did you have a vision or dream about it?" Ahulani asked.

"No. However, arrowheads were primarily tools used for war and hunting. Perhaps, it can help us fight against this unknown force."

"One of my warrior guides mentioned a remote connection using Moldavite," she said.

Joe nodded. "Yes, Moldavite can be highly effective when it comes to that sort of travel. After all, it does come from outer space."

"I traveled to Kuelap once, though I'm pretty sure it

was due to a subconscious connection with David when he was in Elden Pueblo."

She let out a heavy sigh. "I believe Eric and his parents are in different places."

Should she go on to tell David and Joe about Bahlam? It was the jaguar god who had confirmed their separation.

"You've had numerous visions and journeyed to the Marble Caves," David said. "I wonder if that's where they could be."

"My feeling is that they aren't on Earth," she said firmly.

Joe handed the arrowhead to David, who also turned it over in his hand. Joe pointed out the inside spiral at the tip to him.

Ahulani leaned forward in her chair. "I was told that identifies the arrowhead as one of three on Earth with powerful properties."

"Wow." David closed his eyes while still holding the arrowhead. "I don't think this is from the Painted Desert region. I wonder where our friendly spirit healer got this."

Joe removed his phone from his back pocket and glanced at the display. "Aren't we missing someone?"

Ahulani stared at him. "What do you mean?"

David stood up abruptly and stared at her back door. "What the hell is *that* doing here, in Sedona and at your house?"

She followed his gaze to see Bahlam in jaguar form staring into her home.

Joe also stood up and took a few steps toward the door.

"It's okay," she said. "It sounds nuts, but that's Bahlam. He's a shapeshifter, so be prepared."

David and Joe followed Ahulani to the sliding glass doors.

After she opened it, the animal walked into the house. Bahlam immediately transformed into a human.

David took a few steps back toward the couch. He observed the jaguar-turned-man with apprehension.

"I suppose this is the person we've been waiting for," Ahulani said.

David stood in front of Bahlam, watching him closely. "How come neither of you are in shock?"

Ahulani guided David to the couch. "I've seen him before. Plus, I saw him change between forms yesterday." She pointed to David. "Bahlam, this is David."

She looked at Joe. "And Joe, who I met recently."

Joe took a step toward Bahlam. "We have been introduced. Long ago."

Bahlam stepped up to within an inch of Joe's face. "Yes, on your journey to retrieve a power animal for one of your patients. I remember. I knew we would meet again."

"That spirit animal was you," Joe whispered.

Bahlam observed David while speaking with Joe. "Your client was a powerful healer himself and a true friend. His confidence and abilities were being tested by a bad relationship and negative energy."

Ahulani was amazed at the prior relationship, albeit brief, between Joe and the jaguar god. Though, she guessed she shouldn't be. Joe seemed full of surprises.

Joe looked out at the forest and canyon wall behind her house. "He died a few years ago of a stroke."

Bahlam prowled her home, running his fingers along the walls and counters before sitting on the floor in the center of the living room. The man had the aura and posture of a master yogi. "He never wanted to release that bad energy. It provided a certain comfort, protection."

Joe remained focused on the outdoors while Bahlam watched David and Ahulani. "I do."

She glanced at David, who shrugged his shoulders.

A few minutes later, Joe turned around to face them all. "This is going to take all our abilities and efforts. We have to figure out who placed the bear fetish at Kuelap and why. But first, we must get Eric and his family back home. And any other innocent tourists."

"The fetish was not there when I did my research at Kuelap about five years ago," David said. "I never felt anything negative, nor did any other researchers or students I worked with there that I know of. During my brief soul visit with the pan flute, I sensed something nefarious and saw a dark mass. Initially, I thought it might be the entity from my past that caused my accident. It looked human, but I couldn't see any features."

David watched Bahlam nervously. "I'm thinking that thing from Kuelap probably followed me back. Perhaps, it mocked the evil specter from my youth to torture me."

Joe stared through Ahulani's patio doors again. "During my brief healing session with you at your sister's home, I picked up on two different entities—the main one being the non-human form from your childhood. But I saw a vision of this other thing you recently encountered during your astral visit roaming between Kuelap and the Marble Caves. I believe he had a connection to Kuelap, the Marble Caves, or both. I think that mass you saw is human, and he picked up on your past horrors with the non-human entity. He either brought that forth for you again or created it himself to scare you. I bet he knows of your abilities and is threatened."

Brooding about the topic, Ahulani got up and went into the kitchen. She opened the refrigerator and removed bottles of water, bringing them into the living room. "You said 'he,' so that means you saw a person?"

Joe took a bottle of water from Ahulani. "Sort of. I saw him from the back. Definitely a male. He sensed me and made sure I couldn't see his face."

She handed David a bottle of water and turned to look at Bahlam. For a brief second, she smiled, wondering if he wanted it in a saucer. She set it on the table for him and opened the last one for herself.

Bahlam ignored the water and continued to observe David.

David didn't take his eyes off Bahlam, as if the jaguar god would pounce at any second. "What made you think he could be the person responsible?"

Joe took a drink of water, then said, "This person stood inside the middle of a stone house looking down at the bear. I was seeing it from his perspective. He was chanting, and I saw dark energy emanating from him and the ground. The fetish looked as if it were increasing in size by the minute. Then, a moment later, I saw him in the Marble Caves."

Bahlam sat on the carpet with his back completely straight. "His strength grows," Bahlam said. "He is using the fetish to empower himself and to send visitors to other dimensions. That moving mass you saw could be negative energy he's created, or he could have transformed himself to scare you."

David glanced from Bahlam to Joe and then Ahulani. "Fantastic," he said sarcastically. "How can we save Eric, his parents, and any others? Do we have any ideas as to where they are being held captive?"

Ahulani usually had trouble accepting help, whether from strangers or friends. This time, she couldn't let pride get in the way of saving lives. "Bahlam mentioned to me yesterday that they could be in places or dimensions associated with their past lives."

"That's true," said Bahlam.

"We almost have to get inside the bastard's head to figure out where the victims are," David said.

"I doubt *he* even knows," Joe said. "He used the power of the bear to create chaos. He thrives on it."

Joe observed the crystals and stones on Ahulani's bookshelf. "David, you have the bear as your animal totem. It is one of the most ancient worshipped animals. Since this fierce mammal is often associated with shamans in many traditions, it can symbolize healing abilities and stepping into the role of the healer."

Bahlam transformed into a jaguar, strode up to David, sat against his leg, and looked up at him. "You worked there and are familiar with the landscape."

Hesitantly, David placed his hand on Bahlam's head and stroked it. "This is so cool. I feel like I'm dreaming."

Ahulani realized David was starting to cool off and make the case the focus now, instead of his fear of Bahlam. She took the moment to search for the picture of Eric and his parents that Tabitha had sent. There were two—one of Eric by himself and the other with his parents at Kuelap. "I can use a picture of Eric and his parents taken before they disappeared to see if I can locate them. Maybe we can do a group remote viewing. What do you think?"

Joe smiled. "Great idea. I think the viewing session needs to start at Kuelap—at the place where the bear fetish is. We might be able to use the entity's magic against him to reverse whatever is happening."

"Help me!" a child yelled.

Joe and David stood quickly.

Ahulani glanced around. The words were loud and distinct—definitely a child's voice. "That sounded like Eric's voice. I recognize it from my Amazon dream. It sounds different, hoarse."

Ahulani raced from the living room searching every room with Bahlam in tow, but she didn't find anyone. "I can't be hearing things."

"No," he said. "We all heard it."

Back in the living room, Ahulani grabbed the arrowhead and stood in the center of the room. "Eric, where are you?"

Bahlam leapt up to Ahulani. For a second, she thought she was being attacked. His strength nearly knocked her over. He placed a front paw on her arm that held the arrowhead. "Place that on the ground. Eric's trying to get through."

A small figure immediately appeared where the arrowhead lay. He was a beautiful boy with light brown hair, but she couldn't clearly detect all his features.

Joe approached Eric and knelt in front of him. "We're going to help you get home. Do you know where you are?" he asked the child.

Eric shook his head. "It changes. I see jungle and forest, a river and mountain, sand dunes. It's sort of like switching channels on my TV."

Ahulani noticed people dressed in animal skins near Eric. She spotted tall, well-built men—possibly warriors—along with a couple of women wrapped warmly in some sort of fur. "Eric, are you aware that you have some protective spirits with you?"

"Yes," Eric said. "I talked to them at Kuelap before I got lost. They used to live there a long time ago."

Ahulani glanced at Bahlam. The jaguar god had mentioned how special Eric was, proven by his ability to communicate with the Chachapoyan spirits.

Eric turned away. "One of them lived near the home with the bear."

She wanted to grab him and pull him into her world to save him, but Ahulani knew it wouldn't be that easy.

"Eric, do these spirits know how to help you get home?" David asked.

Eric glanced behind him nervously. "I don't think so. I don't know how I found you guys."

Ahulani wondered if Eric had found her, Joe, and David by accident. Perhaps a connection with him had been established when she and David traveled to Kuelap in a spiritual manner.

"Something's wrong," Joe said and touched Ahulani's arm. He looked down at the arrowhead. "That shadow thing from Kuelap and the man in my vision performing the ritual at the bear fetish—they *are* the same. He's found Eric, and he knows about this temporary portal."

Ahulani peered at one of the warriors, who moved in front of Eric and attempted to speak to her. She watched his lips move but couldn't hear a voice. The ancient apparition waved his hands frantically, then put his large hands on Eric's shoulders.

"What? I can't hear you!" Ahulani knelt down.

Another Chachapoyan brave stepped forward. "He's coming!"

Chapter Sixteen

David received a distinct vision of a six-foot man with hair to his shoulders as Eric appeared in Ahulani's home. The mystery man wasn't in the room but glared intently at David from within the recesses of his mind. David took a step back, nearly falling over the coffee table in front of the couch. He had never seen this person before, yet he felt familiar. Within a few seconds, the vision faded.

Eric kept looking over his shoulder.

David realized the child could see the mysterious people from Kuelap who had established such a magnificent city. Were they watching over Eric? Or was it someone else?

Ahulani's home started to take on a more sinister sensation the longer Eric remained with them.

The way Ahulani glanced around the room seemed to indicate she had picked up on something negative as well. The jaguar had lowered its back and stared menacingly at something beyond Eric.

Joe did a 360-degree turn. "He's here. The magician from Kuelap is here."

"Eric, have you seen anyone other than the nice spirits who are with you?" David asked.

Eric started to cry. "No. I climbed into that cool house, and then everything began to turn dark. Next thing I knew, I was in the jungle. And my mom and dad were gone."

"It's okay. We're going to help you and your parents," Joe said. "That ancient home you stepped into is a portal. Your parents disappeared trying to find you, but I'm sure they're safe."

David wondered if the man that Joe referred to as the magician was in Ahulani's home, or near Eric. Either way, they needed to be careful.

Eric's eyes followed Bahlam as he circled the child's body inside the portal. "I don't know how I got here."

As soon as Eric said the word *here*, he vanished from the room.

Ahulani attempted to grab the arrowhead off the floor, but another presence started to reveal itself.

David pulled her back from the incoming figure.

A man about six feet tall with dark hair materialized in the spot where Eric had been. Unlike Eric's vague and more transparent form, David could see his distinct facial and body features. The man had straight black hair to his shoulders, a brightly colored tattoo extending the length of his right arm, and a sinister grin that made David's blood run cold.

Ahulani pulled away from David and stood face-to-face with the intruder. "What have you done with Eric and his parents?"

The magician did not respond. He looked from Ahulani to Joe, David, and stopped at Bahlam, where his gaze remained for several seconds.

Bahlam stepped next to Ahulani and growled—a deep, threatening growl that seemed to vibrate David's entire body.

Ahulani didn't back down.

And David was scared for her. The malevolent force from Kuelap had found her home and could come back at any time. What was this being capable of?

Joe glanced down at the arrowhead below the man's feet. "You don't know the people you're dealing with." He stepped up to the magician's face, glaring at him. Joe quaked in anger, his fists clenched tight. "I've dealt with others like you, hungry for power, gaining enjoyment out of suffering, but you won't win. Not this time. Eric, his parents, and the other victims will be saved." Joe glanced at his friends. "We will all make sure you end up somewhere never to return."

The magician grinned and it reached his dark eyes showing untold stories of horror.

It made David's hair stand up on his spine. Then, unfamiliar symbols surfaced in David's mind—distinct images that scrolled through his vision in a horizontal line. Odd.

While the magician and Joe had a stare-off, David grabbed a small notepad from his back pocket and looked around for a pen. He couldn't find one. He hoped he'd remember the symbols. Maybe they were a clue to helping solve the mystery, and perhaps locate the missing victims or close the portal at Kuelap.

The symbols repeated themselves in groups of ten. Some were similar to music notes and a few others were entailed with triangles in particular patterns.

Is the magician doing this? David wasn't sure.

The jaguar circled the man stealthily. Before anyone could stop it, the black beast leapt into the portal with the magician.

"Bahlam," Ahulani shouted.

The jaguar god and magician vanished as the portal closed.

David couldn't believe what he had seen. The beautiful animal had probably made a desperate attempt to help Eric.

Joe threw his hands up. "Not sure what that stunt on Bahlam's part is going to achieve, but I hope he'll be all right."

The symbols still scrolled through David's mind in the same manner. Intuition told him that the magician had nothing to do with it. He touched Ahulani's arm. "I've been getting these weird signs and images repeating themselves in my head since that man showed up. I want to write them down."

Ahulani walked into the kitchen and brought back a pad and pen. She handed them to David.

He sat down on the couch and started to record the images. Joe sat next to him, watching.

David recorded all the symbols he could remember.

The first three images resembled various music notes, the fourth a compilation of three triangles, with an upside-down triangle fitting snuggly into the middle of the other two. The fifth looked like a Chinese symbol, and the last, a cloud. He struggled to remember the seventh through the tenth, but he couldn't.

Ahulani stared at the spot where the arrowhead had been. "It's gone. The arrowhead is gone. I didn't even see anyone take it."

Ahulani collapsed onto her knees on the floor, her head in her hands. "I thought that would be the key to solving this, to helping us find everyone."

Joe placed his hand on her shoulder. "Unless Bahlam took it when he jumped into the portal. Or it accidentally slipped in with him. If Bahlam has the arrowhead, he might be able to help us on this dimension."

Ahulani yawned. She could barely stay awake. "I hope so," she said. "We can only pray that the magician didn't get hold of it."

David got up and paced the length of the couch. He recalled a star symbol as one of the missing signs he'd seen and jotted the image down with a question mark between the seventh and tenth pictures. He knew Ahulani desperately wanted to save Eric and his parents, but supernatural mysteries didn't come with evidence or practicality. The universe had its own mysteries that didn't align with common sense.

David dropped the pad of paper and pen on the coffee table and knelt next to her. He placed his hands on her face. "You aren't in this alone. I will do what I can, along with Joe and the medicine woman. Not to mention Bahlam."

She put her hand on his arm. "I keep thinking of how frightened his victims might be. Bahlam mentioned they could be going between past lives, but that could be putting them in danger. We have no idea what positions they are being put into. I don't have the answers."

David kissed her on the cheek. "I have a feeling these

crazy symbols mean something. We can do a group remote viewing and meditation using them." He put his hand out to help her up, then standing, held her close, reviving her spirit.

Joe smiled. "I hate to interrupt this lovely moment, but how about we get this party started?"

David said, "I don't remember all of the signs."

"They will come," Joe said. "Let's form a small circle. I believe the portal's residue should help. I want us to concentrate on the bear fetish at Kuelap and the man who was here. Perhaps his leftover energy and our talents can help. Let's surround the spot where the arrowhead was placed."

David sat down next to Joe while Ahulani opened the patio doors. A refreshing breeze gently kissed the back of his neck. The trickling waters of the nearby stream combined with the chattering of hummingbirds.

Ahulani sat between Joe and David.

Joe took Ahulani's hand first and then David's. David placed his hand in Ahulani's. He could feel her trembling.

"Wait." David picked up the notepad behind him and placed it in front of him in case he recalled the other signs.

Joe gave David a stern look. "Don't break the circle by recording anything. The symbols will probably repeat themselves again."

Ahulani tightened her grip on David's hand.

"Let's close our eyes and take three deep breaths together," Joe said. "With each breath, focus on Kuelap and the bear fetish. I've never been there, but I can pick up on its energy through the both of you and the universe. I'm hoping we'll all be able to see or sense each other once we're there."

David, Joe, and Ahulani closed their eyes and started to take the first deep breath.

"Wait," Ahulani said. "Not yet." She got up, took the two chunks of Moldavite from her bookshelf, and sat down again.

Joe smiled. "I almost forgot about those. The most important objects to work with, besides the arrowhead."

She fit the two sections of gemstone together in the center. "These two pieces have been reunited with each other. Let's hope this beautiful stone can help us bring together Eric and his parents, and bring the other victims back home."

David took the first deep breath, along with Ahulani and Joe.

He two took more breaths in tune with them.

By the end of the third breath, David had placed himself inside the prehistoric Chachapoyan structure with the bear fetish. He thought of the magician while he stood over it. It took some time, but he felt another presence and glanced up to see Ahulani next to him.

"It's working," Joe said. "I can see both of you at Kuelap."

Seconds later, Joe showed up between he and Ahulani. They were in the same positions as in the circle at her home, and all were holding hands.

The spot where the arrowhead had been sitting could really be a portal, not to mention the amazing properties of the Moldavite. Or could Ahulani's house be a gateway to other dimensions?

David focused on the bear fetish—observing it closely and trying to pick up on its energy. He envisioned the first three music-like images and the triangular sign over and over, hoping it would initiate a replay of the others. Without thinking, he removed his hand from Joe's, knelt, and touched the fetish inside the circular stone structure.

Joe and Ahulani watched him closely.

The symbols showed themselves again in his mind, only rather than in a row, they were now in a circle. As the images moved clockwise, David saw a spiral sun, star, feather, and a thunderbird sign after the rain cloud. The circular motion made it harder for him to focus on where each symbol should be in relation to the ones he had memorized.

He began to hear muffled voices. Could it be Ahulani and Joe? Or was he hearing the ghosts from Kuelap?

Seconds later, David heard a woman crying. The melancholy murmur turned into a vision of a blonde woman in her mid-twenties standing alone amid a wide-open expanse of prairie. Her legs were barely visible among the tall grasses. She wiped her eyes and stumbled through the foliage. A massive herd of bison grazed in the distance.

The woman stopped and performed a slow 360 turn through the tall grasses.

This young lady didn't belong among these open wilds. Who was she, and how long had she been here?

Chapter Seventeen

The prairie grasses swayed in response to a breeze David could not feel. Thick black smoke hung in the air. The woman watched with apprehension. As the smoke drifted in her direction, flames transformed the horizon into a reddish-orange blanket. The winds picked up, and the bison began to run. The fire was coming her way—fast.

There wasn't anything he could do but watch. He prayed the wind would switch direction or she would end up traveling to another life. Or go home.

Two men on horseback rode rapidly in her direction from the opposite direction as the fire. As they got closer, David could see they were Native Americans and wore leather pants with breastplates made of bone over their chests. He hoped they were friendly.

She glanced from the raging blaze getting closer to the approaching men and back to the fire. The taller of the two men rode up to her and jumped off his horse. He lifted her up onto his white steed, got in the saddle, and rode off in the same direction he had come, with the second rider following behind.

The vision ended.

David opened his eyes. He was still in Ahulani's living room. His watch read 4:15 P.M.—over a half hour from when they formed the circle.

Joe and Ahulani still had their eyes closed. David attempted to go back to Kuelap, but he couldn't concentrate. He didn't release his hold on their hands since it could break the bond between Joe and Ahulani at the scene of the crimes.

Had they noticed his disappearance from Kuelap?

Joe's cell phone rang.

David glanced at Joe and Ahulani, but they were unaware. He had told Shelly that he would be at her place for dinner at 4:30 P.M. She and Larry had insisted that David stay with them for a couple of weeks to ensure his health was up to par. His sister would be rather worried to see him putting himself in jeopardy, especially considering the magician's possible role in the accident.

Ahulani squeezed his hand involuntarily and her face twitched repeatedly. He wondered if she had discovered a victim or if she and Joe had encountered the magician.

David prayed for the woman he had seen on the prairie. Maybe she had journeyed to a past life involving Native Americans. Had the traumatic fire scene been from her past life? The men on horseback hadn't seemed phased by her modern appearance, which was odd to him. Had they seen her as a Native woman?

Joe opened his eyes and looked at David. "We wondered where you went."

"I've been sitting here for a few minutes. I didn't want to break the hand hold since I didn't know what was happening."

Ahulani gasped and opened her eyes seconds after Joe. David searched her face. "Is everything all right?"

She nodded, stood, and stretched. She looked at the pad of paper with the six symbols. "What happened to you?"

"I think I saw one of his victims. I believe she found a past life associated with a Plains tribe. There was a huge fire coming in her direction, but she was saved by Native men."

David stood and picked up the pad of paper and pen from the floor, then moved to the couch where he drew the missing four signs.

Joe continued to sit cross-legged on the floor. He looked up at David. "How did you find her?"

"I think it was the symbols. I envisioned the six I had seen during Eric's appearance here, then the others came into focus while I was at Kuelap with the both of you."

Ahulani threw her head back and walked around the living room. "You also have the bear as your power animal. We saw you kneel down and touch it. You must have transported elsewhere. That had to be what helped you."

"Maybe. Did either of you figure out where Eric or his parents are?" David asked.

Joe finally stood and took a long drink from his water bottle. "No."

David glanced at his watch. "Unfortunately, I need to go. My sister is expecting me for dinner."

He looked at Ahulani and then Joe. "You are both welcome to join me." He hoped Ahulani would accept.

Joe removed his phone from his pocket. "I need to get home to Mandy. I plan on fixing her a special dinner." Joe placed his hand on Ahulani's shoulder. "But I'm sure this young lady can make it."

Ahulani smiled. "Sure, I would like that."

David's insides jumped up and down. He wanted to leap for joy but didn't want to scare her away. He'd need to take things slow.

Joe headed toward the front door. "We made a major breakthrough today."

"I found one of the victims, but not Eric or his parents. There is still the question of how to get them back home," David said.

Joe stared at something behind David. "By the way, you returned the woman from your vision. She is home now in Colorado—ridden there by the Native man who saved her."

David wasn't so sure. "That guy couldn't have returned her to her home on Earth. He was from her past life, another time and place."

"*You* rescued her, David," Joe said. "The woman you saw may not have been able to see you. However,

126

your presence made a difference. Those symbols you keep seeing somehow lock onto the victims. They also appeared in my mind during our time at Kuelap, probably due to the remote viewing connection.

"David, those signs also appeared in my vision while at Kuelap and when I first arrived back home. Joe and I found that out right before our souls returned here."

Joe glanced at his phone. "You witnessed the woman riding off on a horse with a figure from her past, but she ended up safe and sound at home. I believe the Native man was returning her to their tribe—her past life family. That could have been a trigger for her return to her true home in this life."

David ran his hand through his hair. "How the heck do you know?"

Ahulani approached David and put her hand on his shoulder. "She showed up at the ruins right before she returned home, whether that's because she vanished from Kuelap or because you had been there. You just missed her. I don't think she saw Joe or me, but she kept saying she could see home. A moment later, I had a vision of her standing in the center of her living room, looking around in shock. She collapsed on the floor, crying."

"You could have been the ones who sent her home," David said. "After all, you were the last to see her."

Joe sighed. "That was *after* you released her from her past life torture by using those signs you keep seeing." He lifted David's arm at the elbow and showed him.

David hadn't noticed it, but the underside of his left forearm had the ten symbols lightly etched on the surface of his skin.

He started to shake, wondering if the marks were permanent. "Where did these come from?"

"Probably at Kuelap when you began seeing the motifs," Joe said. "There's some overwhelming energy at those ruins. I believe they enhanced your abilities."

Ahulani turned David's arm gently upward to get a better look. "They seem to be fading."

"Those signs are a part of you, not sure from where, but they are coming out now to help you solve this case. They released this one woman and I have no doubt they can help with Eric and his parents," Joe said.

David glanced at Ahulani. "I'm sorry. This is your case, and I feel like I'm creating more confusion."

She hugged him lightly. "It doesn't matter. What matters is saving lives. I was at my wits' end trying to figure out what to do, and you've managed to send someone home. Now we know it *is* possible."

Ahulani grabbed her keys and purse from a hook by the front door. She followed David and Joe outside, then she locked the door behind her.

As she stepped away from the house, Joe hugged her.

"Don't forget, Lani. You're the one that got us to Kuelap so that David could save that tourist. You're critical to all of this with your remote viewing and psychic abilities."

Joe waved and walked to his truck. "I'll be in touch." He quickly got into his vehicle and drove away.

She walked side to side with David. He couldn't believe everything that had occurred in the past week, and he had doubts about saving a person's life simply by seeing visions of symbols. The shapeshifter, the medicine woman, and the fair-haired, fair skinned beauty by the stream—he felt like he was trapped in a dream.

Ahulani smiled at him.

I hope I never wake up.

"Amazing how things change in an instant," he said. "The next thing I know, I am traveling to ruins in a manner most people aren't aware of. It's hard to believe I might've saved a life."

Ahulani picked up a small pebble and threw it into the stream. "Too much change, perhaps. Not sure you would have ended up in an accident if it weren't for me."

David stopped and placed his hand in hers. "That wasn't your fault. I might have ended up at Kuelap because of my experience working there. You are the best thing that's happened to me in a long time, and not because of this adventure." He stepped closer to her, expecting her to pull away but she didn't.

"I am coming to terms with my past lives, particularly the one where I murdered your lover. We both know that is one of the reasons why I am here, why we met."

She looked at him in awe, her emerald eyes were pools drawing him in to their depths. "How did you know? I only found out about that when I met Joe, at Palatki."

Among the trees across the stream, David thought he caught a glimpse of the lovely nymph-collector of stones.

"I dreamt it. I was a pretty messed up person then, and I brutally murdered your lover." He didn't want to wait anymore. He didn't want to be afraid. He bent his head and leaned in. David kissed her on her lips, a soft kiss that left him lightheaded.

She'd closed her eyes and her lips were slightly parted. Ahulani put her arms around his waist and tilted her head against his chest.

In response, David held her tight with one hand and placed his other hand in her silky hair. He wanted to tell her he would love her forever. He wanted to tell her not to be afraid, that they were meant to be together.

Saying it now didn't feel right, so he just held onto her.

They remained that way for a while until a woman's voice startled them both.

"We've been waiting on the both of you."

David turned to see Shelly and Larry, holding hands and grinning. He hoped they didn't make a big deal of what they had seen.

His watch said 4:40 P.M. They had been holding each other for ten minutes. He wasn't ready to let her go.

David took her hand, grinned at her for assurance, and they followed Shelly and Larry.

They walked in silence for a while until Shelly stopped and pointed to something across the stream.

Ahulani gasped.

The beautiful, ghostly nymph stared back at them. She floated above the forest floor, holding onto a tree.

The youthful medicine woman appeared next to her.

Ahulani gazed at both spirits in childlike wonder, her eyes twinkling like the light of a first Christmas.

The medicine woman crossed through the stream and moved toward them, carrying a bunch of flowers. It included daisies, Indian paintbrush, and a stately sunflower bursting from the center. As she reached the group, she smiled and handed the flowers to Ahulani.

Tears flowed down Ahulani's cheeks. "I don't believe it. I'm not seeing her as being old anymore. She's young and gorgeous."

David realized that by Ahulani opening her heart to love, the medicine woman had gifted her the sight of herself in her prime. Or had the beauty been there all along, waiting for a new perspective?

Chapter Eighteen

Ahulani watched the medicine woman approach. The healer treaded through the stream, easily stepping over the large river stones. There was no sign of the much older woman she'd once seen from the Petrified Forest, who had been so hunched and wrinkled. Ahulani had begun to open her heart to David. The prehistoric spirit had told her she was on the right path by giving her the flowers—and the sight of seeing her beauty.

Ahulani stroked the narrow leaves of the bright yellow sunflower and breathed in the scent of the bouquet. Red and orange Indian paintbrush was interspersed with white and purple plants. A sweet smell wafted through the air as the ancient spirit stood in front of her. Ahulani wondered if the woman in white and the medicine woman were any relation.

David had mentioned this ghostly spirit of the forest was the one who had given him the heart-shaped stone. Ahulani sensed the goddess was part of the trees—an elemental that resided in Oak Creek Canyon. There were many types of elementals—fairies, elves, and gnomes to dragons, nymphs, sylphs, and mermaids. Such creatures protected the forests, plant life, and trees, acted as guardians of the wind and air, and purified and protected the rivers, oceans, and other bodies of water.

The medicine woman vanished.

Ahulani glanced over at the floating elemental. Within seconds, small, sparkly blue beings surrounded the lithe, angelic beauty, who now had her feet in the water.

Tiny squeaking noises emanated from them as they danced and splashed in the stream.

"Do you see them?" Ahulani asked.

David, Shelly, and Larry stopped to watch the woman in white.

David looked at Ahulani. "See what?"

She heard the words "water sprites" as a whisper on the wind. Ahulani had studied elementals as part of her spiritual journey. The little beings inhabited water all over the earth and added an energetic frequency to the waters. In healing waters, such as sacred wells, certain sprites added the healing frequency and played a vital role in the energy systems of ecosystems.

The dazzling arrangement wasn't the only gift she had received. Mother Earth allowed Ahulani to see a realm that was closed to most humans—the elemental realm. Or had the surreal forest specter helped her see the spritely beings?

The floating woman disappeared behind a tree. She playfully peeked out at Ahulani and the others, and then half-floated, half-walked deeper into the forest. The blue sprites remained by the water. Some dived in off river rocks and others chased each other along the edge of the stream.

David took Ahulani's hand. She realized he'd noticed her focus on the stream, even after the fair-haired woman disappeared into the trees.

"Do you know what elementals are?" Ahulani asked.

"Yes," David said, "though, I've always doubted their existence."

Shelly and Larry focused their attention on the tree where the lovely phantom was last seen.

"Trust me, they exist. I am seeing water sprites the size of fairies but without wings. They exist to help protect the waters."

Ahulani wanted to get closer but was afraid she'd scare them. She took a few cautious steps forward. The creatures continued to play in the stream, the trees, and among the foliage.

132

"Be careful. You don't know what they'll do," David whispered.

She took one more step. A couple of the sprites stopped playing and watched her.

"I won't hurt you, I promise," she said softly. She thought her guides would tell her to back off.

They didn't.

A group of twenty sprites gathered together. They whispered among themselves, peeking at her every few seconds.

More sprites emerged from the forest. Some had ceased their play.

"Stay still," a female guide warned Ahulani. "They are picking up on your energy."

Then, the same spirit guide told her to proceed with caution.

Ahulani wasn't sure if the tiny sprites understood English. *How many others have seen such beings?*

She made her way to the edge of the stream. The elementals moved backwards to create a clearing next to the water.

Realizing she still held the flowers, Ahulani knelt and set the bouquet on the ground. One of the larger sprites leapt onto her hand and ran up to her shoulder, tickling her in the process. It waved to the others in the stream.

Ahulani forced back a giggle so as not to scare them.

Is this their leader? Is there such a thing among elementals?

David, Shelly, and Larry had remained quiet behind her. They probably thought Ahulani was nuts, playing with creatures that only she could see.

Another sprite had moved within a few inches of her knees. It stared up at her.

She reached her hand out to touch it.

"No!" her female guide yelled close to her ear. "They have never experienced a human touch. The brave being on your shoulder has immunity."

Ahulani pulled her hand back.

The sprite on her shoulder jumped onto her head and then to the ground in a split second.

Ahulani smiled. This sprite was showing off for the others.

Another creature revealed itself. A fairy, whose body was ten times larger than the sprites, peeked out from a nearby tree. The female fairy had wavy blonde hair tied in a gold ribbon. She wore a light blue dress with a fluffy skirt. Now, she flew around the tree and hovered above the water like a hummingbird. The sprites looked up at it in curiosity.

A whole new world had opened up to Ahulani. Could it be because *she* was opening up to David and new adventures?

The fairy darted toward her in a circle around Ahulani's head and then disappeared behind a tree.

All the sprites jumped out of the water. Others popped up from between the leaves on the ground. They raced into the trees, climbing up onto branches, taking refuge in holes in the ground, or diving under large rocks. A couple of them found hobbit-like knobs at the bottom of trees.

Ahulani didn't see any threat. Had they decided *she* was a threat?

"That is their way," a male guide said.

Ahulani looked behind her, but didn't see David, Shelly, or Larry. They had been standing about ten feet away. She stood and slowly stepped back to the spot where she had first seen the elementals.

She took a few more steps and saw David walking along the stream, calling for her.

"David," she yelled back.

He smiled when he saw her. "Thank God, you're safe. We watched you walk to the water and kneel by the stream, then you disappeared."

"What? I must've walked into their realm."

David hugged her. "I believe so. None of us could see them, but you were focused on something. Shelly and Larry are still downstream looking for you."

She followed David's gaze downstream to see the couple. She waved at them.

They waved back at Ahulani and David, making their way toward them.

Shelly said, "Told you she'd be okay. I've never sensed any negative energy in these woods." She took Ahulani's hands in hers. "You saw them. I'm so jealous."

"You mean the little blue creatures that live near the water?" Ahulani asked.

"Yes. There was a little girl camping with her family a few months ago who spotted them. At first, her parents thought their child was imagining things, but they saw them while fishing one day."

Since water sprites were guardians of rivers and streams as well as for the creatures in it, Ahulani wondered if the elementals had a problem with people removing the stream's inhabitants.

"The parents didn't have quite the same positive experience that the child did," Larry said as he glanced toward the stream. "They kept hearing what they called 'angry chatter,' and the bait got removed from the line a few times. The father thought he might be getting bites from fish, but one sprite grabbed his pole and yanked the worm off."

Shelly laughed. "Yeah, and they left Oak Creek the same day."

"Well, I don't know about the two of you," Larry looked at Ahulani and David, "but I am starving."

Shelly took Ahulani's arm in hers. "Hope the food isn't too cold."

In less than five minutes, they were at Shelly and Larry's house. Larry opened the door and let Ahulani and David inside.

Shelly had other guests—not of the living visiting. A distinguished Native American male with long, dark grey hair waved at Ahulani and smiled.

Ahulani heard the word "grandfather" whispered from one of her guides.

Other Native spirits surrounded the grandfather. Some were in brightly-colored regalia of yellow, orange, green, and blue. One woman wore a purple jingle dress lined with metal cones. A short bulky man with long braids wore grass-dancing attire with yarn-fringed strips hanging from his outfit. When he moved, it sounded like grass blowing in the wind.

Shelly watched Ahulani. "What's wrong? Don't tell me you're seeing those creatures here?"

Ahulani laughed. "No, but your grandfather is here, along with other spirit guides."

Shelly was stunned. She stared at Ahulani. "Are you sure?"

Ahulani nodded. "I'm sure."

"I thought he might be." Shelly went into the kitchen to warm up the food on the stove.

Larry put his arm around Ahulani's shoulders. "They were very close, and he died rather suddenly of a stroke over a year ago."

"I'm so sorry," Ahulani said.

"Thanks," Larry said, and dropped his arm. "I'm not a medium but I do sense him here quite often. I think he's the one responsible for taking my keys off the kitchen counter and hiding them. I found them in the toilet once."

The grandfather smiled, then winked.

David pulled out a chair for her at the rectangular oak table in the dining room. The table had southwestern style cutouts in the center, which gave it a unique look. She noticed the table was set for four.

She raised an eyebrow at David, but he shrugged.

"We were hoping you would come," Larry said.

Shelly's grandfather and the other spirits had disappeared. It gave Ahulani a chance to observe the home while they waited for Shelly to bring in the food.

The home had a log cabin atmosphere with warm wood tones and trinkets; a deerskin rug on the floor, stunning Navajo rugs on the walls, and Native American baskets, drums, and rattles throughout the home.

David took an oven dish of baked chicken from Shelly, placing it on the table. "Cozy, huh? I love staying here."

Ahulani smiled. "Let me help." She started to get up, but Larry gently pushed her down.

"We don't allow guests to work, unless it's David." Larry gave David a friendly smack on his back.

Shelly and David placed more bowls of food down, including a mixture of squash and zucchini, scalloped potatoes, small ears of corn, a big bowl of salad, and bread rolls. Larry put a platter of sliced pork roast in the center.

Ahulani's stomach growled and her mouth watered. "Wow. This looks fantastic. I haven't been eating much since this Torres mystery started. I'm feeling guilty for just being here right now."

David took her hand. "You have to eat. We're going to find Eric and his parents next. I think we should try tonight, after dinner. Joe is great, but he has a family. We can do this together."

He was right, but perhaps she should perform a remote viewing session at Kuelap to find any other victims.

Even though she was hungry, she felt uncomfortable about having a good time when Eric and his parents were still lost. What if the magician's victims were starving or suffering? She continued her prayers to her angels.

Finally, Larry and Shelly sat at the table. They all held hands and Shelly said a prayer. "Thank you, God, for this meal, for our health, and for the fortunes you have brought us."

Shelly glanced at Ahulani, and Ahulani smiled back at her.

"Amen," Larry said.

Larry passed the platter of pork to Ahulani.

She took two slices of pork roast, then a small breast of herbed chicken that Shelly sent around.

She glanced up from the food to see Shelly and David's grandfather standing behind David, his hands hovered on David's shoulders.

The grandfather looked at Ahulani and said, "He is destined for greatness."

David didn't seem to feel the weight of the man's hands as the remainder of the food was passed around the table. If he did, he didn't react.

She watched as the grandfather took a slice of the roast and a roll from the table. He ate the food and gave a thumbs up.

Ahulani smiled to herself and continued to add veggies to her plate.

"I forgot the wine," Shelly said and got up from the table. She brought two open bottles, placing them in the center of the table.

David picked up Ahulani's wine glass. "What do you prefer?"

"Um, red is fine, thanks," she said. One of Ahulani's female guides loved to drink. She started jumping up and down when David poured some for Ahulani.

Ahulani smiled. "Thanks."

Her guide took a drink from her glass before Ahulani had a chance.

Larry poured a glass of white wine for Shelly, but he didn't partake himself.

Neither did David.

Larry reached for the bowl of mashed potatoes. "I am a recovering alcoholic for over six years, but I feel that Shelly should still enjoy her favorite pastime."

Shelly grinned. "Yes, I like to have at least one glass a day."

Ahulani suspected David was probably avoiding the wine to support Larry's choice.

After dinner, they stayed at the table and continued to talk when Ahulani felt a knife being twisted inside her stomach. She doubled over in her chair. "Ouch," she cried.

Am I feeling what one of the magician's victims are going through?

David and Larry quickly pushed back their chairs and got up to help her.

The agonizing sensation lasted only a few seconds before it went away. Ahulani held her hand up. "I am fine now."

138

Larry knelt next to her. "Are you sure you're all right?"

"This happened once before, right after the case started," Ahulani said.

"Do you think the magician could be responsible?" David took her hand in his.

Ahulani hadn't thought of that. He could have developed a connection with her during the remote viewing sessions. "It could be. Either that, or I'm picking up on something the victims might be experiencing."

"Just in case," Shelly said, and ran into the hallway. She returned with a branch of white sage and a lighter. She lit the sage, and a sweet, earthy aroma enveloped the room.

Ahulani imagined an angelic light around her.

I call upon Archangel Michael to protect me and this house from that which has evil intent.

"I'm okay," Ahulani said. "I think it has stopped."

David put his hand on her shoulder in comfort.

The sharp pains had ceased, but a wave of nausea overcame her. She bent over again, holding onto her stomach.

"Is it happening again, Ahulani?" Shelly asked, concerned. "Can I get you anything? Water?"

Ahulani shook her head and stood up. "No, thanks. I feel like I'm going to be sick."

David guided her to the bathroom in the hallway.

After a few minutes of leaning against the wall, the nausea subsided. She'd become so tired she could barely keep her eyes open.

Shelly peeked in the bathroom at her, then spoke to David who still stood in the hallway. "Have her lie down in the spare bedroom."

"No, I think I'll head home," Ahulani said. She stepped toward the bathroom doorway but fell down, nearly hitting her head against the wall.

David picked her up and took her into his room. He laid her on the queen-sized bed, then sat next to her, holding her hand. "Take it easy. You can stay here overnight."

139

He got up and placed the comforter that was at the end of the bed over her.

Shelly and Larry had come into the room and stood next to David.

Ahulani rolled her head back and forth across the soft pillow, trying to get comfortable. Across from her, a yellow pow-wow dress lined in purple was framed in glass hanging on the dark beige wall. "I don't have time to be sick."

Shelly's grandfather stood on the opposite side of the bed from David. His deep voice resonated throughout the room. "You are not ill. You are detecting pure evil from the one you call the magician."

Ahulani lay still and stared at the old man. "Is this what the victims are feeling?" she asked.

Chapter Nineteen

*O*bscurity created fear. The darkness that surrounded him made David feel off-kilter, confused. He couldn't discern between up or down, left or right. The air felt damp, and a small breeze blew above him every few seconds.

He touched the top of his head, and his fingertips caressed a tiny furry body as it flew off with a few strands of his hair. Bats.

He reached his hands out but didn't feel anything, so he took small cautious steps to try and find something stable in the gloom.

Water dripped nearby, echoing into the dark wasteland. Slowly, he walked toward the comforting sound and discovered a hard surface in front of him. His eyes had started to adjust to the darkness, and now he could detect tall shadows. He continued to use his hands as his eyes and found smooth, twisted columns in various sizes.

With nowhere else to go, he felt his way toward the largest pillar. As he got closer, he could see an opening at the bottom—a concave hole big enough for a large dog to fit into it.

David bent down to see into the strange aperture. A gust of wind blew through and rustled his long hair. What sounded like a howling wind had come from inside, along with other unfamiliar disturbances.

Scraping noises and footsteps came from behind. He turned his head to look but saw nothing but blackness.

The chasm in the column drew him in. Pulse racing, heart pounding, he crawled into it on his hands and knees. The ground seemed level, but his arms scraped against the closely confined walls.

The haunting howling took on a life of its own. David wondered if that meant there was an exit coming up.

He moved faster, and the tunnel walls widened. The top of his head hit the ceiling hard. He rubbed it and waited until the pain subsided.

He pulled himself up gradually until he stood at his full height. His eyes adjusted to the dimness after a few moments.

David stood for what felt like an eternity until he started to see the outline of a massive chamber. A ceiling at least fifty feet high with moist stalactites hung down above him. Nearby, a narrow, spiral stairway of limestone rock led up to the unknown.

He approached, and slowly ascended the stone stairs. Round bulbish formations were on his right and a wide crevasse could be seen on the opposite side.

David looked down into the void but couldn't see the bottom. The spiral stairs continued for about a quarter mile and ended at an eight-foot long by four-foot-high concave niche.

He wondered why stairs would lead to such a place with no apparent purpose. It didn't make sense, but maybe there was more to this place than he understood.

David knelt, then crawled along the back of the niche. His hand touched something roundish and smooth.

He yanked his hand away when he felt eye sockets and deteriorated teeth.

He picked up a long object, mostly smooth except for a few indentations. His opposite hand fell into a pile of debris and was poked by something sharp. When he moved, it sounded like he was stepping on a pile of bones.

He rubbed his palms together repeatedly to try to get rid of the smell of death.

"Please forgive me."

As he stared into the dark niche, he started to see other things on a smaller ledge above where the body, or bodies, had been laid. A wooden staff was also there, surrounded by various stones, fetishes, jewelry, and what he thought might be prayer sticks. Leather was wrapped around the bottom of it. The top had been carved in the shape of a bear's head. David suspected this had been the grave of *an important person, possibly a shaman.*

He could hear someone climbing the narrow stone stairs below. He waited and waited, but no one appeared.

Have I angered the spirit of this person?

David backed away from the altar and out of the niche, then climbed back down the stairs. He found an open pit about ten feet deep within the center of the cave. It contained fallen rocks, debris, and large pieces of pottery.

David bent over and stared into the pit.

Hands pushed him from behind.

He yelled and landed face down on the hard ground, his face close to a large grouping of dark yellow broken pottery.

He slowly stood, gathering his bearings. David looked up the stairs. Had the spirit associated with the burial been offended by David's actions? Or could there be something or someone else following him?

He saw a fractured crack approximately a foot wide running along the wall of the cave near the pottery sherd. A ray of light came from its depths, enabling him to see the layers of rock and additional levels of the cave far below.

As he stood in the open pit, movement came from all around him—the upper section with the burial chamber, above him in the main cavern, and within the pit. It wasn't footsteps, more like settling noises.

The darkness hid any secrets, but he felt eyes on him— many pairs of eyes. Too scared to move, he searched the area all around him. A small shadow low to the ground raced across the pit before it vanished. Figures swayed back and forth in rhythm above from where he had been pushed.

A myriad of pottery pieces surrounded the cave. A ring of primitive looking dancers painted in black encircled a portion of what looked to have been a wide-rimmed bowl. A bear fetish had been painted on a section of a large plate, though he wasn't sure why.

The rocks and potsherds around him skipped and danced. The vibration worked its way through David's body from his feet to his head. It became stronger, and the mysterious shadows that had been observing him took off.

He imagined a fire-breathing dragon or some sort of lava monster pushing itself up through the core of the cave system to get to its unlucky human meal.

Realizing the pit had probably been created by such vibrations, David wondered if the ground would continue to hold or if he would be swallowed alive.

For survival's sake, he explored the pit, trying to find a way to the surface. Every direction led to a dead end. The only way seemed to be the wall fracture—straight down.

David remained frozen, waiting for the quaking to stop. When it finally did, a new crack, a few inches wide, split the ground behind him, burying some of the smaller pottery pieces within it.

The wide plate with the bear fetish painted on it stuck up through the crack. He bent down and removed it before another tremor devoured it.

The bear staff was on the left side of the plate. He looked around and found another large plate piece in the corner near the fracture. When David matched the two sections together, another small shadow ran by him in the pit and leapt up to the level of the cave. He was missing the last piece.

He walked up and down the length of the pit, peering closely at the ground.

It could be anywhere! Even in the bowels of the Earth.

He took another look into the newly formed crevasse but didn't see any ceramic art. It could have been lost during the recent tremor or already buried in the depths of the cave. Intuition led him to the wall fracture.

He knelt at a section closest to where he had discovered the first part of the plate and squeezed his hand down into the fracture. He felt a ledge with something resting on it. He grabbed the smooth object and carefully pulled it up from its hiding place.

I don't believe it!

Laying the ceramic sections on the ground, David matched the pieces. In the center stood a shaman with a staff held high and stars shining above. There were two bear fetishes, one on either side of the plate.

He looked closer to see other images around the circumference. The first three looked similar to music

144

notes, the fourth was three triangles—the top one pointed down to fit into the bottom two—one that resembled a Chinese symbol, a cloud, a spiral sun, a star, a feather, and last, a thunderbird.

There was something very important about the ten symbols, but David couldn't remember, just that they were familiar.

Sensing something behind him, David turned to see two short shadow people. He recalled the size of the opening in the spiral column. It was the height of the creatures standing in front of him. It appeared they had transformed from shadows into beings that matched the color and texture of the cavern. They were human-like, with two arms and legs and seemed to be hairless. Round, thin, straw-like formations covered parts of their bodies, similar to the ones created by the moisture in the cave. Some had bulbous formations on their heads and bodies.

He slowly backed away from the plate.

The creatures looked at each other and emitted a series of grunts, then they began to seep water from their bodies. It flowed from their little forms, shining on their skin, and flowed down onto a combination of rough and smooth scales.

One of the creatures jumped up and melded into the rock. It blended perfectly, its own moisture dripping in rhythm with that of the cave wall.

David looked closely at the rock, wondering how much of the environment was cave rather than creature. Curiosity kept his feet bound to the ground. He could run but there was nowhere to run.

Another one leapt from the pit to the ceiling high above. It expanded, creating a slimy globule that dripped slowly into a shiny stalactite.

He didn't know what had pushed him into the pit, but David didn't think it was these indigenous beings. They didn't seem to think in terms of harming anyone, only of themselves in relation to the environment.

His skin tingled. David was in danger. He saw a tall human figure in the corner of the pit who didn't appear to be friendly.

The cave dwellers began to grunt, squeak, and squawk. A shadow dropped from the ceiling. It was the same creature that had made the stalactite. But the newcomer didn't notice. The person stepped forward toward the plate.

David could tell it was a man by his stature but found it hard to detect any other features. Cave dwellers gathered around the rim of the pit.

The male figure bent down to pick up a piece of pottery. When he touched the section with the staff, two of the creatures jumped into the pit and revealed themselves from shadow to cave form. They stood between David and the intruder.

The unidentified male backed off a few feet.

Two more shadows appeared, one on either side of David.

The intruder glanced from the ones in cave form to the shadows. He looked at David.

For a few seconds, David saw straight black hair and an elaborate tattoo on one arm that looked to be vines, trees, and a parrot.

The plate had held much more than food. David sensed its creator had instilled powers with the paint and clay.

This stranger felt familiar, dangerous. David detected this individual sought power from the cave in order to cause chaos, not only on Earth, but in other worlds and dimensions.

Chapter Twenty

David sat up quickly, glancing around the room. It took him a few seconds to reorientate himself. He was back in his sister's house and Ahulani was in his bedroom. He threw off the blanket, left the couch, and ran into the hallway. The door to the room was open and the bed was made.

The clock on the wall showed 7:10 A.M. The house was quiet, and Shelly was always up before 7 A.M. Her bedroom door was open, but David didn't see her or Larry.

He went into the living room, then out into the back yard. Larry and Shelly were showing Ahulani some dance moves.

As he approached, Shelly smoothed strands of his long hair. "Hey, sleepy head. You must've had one heck of a dream. You slept through breakfast."

David hugged Ahulani. "How are you feeling?"

"So much better. I think your grandfather helped me rest."

"I'm so glad. What if you keep feeling the magician's negativity?"

Larry smiled and put his arm around Shelly. "I don't think that'll happen. Both of these beautiful ladies had the same dream of your grandfather healing Ahulani. He was playing the drum by Ahulani's bedside, and they both smelled white sage in their dreams right before waking."

"I almost forgot Grandpa had those abilities," David said.

Ahulani took David's hand in hers. "You saw the magician, didn't you? In your dream."

A black-chinned hummingbird hovered above Ahulani's head. Easily recognized because of its black head, royal blue stripe around its neck and white breast, this one seemed to take a liking to the dark-haired beauty.

A phone rang from inside. Larry ran into the house. He came to the back door and waved Shelly in, holding a mobile phone in his hand.

David watched the hummingbird. "Yes. I didn't realize it in the dream, but it was him. How did you know?"

"He showed himself in mine briefly. I think your grandfather might have scared him away."

Why hadn't his grandfather helped David? Or perhaps he had.

The tiny bird shot off into the trees. Seconds later, there were three hummingbirds—two black chinned and an Anna's hummingbird with its brilliant emerald feathers and bright pink throat. All three birds flitted and circled around her.

"I've never seen anything like it," Shelly said as she watched from the porch. "I am out in the yard all the time, and they've never reacted that way for me."

Ahulani remained still, observing the colorful creatures flying around her. She looked stunning with the morning sun shining down on her. She had never told David where she was from, but he could tell she was part Hawaiian, Polynesian, or possibly both. Yet, he thought he detected Peruvian features as well. If that was the case, why hadn't she mentioned it, especially knowing David's background?

She had let him hold her hand yesterday during the walk to Shelly's house, but he wondered if she would retreat again. He still detected a certain amount of sadness within her, but her experience with the water elementals seemed to have lifted her spirits. He hoped one day he would be able to see such creatures. Perhaps she had numerous spirit elementals that were opening up their world for her.

David watched Larry and Shelly sit next to each other on the swinging porch chair, with Larry putting his arm around Shelly's shoulder. Larry had been the best thing that had ever happened to his sister. He knew in his heart they would always be together. Would that be the case for David?

He gazed at Ahulani as the birds continued to hover around her. She put a finger slowly in the air—the Anna's hummingbird landed on it and perched for a few seconds.

"Does this happen to you often?" David asked.

"Never. There are times when they fly close, but nothing like this."

The birds flew off, abandoning Ahulani.

"David, I think we should go back to the place where I saw the water sprites and the fairy," Ahulani said. "Such a place could help with the connection to Eric and his parents."

"Through remote viewing?"

Ahulani glanced around the yard. "I want to try something different. Those ten symbols of yours represent some sort of tie to Kuelap and the victims, I know it. Some of the signs you've been seeing are important to Native culture and to Mother Nature—the cloud, star, spiral sun. Not to mention, elementals have a pertinent connection with the Earth—air, water, fire, and earth itself. Your energy, combined with Mother Nature, could provide a powerful force."

She stepped closer to him. He didn't want to think about the case anymore. He only wanted to take her in his arms and kiss her until he convinced her of his love.

A hummingbird returned and floated above Ahulani's head for a few seconds then flitted off. "Considering the bear fetish in the stone house," David said, "this man is drawing on the environment of the ancient culture and possibly even nature itself. Most magicians and witches rely heavily on nature and the elements. Maybe these beings you saw at the stream can help us break down this strange spell of his."

She observed something behind David. "Maybe."

David turned but saw only Larry and Shelly. "Is something wrong?" he asked.

149

"I thought I saw fairies in the trees. That might be a confirmation."

David wondered about the bear fetishes from the plate in his dream. Did that power animal have something to do with the caves?

With himself? Or with the magician?

Three turkey vultures floated high on the currents above the cliff. "In my dream, I saw the magician standing in front of me, in a cave. He had straight dark hair and a detailed tattoo of a jungle scene. I found an amazing plate, though I had to piece it together. I think it was instilled with special powers. This plate had the ten symbols around the circumference, and the magician attempted to take it."

Ahulani observed him with curiosity. "A cave, really? Did it look like the Marble Caves?"

"Hmm, yes... I found myself in an underground realm with several caves and tunnels. And yes, the first had columns like those in the Marble Caves. However, I didn't see any water."

"I want to hear more when we have time, but we need to get to the place where I saw the sprites. I want to run home and pick up some stones. Meet me there in half an hour?"

David felt guilty for not describing the whole dream. He watched Ahulani run through the wooden gate in the yard.

"What's going on?" Larry asked and stood.

"Ahulani has to get home. We're meeting in a bit at the place where she communicated with the elementals. She thinks we can use their powers and connection with nature to help solve the case."

"We've been praying every night," Shelly said. "If anyone can bring the victims back, you can. Along with Ahulani, of course."

"Why do you say that?" David asked, curious.

Shelly stood. "Before your grandfather died, he helped you initiate your powers, which were the same as his.

He *knew* you could handle it. Before he passed away, he told me the day would come when it would be appropriate to tell you the truth."

"Tell me what? I can travel with my pan flute, but I didn't know Grandpa played any instruments."

"No, not that, David. It's those symbols you're seeing," Shelly said. "Like Grandfather, they are innate in you, and they control and create portals. Certain combinations of the signs open portals for you to different worlds."

Panic set in. David felt short of breath.

Kuelap. What if I unknowingly opened a portal during my research trip that the magician is using to get new victims?

Chapter Twenty-one

A hulani sat by the stream in the spot where she had played with the water sprites. Her eyes were closed, and a warm breeze rustled her hair. She hoped she would be able to see the elementals again, but if not, Ahulani could still draw upon their earthly energy.

Her dreams had been overrun with images of David, including memories of when they'd first met at the Painted Desert.

Joe, Shelly, Larry, and the medicine woman weren't the only ones pushing her toward a relationship. Her spirit guides also seemed to be directing her to romance. The more time she spent with David, the more she wanted to be around him.

Ahulani didn't want to have to rely on anyone to help with a case, but this time was different. This mystery was too complicated and involved for her to figure out on her own. She needed the assistance of someone who had worked at Kuelap and had been blessed with knowledge of the special symbols that could bring people back home.

Footsteps crunched through the leaves and twigs. She glanced up to see David approaching, head and shoulders bent, his hands in his pockets. He had a backpack strapped over his shoulder.

Where was he planning on going?

She stood as he met her.

"Grandpa said I might need this." David lifted a strap of the pack. "Some basic survival stuff and a bit of food." He smiled—a forced grin.

"Is everything okay?" Ahulani asked.

"No. I don't know... Shelly told me that my grandfather gave me those symbols upon his death. The symbols can open portals. I was doing research at Kuelap. Ahulani, what if I unknowingly opened a portal that the magician is now using?" He stared at the ground. "Even worse, what if I am responsible for all of this? All of the victims disappearing?"

Ahulani placed her hand on David's shoulder. "You would never do anything to deliberately harm another." She listened intently to see if her guides would indicate David's involvement, but they were silent. "You said yourself that nothing unusual was happening when you were there. If you had accidentally accessed a vortex or portal at Kuelap, there would've been a sign. Maybe your grandfather merely helped *initiate* your abilities. They could have been lying dormant since you were born."

After Ahulani finished speaking, David's grandfather showed himself standing behind David. The man was intelligent and powerful, yet humble. Something told Ahulani that his grandfather had more talent than Shelly realized—maybe more so than he himself understood.

David noticed. "Is he here?"

She nodded. "I think he just got here." His grandfather was dressed in a cowboy hat, jeans, denim dress shirt, and vest.

Ahulani stepped around David and approached his grandfather. "With those symbols comes great power. Did David open a portal in Kuelap?"

The grandfather placed his arm around David. "No. It was already there but kept dormant by the shaman of the village."

Ahulani took a deep breath. She needed to tell David the truth. "David, you aren't responsible. He told me you didn't create an opening. It's been there for centuries. The magician must've done something to activate it."

David looked up at the clouds. "Thank God. I mean... there is no way I could have dealt with that possibility."

His grandfather placed his hand on the tree next to him and looked up into its luscious green canopy. "It is impossible for David to open a portal without knowing. He has to tap into the power of those images, and not all ten are used to open every portal. A specific combination is used, depending upon the purpose and travel location. David has only been given ten to start with for now."

"How many more are there?" she asked.

"Hundreds. The ones he has seen are the primaries that will help save the victims. The living cave from his dream has the answers for them all."

Ahulani looked at David in awe. "There are more symbols, hundreds, he said."

David rolled his eyes. "Fantastic."

He had mentioned a plate with the ten primary symbols in his dream the night before. She wondered if his dreams would provide information about some of the others.

Before she could ask any more questions, his grandfather vanished. She sensed he was still present, but like her spirit guides, he wasn't providing all the answers. It was up to David to figure out.

"I can't see him, but I think he's still with you. Not sure what your grandfather meant, but he said that cave you dreamt about contains knowledge of all of the symbols."

David took a step toward her. "There were creatures there. Odd creatures I've never seen before. They resembled features, formations of the cave, and I saw them merge with the environment. It was the most intense vivid dream I've ever had."

"You saw nothing that showed any new symbols?"

"No, just the broken plate with the images I've already seen."

Ahulani thought of the Egyptian hieroglyphs scribed into walls of pyramids and tombs. She took his hand. "It was dark, I assume?"

"Of course. I couldn't see until my eyes adjusted. Even then, it was like walking around in a dimly lit room."

"Perhaps, the cave walls held the hidden symbols."

"It's possible, but I'm not sure I can ever go back."

One of her female spirit guides spoke to her. "The elementals are waiting."

"David, my guides are telling me the sprites are ready to communicate."

"But you are the only one who saw them."

"It doesn't matter," Ahulani said. "They are all around us. We can use their earthly energy. I will ask my guides to bring them forth again, if only in my third eye."

She removed a picture from her back pocket and handed it to David. "I need you to concentrate on Eric and his parents. Maybe you will be able to see where they have been transported to with the help of the symbols."

She looked closely at the water to see if any of the water sprites would show themselves, but she could not see the little blue creatures in the stream. David could be the reason for them hiding.

Something large, about thirty feet away from the stream, walked heavily through the brush, snapping leaves and branches, crunching its feet through the undergrowth. The height of the unseen creature seemed to be nearly to the top of the tallest sycamore. It sounded like it would trample the whole forest.

Ahulani stood next to David, who stared nervously into the trees.

"What the heck is that?" David asked.

The trees closer to the stream swayed. Whatever was out there was only twenty feet away. David stared at the disrupted sycamores.

The hairs on Ahulani's arms went up. A tingling ran down her spine. She got to her feet. "It's watching us."

David tossed his hair back. "What could be that big?"

"I don't know." She shivered.

David put his arm around her waist. "Maybe we should get out of here."

She wanted to stay to see if it would show itself. "No. I don't think we're in danger."

Ahulani stepped into the slow-moving stream to cross

it, hoping to get closer to the creature. David grabbed her arm.

As soon as she stepped into the water, the hidden anomaly appeared.

A pure white horse stood watching Ahulani and David. It was the biggest horse she had ever seen—at least ten feet tall.

She smacked David's arm without taking her eyes off the horse. "Can you see it?"

He didn't respond.

The large animal stepped forward a few feet. It wasn't a horse at all. A twisted horn on the top of its head was clearly visible, having been blocked by a tree branch.

She looked at David, who had collapsed to his knees, staring at the mythical beast. His jaw dropped—he seemed to be trying to speak.

Ahulani couldn't take her eyes off of it, either. *Everyone is aware of portals in Sedona. But water sprites and unicorns? What else is out there waiting?*

One of her female spirit guides spoke up. "Unicorns are the consciousness of pure love radiated out onto the land. They can have profound healing roles to help humans. Their gift to us as a race is unconditional divine love, which can be accessed by all who ask."

The forest became still—no birds, insects, or even a breeze.

Ahulani glanced at David, who had gotten slowly off his knees and continued to stare at the beast.

"Maybe I should cross the stream and say hello," Ahulani said.

A voice spoke but this communication was not through telepathy. The male was next to her, and the voice sounded familiar. "Wait for it to invite you into its space."

David glanced around, trying to find the source. "Sounded like Grandpa."

Ahulani nodded.

Frustrated, David threw his hands up. "Is this thing supposed to invite her to lunch?"

A quick response came through. "Yes."

David rolled his eyes and smiled.

Ahulani laughed out loud, then covered her mouth with her hand. She was afraid she had frightened the unicorn. It had taken a few steps back but continued to watch Ahulani and David. It stepped toward them and stopped at the edge of the stream.

The unicorn bent its front knees and knelt on the ground.

"I think that's your invitation," David said.

She started to cross the water, then waited for David.

"It's your invitation, also," his grandfather said.

David was pushed toward Ahulani.

He did a 360-degree turn, attempting to look at the force that moved him. Then, he took her hand and led her over boulders that were peeking above the water. As they crossed, the animal rose.

Ahulani held her breath.

David cautiously approached the unicorn and put his hand out to touch the top of its head.

She had hoped to communicate with the sprites, but perhaps this pure of heart mythical creature was here to help. One of her guides had mentioned these beasts were the *consciousness of pure love*, and that they also had *profound healing roles*.

The animal shook its head and whinnied as David moved his hand to its nose. It didn't back away. Next to the unicorn, stroking its side was his grandfather.

Ahulani approached and stood on the opposite side of the beast.

David's grandfather said, "I think it's time you knew my name. I don't think my love-stricken grandson will tell you."

He didn't open his mouth, but she heard the word Rafael.

"Like the angel?" she asked.

He nodded.

David glanced at her. "What?"

Ahulani looked at him over the unicorn's back.

"Was your grandfather's name Rafael?"

"Yes. He's still here?"

She pointed to the other side of the unicorn. "Over there. Not sure why you heard him a few minutes ago but can't now."

"It depends on where you are in the forest," Rafael said, and picked up a large leaf off the ground. Then, he went to David and used it to tickle him on the cheek. Rafael smiled as David itched that side of his face.

"My grandfather was a miracle worker. Cured a number of people of cancer, including a thirty-two-year-old diagnosed with ovarian cancer. She only had a month to live."

Ahulani smiled and watched Rafael. He blushed, listening to David.

"I think my grandpa's mother knew of his healing abilities when he was born. From what I've heard, she was a remarkable woman and could detect people's ability to heal."

An angelic light began to surround David. She had never detected it as part of his aura before, but it was very strong. Could the unicorn be enhancing his healing talents? For that matter, it could be working its magic on her.

David's hand became still as he rested it on the snout of the beast. He closed his eyes and stood, but remained completely still for a few minutes.

Ahulani glanced at Rafael who watched his grandson, not with curiosity or concern, rather with knowing. "Is David all right?" she asked.

Rafael placed his hand on his grandson's shoulder and stared at David intently.

Ahulani's third eye showed her a dark cavern with stalactites and stalagmites. A set of stairs wound its way up—to what she couldn't tell. One of the larger stalagmites moved. At first, she thought it was the way the water dripped down the smooth limestone formation. It moved again. This time, it separated itself from the ground.

She gasped when she saw a short creature that had the appearance of a stalagmite, but with small slits for eyes. Its skin matched the browns and dark yellows of the cavern. That wasn't all. A bizarre image was etched into the center of its stomach—a stalactite and a stalagmite joining together. Her gaze was drawn to the perimeter of the cave where she could see other faint symbols on the walls.

Within seconds, her focus was snapped back to the forest. However, the unicorn, David, and Rafael were gone.

Had he returned to his sister's house?

"Look behind you," a male spirit guide whispered.

She saw David facing her with both hands raised in the air, as she had seen many Native Americans do in prayer. He looked handsome. Not just handsome, but hot. The sides of his hair blew in the breeze and his eyes were closed with the sun's rays cutting through the trees and shining on his face. Rafael stood next to him with his head bowed.

Ahulani stayed put, afraid to interrupt. Could David be seeing more symbols initiated by the magic of the unicorn? Was he in the midst of a journey to the cavern?

Observing David in prayer made her feel vulnerable. Every day, she found herself letting go a little more. She had sworn she would never allow such a thing to happen, but her heart was rapidly overtaking her mind, falling for David.

He opened his eyes and lowered his hands. David saw Ahulani and smiled. As he did, she had the most distinct vision of her life.

She saw herself and David in the midst of a wedding ceremony. They were facing each other, holding hands. He wore dark dress pants, a navy shirt, and a vest embroidered with yellow, black, and navy designs. His hair hung in two braids on either side of his head.

She wore a white floor-length Native dress decorated in the same color bead work as David's vest with a southwestern style cutout above her cleavage. Beautiful moccasin boots adorned her feet with yellow, black, and navy beads. Yellow ribbons had been interwoven into a single braid that hung over her shoulder. A modest turquoise and abalone necklace put the final touches on her extravagant attire.

She and David were surrounded by a small crowd with Shelly and Larry standing next to them. Deep drumming started, accompanied by flutes. The shadow of a massive bird flew directly above David and Ahulani.

Ahulani could feel tears on her cheeks as the lifelike vision ended. This was not her imagination; it was the pure power of the unicorn. Could it be her future? She hadn't noticed David move due to the scene unfolding before her, yet here he stood a foot in front of her. Had he seen the ceremony, too?

A large winged shadow flew above them.

Ahulani stepped closer to David, and he turned to face her.

Something was different. Not bad, just peculiar. His eyes shifted from the usual brown to dark grey, watching her.

He's being channeled.

"They are safe," David said.

Yet *his* voice was much deeper than David's normally was. She wondered if his prayer had invited this newcomer in. "*They.* Are you talking about the victims from Kuelap?"

"Yes."

"We have to bring them back home. I don't know whom I'm talking to right now, but David is very important to solving this mystery. I need him back."

"We are one," the voice said.

Ahulani threw her hands up. "Of course, because you're using him as a vessel for communication."

"David and I are the same. I brought him to the cavern of the cloaked mineral beings because he lived as myself, hundreds of years ago. My ancient remains are those at the top of the stairs."

Shocked, she recalled the winding steps leading up from the vision.

Had David unknowingly invited his past self to help?

"David's grandfather mentioned there are hundreds of symbols at that place. What about you? If you really are from the cave, you probably know what many of those symbols are for, don't you?"

David's bodily intruder said, "The gate has been opened. You don't have much time."

David's eyes turned back to brown, and he placed his hand on her shoulders. "He's gone."

She nodded. "Are you okay? Do you know who you were channeling?"

Dropping his hand, he got his bearings. "Yeah, I'm fine. It was the shaman from the caves I told you about. We have to move fast. Eric and his parents are on the opposite sides of the same planet, though in much different environments." He took her hand and pulled her to the area where the wedding ceremony had taken place.

"David, I think I met you so *you* can solve this case— and only you."

He hugged her tight. "No, Ahulani." He shook his head and looked deep into her eyes. "The victims need both of us. You, Joe, and I worked together remotely at Kuelap. You were the one who figured out the power of the bear fetish. During the prayer, I was able to see the symbols I would need to access the location where Eric and his parents are. You had the picture of Eric and his family. All I did was hold that picture. Grandpa helped me to connect with the strong personae who channeled me to relay the message. And Joe…"

"David, wait. You know you and he are the same, that you were this man, the shaman, in a past life?"

David nodded. "I do now."

She smiled up at him. "I'm glad." She was happy for David but wondered about her part. Would they be able to bring the victims back safely? What danger would they be putting themselves in to rescue them?

"Remember, you were the one who managed to return that woman to her home in Colorado."

"I remember." He held her close next to him. "Stand right here." The birds stopped singing. They were entering the dimension of the water sprites. She and David were in the portal.

David took her hands in his. "Stay close. Eric and his parents have stepped into the same dimension and on the same planet, but they are leaving an imprint in entirely different parts of this world, which is why they are having such different experiences. We have to work together to bring them to us—in Sedona. This tree," David looked up into the branches of a tall cottonwood, "and this spot in the forest is a prominent vortex."

Ahulani nodded in understanding. "David, Bahlam said that the bear fetish was transporting people to their past lives. For Eric and his parents, that's Central and South America. You're talking about an entirely different world."

A leaf fell onto David's head. It remained there for a few seconds before he flicked it away. To Ahulani, it was a crown.

He put his hand on her face. "Yes, but I believe the energy, magic, strength of the portal is changing, morphing dimensions and reality—including that of the victims."

"What about remote viewing?" Ahulani asked. "Wouldn't that be safer? You were able to bring that woman home from within the stone house."

"Yes, but this is different. The shaman instructed both of us to travel to this planet. They need our energy, our full form, to help them. Not to mention, my grandfather said we have our own lessons to learn."

She trembled just thinking about such a journey. This would not be as quick as the trip to Kuelap. "David, are *we* going to be able to return home?"

"Of course, but it will take both of us to help all of the victims."

She smiled. "Makes sense as to why you were supposed

to bring the backpack." Ahulani looked down and saw the picture of Eric and his parents laying on a pile of leaves.

David knelt and traced his finger over the image of the Torres family. "It's time."

He stood up, held onto the tree next to him and guided her hand to another spot below his. He took her other hand and held it tightly. "Keep your hand on the tree. It will ground us to this place. I think their family picture in this vortex will combine all our energy, and hopefully, make it easier to find them."

She felt as if she were in earthquake mode. "I am not going to lie, I am terrified. I don't feel prepared for this."

He leaned in and kissed her on the lips—a gentle yet persuasive kiss that made her forget about the potential danger, if only for a few seconds.

"I know. I'm afraid, too, but we'll be together. Not to mention, we are both well protected."

Ahulani heard leaves crunching and saw Shelly and Larry watching them—not with worry or shock on their faces, but rather with acceptance.

"It's time." She heard the voice of the shaman. Rafael stood behind her and David with one hand on her shoulder and the other on David's.

Ahulani felt herself fading. She felt the rough bark of the sacred tree disappear under her hand. The last thing Ahulani saw was Shelly holding her hands in prayer.

Chapter Twenty-two

David didn't want to bring Ahulani. He didn't want to put her in danger, but he had no choice. They were in it together, and it was her case. During his prayer to the heavens, his grandfather and the shaman told him that Ahulani needed to travel with him. If she didn't, she wouldn't be able to live it down—especially if David were to be hurt or if he couldn't rescue the victims.

Ahulani was the strongest, most interesting, and most intelligent woman he had ever met. He knew she'd be able to handle the journey.

He watched her close her eyes before he closed his.

He focused on the faces of those lost in another dimension, on the rough bark of the Cottonwood tree, on the feel of Ahulani's hand in his, and on the series of eight symbols that had scrolled across his mind during the prayer—some of which were not of the original ten he'd seen. It had opened a gateway that he was told would lead him to Eric.

I call upon the power of Kuelap, the Marble Caves, Mother Nature, and the Universe to lead us safely to the world where Eric and his parents are located.

The images revealed themselves again one at a time. As soon as the eighth one appeared, the ground vanished beneath his feet. He could still feel Ahulani's hand and prayed for a safe journey.

Seconds later, he opened his eyes to a landscape of red sand dunes on one side and endless harsh, cracked earth on the other. Was it a dried-up lakebed? He wasn't sure.

Yet the atmosphere did not feel overly warm, like that of a desert. It was cool with no breeze. The planet's sun was low on the horizon, and blocked by the yellowish, hazy sky.

Ahulani let go of his hand and did a 360-degree turn, soaking in the scenery.

A bright blue lizard scrambled up the nearby embankment of a massive dune, its tracks temporary reminders of life on an unfamiliar planet. The lizard stopped to look at David and Ahulani, then ran to the top of the sandy dune and disappeared.

Ahulani looked at him. "I am surrounding us with light, love, and spiritual protection, though my guides say we should be safe."

No symbols appeared in his mind, but he continued to visualize Eric's face. He wasn't sure how the symbols worked or how they would help save the Torres family, but he knew his grandfather was watching over him and would provide guidance when it was needed. He had to believe that, for the victims' sakes.

David watched Ahulani as she absorbed her surroundings. Would he and Ahulani need saving as well? He hoped not. Would she rely on him—and only him to save everyone? He knew the answer, yet David felt tremendous pressure.

She crossed the lakebed quickly, her feet crunching on the lifeless surface. She glanced back at him to see if he followed.

He knew her intuition was guiding her, but he wanted to take a few seconds to look around. Besides the lizard, there was no other life—at least as far as he could see. David prayed they didn't come across anything dangerous.

He ran to catch up with her, and they walked hand-in-hand together in silence.

The horizon revealed a dull haze. He wished his grandpa had prepared him for this place. Or could anyone be ready for such a journey?

Ahulani stopped and pointed to a tree about a quarter

mile in the distance. "This tree could be somehow connected energetically to the one at the vortex on Earth. I say we check it out."

"Sure, let's go." She was right. It looked similar to the baobab tree of Africa. The massive, smooth trunk held bare branches that were shaped in a perfect half circle.

She pulled free of his hand and ran to the tree, nearly tripping over a large rock. Stepping around it, she glanced down at it before she continued toward the tree again.

Bizarre etchings were on the rock, as if someone had been marking the days. Is that why she had taken a second look?

She walked at a rapid pace and was nearly thirty feet ahead of him, standing by the tree.

"Lani, wait!" David raced to her. He didn't want to let her out of his sight.

He stopped in his tracks within a few steps of the tree. A child stood under the canopy of its gnarled, thick branches, peeking from behind the huge trunk. A small, stray tendril extended from the trunk and onto the child's shoulder.

The little boy had ruffled brown hair and light skin. For a second, David thought he saw a golden aura around the child.

"Eric," David whispered.

He couldn't believe how quickly they had found Eric. Perhaps, Eric had stayed in the location of his arrival, which could have been the tree he seemed attached to—though Ahulani had mentioned hearing Eric and his father in a jungle.

David was relieved to see Eric. The child's hair was messed up and he had dirt smears on his face and body. Otherwise, he seemed to be in good shape.

Ahulani had put her hands on Eric's shoulders and was looking him up and down. Tears rolled down her face as she hugged him tight. "Are you all right, Eric?"

Eric nodded repeatedly. "I'm okay, and I remember you!"

David ruffled Eric's hair. "Yes, this is Ahulani and I'm David."

David didn't know if he should ask Eric about the magician. Had there been an encounter between him and the child? Or did Bahlam prevent such an incident? Would his questions ever be answered?

No one else was there. He knew Eric's parents were on another part of this planet, but how the hell had the child managed to make it alone for so long?

A barely discernible humming emanated from the ground. David took a step toward the tree and the sound became louder. He touched the tree, and a sharp vibration emanated through his hand and down his arm. What was happening?

His gaze followed Ahulani's to a large animal twenty feet away. It trudged toward them on four long legs. David noticed it had an elephant's trunk. As it got closer, he realized the trunk was the only commonality with an elephant. *What was this creature?*

It was thinner than a normal-sized adult elephant, but with saggy folds of skin and long ears that went from a rolled-up position against its camel-like head to a straightened position in the air.

Eric ran toward it despite Ahulani's attempt to stop him.

"It's okay," Eric yelled as he approached the beast.

It didn't seem scared of Eric, David, or Ahulani. The bizarre animal lumbered up to the tree, using its thin trunk to strip the bark. Immediately, the tree started to emit moisture.

Ahulani traced her finger down a trickle of liquid. "Amazing."

"It's water," Eric said.

"So that's how you've been able to survive," David said.

Eric touched a knob on the trunk that was covered with a faint spiral. "It's the tree of life."

Bright green leaves and buds began to fill all the branches. The tree had gone from lifeless to sustainable within minutes.

Eric plucked a fruit hanging from the lowest branch. A small mango? The child took a bite and handed it to David.

Ahulani stroked the trunk. "If we could take one seed from this tree and bring it back to Earth, just imagine."

"I don't think so," David said. "Considering how we manage to wipe out species of plants and animals each year on our planet."

He took a bite of the fruit. It was juicy, sweet, and without seeds. Fleshy, the fruit tasted like it'd been crossed between an orange, mango, and banana. He wiped off juice dribbling from his chin, then handed it to Ahulani.

She took a small bite, then handed it to Eric. "Mmmm, that's the best thing I've ever eaten. Talk about a miracle fruit."

"This fruit, if that's what it is, beats the snacks I brought from Earth." David patted his backpack. "I did bring some water, just in case."

The animal grabbed a fruit from a higher branch and sucked it down through its trunk. The tree replaced it with another one immediately.

David's grandfather was still with them. "Your job is not done, David," he said. "You and Ahulani have work to do. It is important you get to somewhere safe before nightfall."

David clearly heard Grandpa's voice now. Could it be due to the atmosphere of the planet?

"We need to move," David said.

"I know," Ahulani said. "I heard."

David put his arm around Eric. "We have to find your parents. They are here somewhere. My friend and I are going to get you all out of here."

"Friend?" Eric gave David a sideways glance then looked at Ahulani, then back at David. Humor was in his eyes. "You are more than just friends. My parents look at each other that way!" The boy giggled.

Ahulani blushed but David smiled. It was as Ahulani had said—the child had an old soul.

Eric diverted his gaze to the bottom of the tree. "It's my fault all this happened. If I hadn't stepped into that house…"

Ahulani got down to Eric's level and gave him a comforting hug. "It's not your fault. You didn't know what would happen. There are other people who were also victims."

Eric swallowed hard, sniffling. "Bahlam told me you would help me find my mom and dad."

David ruffled Eric's hair. "The last time we saw Bahlam was when you appeared at Ahulani's house. He leapt into the portal after you. Is that when you talked to him?"

Eric didn't respond.

"I wonder if Bahlam is safe," Ahulani said.

David ran his hand down the trunk of the magical tree. "Hope so. Maybe we will find him here as well. Your intuition guided you in the right direction to find Eric."

He glanced toward the sand dunes. "What is it telling you this time?"

Ahulani searched the landscape. "Back toward the sand dunes, but we need to travel between the sand and the dry lake. Should we grab fruit for later?"

"No. It's not a bad idea, but I hope we won't have to be here too long," David said. "Eric, want to lead the way?"

"Sure," he said. Eric walked alongside the creature, petting its side as they went.

David followed with Ahulani. "I wonder how long it is until dark," he whispered so Eric couldn't hear him.

"I don't know, but Eric's made it through fine. I'm sure he's encountered the nights."

The slow-moving beast stayed with Eric most of the time, but showed interest in David and Ahulani as well.

Ahulani smiled at the creature as the tip of its trunk explored her head. "This has to be one of the strangest things I've ever experienced."

David laughed. "It likes you."

"I suppose so." Ahulani lifted the creature's trunk off her head, then stroked it. "Eric, does this animal follow you all the time?"

"Only when I wander away from the tree. It's my protector." The large mammal, if that's what it was, never left Eric's side.

They arrived at the edge of the lakebed, then headed around it toward the direction of the hazy sun. David kept watch over Eric and Ahulani to make sure they weren't straining themselves.

Did nightfall on this planet look like that on Earth with darkness and a moon? Or would they simply continue searching *through* the night without knowing?

David noticed the camel beast staring at him. Something about its eyes seemed familiar. "Eric, how long have you been here? Ahulani had a dream vision of you in the jungle and heard you yelling for your parents, but that was over a week ago."

"I don't know. Feels like days. The first place looked like a jungle, but I was only there for a few minutes. I kept traveling to different places—some were scary."

Ahulani put her arm around Eric's shoulder as they walked together. "What do you mean?"

"I was in one place one second and another the next." Eric stared at the reddish sand. "The dark forest was the worst. There were all sorts of strange sounds, and the trees were *watching* me."

David figured it must have been a thick, dark forest with a lot of strange creatures. He wanted to pry but didn't want to bring Eric back to a terrifying moment. He wondered how he would have handled such an experience at Eric's age. He looked at the elephant-camel thing and smiled. *If I had something like that by my side for protection, I suppose that would alleviate some fear.*

"You're safe now. We won't let anything hurt you." She stared intently at the ground as they walked.

"What are you looking at?" David asked.

"Not sure, I think it might be some sort of energy line. I see a solid gold line under the surface. Not to mention the heat I am detecting."

David veered from the beast's trunk as it swayed in his direction. "Have you heard anything from my grandfather?

Sometimes I can hear him, other times I can't."

"Not for a while. I haven't seen him, either."

David hoped his grandpa was still with them and didn't abandon them in such circumstances. He hoped not, at least.

Ahulani stopped, bent her head, and put her hands on her temples.

David stepped behind her and put his arm around her. "Are you all right?"

"Yes. David, I saw Eric's parents. They were by a similar tree as the one where we found Eric."

Eric jumped up and down. Then, he pulled on Ahulani's sleeve. "Are they okay? Tell me they are okay."

Ahulani smiled. "They are fine. Tired, but fine."

"It can help them," Eric said. "The tree, I mean. Did it have fruit?"

"No, honey. It was nothing but bare branches," Ahulani said.

Eric's downtrodden demeanor at the news of his parent's plight didn't go unnoticed.

She tousled his hair. "They probably ate a while ago and the tree reverted to its dormant state."

The temperature had started dropping. Perhaps that was the reason for his grandfather's warning.

Ahulani rubbed her arms to warm herself.

David didn't see any sort of shelter, and it was getting colder. Fast. No branches or anything to create a fire was in range. They were all in danger.

David shivered. "We can't leave until we find his parents. We need to find a safe place for the night."

Eric, who seemed to have been in a trance, looked at David and Ahulani shivering. "I can talk to it," he said.

The little boy walked into the dry lakebed and stood still.

The indigenous creature followed Eric and positioned itself next to the child.

David held Ahulani close, hoping to warm her. He rubbed her arms and back.

She looked over her shoulder up at him. "We are going to be fine. Eric is standing on a ley line that provides heat. I think it leads to that tree where we found him."

Within seconds, heat started to emanate from the ground up. David could feel it on his feet, working its way up his legs and torso. "Do you feel that?"

Ahulani watched the ground curiously. She'd stopped shivering. "Yes. I thought it might be the ley line, but we aren't standing on it."

David's eyes followed her gaze.

Eric stared at the ground intently.

He stood completely still.

Ahulani glanced at David. "A spirit is telling me Eric is keeping us warm using the energy of this planet."

David bent down and placed his hand on the hard surface. The warmth radiated outward rapidly. "We did learn he had special abilities. I can't imagine what else he's capable of."

Ahulani did the same, placing her hand near David's to feel the warmth. "And so brave. Not sure how well I'd be holding up after a week out here."

"You're an amazing woman," he said, standing upright.

"Maybe so, but it'd still be tough." She smiled and stood.

He looked into her eyes. "Ahulani, you can handle anything. I shouldn't have doubted bringing you here."

She snorted, then said, "I didn't know you did."

"I…" David didn't know how to explain.

The sky had taken on a similar hue as the landscape—a light mahogany that quickly spread throughout the horizon.

"Unbelievable," Ahulani said. "Everything is blending together. I almost can't tell where the sky meets the ground."

The friendly beast accompanying them became restless. His front hooves hit the ground hard, repeatedly, and his large head swayed from side to side in agitation.

Eric came out of his trance and went toward them.

"We can't stay here."

David looked from the dry lakebed to the sand dunes and back to the lakebed. "Where can we go? There's nothing out here."

Eric pointed toward the highest hill of sand. "That way."

The beast led the way, walking faster than David thought possible. It stopped and gave a look to Eric, who jumped on its back.

The creature watched Ahulani.

"It wants you to get on as well." David picked her up and lifted her onto the animal. "I'm sensing an urgency, and I have a feeling this thing can move."

"What about you, David?" Eric asked.

"I'll follow behind. I can keep up."

The elephant-camel creature took off at a surprising gallop. David ran behind as fast as he could, his feet sinking into the soft sand. He considered himself to be in decent shape, but his breath came in short spurts as he climbed up the hill. The weight of his backpack made it feel as if he were carrying fifty pounds.

The beast had vanished among the mysterious sand. One second, he saw it running ahead, in another it was gone—along with Eric and Ahulani.

Stopping for a second, his vision became blurry and his head spun. He dropped to his knees to catch his breath.

"David!"

He could hear his name being called, faint but clear. A blood red moon had appeared over the top of the dune, and the sand kicked up in response to something coming his way.

He struggled to breathe. It was as if his lungs were filling with fluid.

I can't die like this. Not alone.

David felt his backpack yanked off, then he was picked up and placed on the back of the camel thing. He collapsed forward onto its head and neck.

His grandfather's voice resounded in his head and in the dangerous atmosphere. "Bahlam, hurry. He won't last much longer."

Chapter Twenty-three

Ahulani could hardly breathe as the enigmatic animal raced up the dune. Its pace and the sand it kicked up made it challenging to take even a shallow breath. The sand should have slowed the animal down, but instead it seemed to urge it forward.

She held on tightly to Eric, hoping neither of them would fall. Ahulani was worried about David. There had been no room on the animal, and she wasn't sure he would be able to keep up.

David's life was in danger.

The minute particles of sand caught in her and Eric's throats, and they began to cough. Her butt was sore from the continuous bouncing.

Are we all going to make it through this?

As soon as the thought left her mind, her Mayan guide's voice resounded loudly, and not just in her mind. "Yes. You will return home. Have faith."

He had said the word *you*. She had a vision of returning with Eric, but she couldn't see David with them.

When she thought she couldn't handle any more punishment, the animal dove *into* the soft sand before reaching the top of the dune. Then, the creature stopped.

It took a few seconds for her eyes to adjust to the darkness. Eric had started to fidget, and she figured he wanted off its back. Her own rear had taken all the abuse it possibly could.

Without waiting for her help, Eric threw his leg over and leapt off the creature. It reared up and tossed her off its back. Ahulani had a soft landing on her rear.

174

David. It needs to go back for David.

The creature took off through a passage.

She stood quickly and assessed the area, brushing sand from her clothes. Eric had disappeared, probably roaming his new environment.

"Eric, where are you?" she whispered.

They were in a massive, open chamber. Large, pyramid style blocks lined one wall. She couldn't see the opposite wall, but Eric was standing in the center of the room.

She wondered how such a structure could exist within a sand dune without the winds exposing it.

Ahulani approached Eric. "Have you been here before?"

"Yes, this is where we sleep. He's been taking me here every night."

"He? You mean the creature with the elephant trunk?"

Eric nodded, then turned away from her. He stared at something she couldn't see.

She put her hand on his shoulder. "What's the matter?"

"I'm waiting."

"For what?"

Eric continued to stare intently into the darkness.

This place must be safe, or the animal wouldn't have brought Eric and her here.

Her guides answered as one. "Yes, you are well protected."

Eric got in a sitting position with his legs crossed, and waited.

"You are in a sacred sanctum."

Ahulani took in a sharp breath when she heard the familiar voice. The creature had returned and stood with David collapsed on its back.

"No..." She ran to David.

He seemed lifeless. His long hair was splayed out over the sides of the animal, and his grandfather appeared next to the beast. Rafael lifted him off its back.

"Please be okay," Ahulani whispered.

The camel-elephant creature transformed into a human form of the jaguar god. It was Bahlam. Relieved to see him but worried about losing David, Ahulani's emotions were in chaos.

Rafael tossed David's backpack on the ground, then lay David gently down and knelt next to him. "The atmosphere is deadly at night." He placed his hand on David's wrist, and his voice cracked with emotion. "I should have had Bahlam take him with you and Eric."

Ahulani felt his pulse. "It's faint, but he's alive."

As she watched, David took in a large gasp of air, opened his eyes wide, but started to choke.

"Help me sit him up," Bahlam yelled.

Ahulani was on one side of David and Bahlam on the other, and together, they helped him rest against the wall. David continued to cough, but the fit subsided eventually. He looked at Ahulani, warmth in his eyes, and then faced Rafael.

"Grandpa," David said.

"You can see him?" Ahulani asked.

David mashed his lips together and started to cry. "Yes, yes... I can see him so clearly."

Rafael smiled, gesturing to the walls. "It is this sacred temple. It is the reason why Bahlam can become himself."

He nodded toward Eric in the center of the room. "And why Eric is able to connect with his parents, if only briefly."

Knowing David would be okay, Ahulani stood when a couple appeared in the distance in front of Eric; it was as if she were staring at a living photograph. The man was a few inches taller than the woman, and to Ahulani, they looked like they could have been brother and sister. Both had dark brown hair of the same length—to their shoulders, and were striking.

In turn, his parents watched Eric from where they sat under a tree of life. Tears rolled freely down his mother's face.

"Can his parents see us?"

"Yes," Rafael said, as he attempted to keep David in a sitting position, but he insisted on standing.

Rafael made a huge sigh of frustration. "Stubborn."

Ahulani stepped closer to Eric. "They are out *there*," she pointed toward the top of the dune. "How can they survive?"

"They are on another part of the planet," Bahlam said. "Their location is far away and somewhat safer, at least as far as the night atmosphere is concerned."

She watched Eric talking to his parents but couldn't hear exactly what they said. "At least they are being helped by a tree of life. We have to find them."

Rafael said, "This planet will mess with your senses, including sense of time. His parents are safe for now. Occasionally, they get sustenance from the tree, but they are in a weird vortex. They are not far, within a couple miles of the dunes, but when they travel, they are led in a circle and back to the tree. The planet itself could be making an effort to protect them from the atmosphere here, or some other force could be preventing them from trying to find their son."

Ahulani went and stood next to Eric, so she could talk to them. Their lips were moving, but she couldn't hear them speak any words.

She glanced at Eric. He didn't seem to care as he soaked up their presence. The child waved and smiled.

Ahulani tried to comfort them with a serene expression on her face. "We will find you and you will all be together soon, I promise."

David came behind her. "Grandpa said they can't hear you. This place could be picking up on Eric's wishes to return home, or merely connecting the few lifeforms on the planet."

Bahlam's voice echoed throughout the chamber. "There is a way to get to his parents."

As Bahlam finished his statement, Eric's parents disappeared.

Ahulani placed her hand on Eric's shoulder. "Is it possible to get Eric home first, Bahlam? Maybe David can send him home with the symbols he discovered."

Eric stomped his feet on the ground and crossed his arms. "No. I want to go with you to find them." He marched over to the wall and slid down until he was sitting on the ground, pouting.

"Where could he go without his parents?" David asked. "He's been kept safe here for so long. At least Eric can see his parents in the temple. I would be afraid to try and send him back to Earth alone. It could be dangerous."

Ahulani was worried, wondering how long they would all be able to survive on an unfamiliar planet. She wanted to help Eric, his parents, and the other victims but she also didn't want to get stuck here with David.

As if sensing her anxiety, David gave her a hug and stroked her hair. "Everything will be fine. We'll find his parents and get home."

She returned his hug and looked him in the eye. "Sounds selfish, but I was thinking about how I wanted to be back home." She kissed him lightly on the lips. "With you."

David played with her hair, twisting the long strands in his fingers. "We'll be fine. We made it to safety. Thanks to you, we found Eric s. This is a life-saving mission, and the Universe will make sure we all make it home safe."

Ahulani held him tight, resting her head against his chest. "I am so tired, David."

Movement against her leg startled her. She glanced down to see Bahlam rubbing against her leg in his jaguar form. "You and David will have help."

She figured Bahlam was referring to himself, Rafael, and possibly the shaman whose bones David had found in the cave.

David pulled her with him and sat against the wall next to Eric. Then, he patted the spot next to him. "I think we'll be here for a while. We should sleep."

She sat next to him and placed her head on his shoulder. "David, I was thinking... You might be able to open another portal using the symbols to get to his parents."

Bahlam lay down in front of her and David. "That cannot be. Those symbols are only used *between* worlds or dimensions."

Ahulani hoped she never had another case like this again. Her saving grace was David. Sweet, handsome David. He was nothing like Will, and she supposed she had known that from the beginning. She hadn't wanted to admit he could be different. That would mean taking a chance.

A line of white light cut across the ground, about three inches wide. It had started from the opposite side of the sacred temple and cut between her and David. It was under the floor of the temple and emanated the same heat as they had felt from the line in the desert.

David moved over a few inches. "Is that a ley line?"

"I think so," Ahulani said.

Bahlam yawned and swished his long, black tail. "This sanctum is a meeting point for the ley lines. There are four lines that extend from each direction and run across the farthest regions. This temple is the center of this world and retains the power of the lines."

Bahlam got up and laid next to Eric. Still awake, Eric rested his head against the jaguar's.

Ahulani yawned and glanced at her watch. It had stopped at 1:11 P.M. She didn't know the exact time they had left Sedona but knew it had been sometime in the afternoon.

David had fallen asleep with his head against the wall and his arm around her shoulder. Eric and Bahlam were also sleeping curled up next to each other.

Drawn to the opposite side of the room, she gently removed David's arm and stood. She followed the ley line's light until she approached another wall stacked with large stones.

She lifted her gaze up to an opening between two blocks approximately a foot above her head. Ahulani slid her hand into the space but couldn't feel anything. *What is it?*

She glanced at the others to see if anyone had woken up, but she couldn't see them in the darkness.

She felt someone watching her. Was it Rafael? Or maybe it was just her nerves.

179

Scraping sounds began from the bowels of the temple. Ahulani stepped back from the wall. Some of the blocks had started shifting. Some blocks went to the left and others to the right, leaving holes in their midst. A couple of the stones sunk into the wall, but others moved up and down.

This looks like a game of Tetris.

Two more stones moved—one to the right and one to the left—two feet off the ground. It left a space twice as large as the others, big enough for a body to fit through.

The radiance of the ley line had diminished, but she could see its faint line on the ground directly below the center of the recent opening. The white energy line climbed the few feet into the crawl space. Then, it stopped moving.

Ahulani stepped forward, and the line started moving again.

It wants me to follow it.

She placed her hands on either side of the opening and peeked into the darkness. A pinprick of light revealed itself deep inside the passage. She wondered if she should let David know about her discovery.

She started to walk back toward the others, but intuition told her to check the line again. The ley line had begun to undulate sideways like a snake. When she took a step toward it, it stopped.

The bizarre line had a life of its own, and it wanted her to follow—now.

The lack of response from her guides was a sign she would be safe. They hadn't warned her of any danger.

Ahulani squeezed into the block tunnel. The line moved again, slowly. It stayed just ahead of her as she wriggled on her hands and knees further into the tight tunnel. She wished she had a flashlight.

A cave crawl tour in Hawaii with Will came to mind. Headlamps that spotlighted bats clinging to the rock. Knees scraped against lava rock and confined spaces above the main caverns had tested Ahulani's claustrophobia while they made their way through fifty feet above the cave floor.

The group had come to a crack in the cave about six inches across. Sharp, monstrous stalagmites rose threateningly from the ground; a drop from her location would have ended her life in a bloody death by *stalagknife*. She froze in place, her body shaking. *Breathe.*

Will had guided her over the fissure, coaxing Ahulani to focus only on him. The cave crawl was something *he* had wanted to do, and she had wanted to impress him.

Crawling through the passage following the ley line, she realized how much her life had changed since the divorce. When she'd lived in Kaunakakai, Molokai, she had loved to scuba dive on the island's south shore. She had nearly forgotten the beauty of the underwater life and the vibrant array of corals. Dolphins and manta rays would swim around her, and only her, as she explored the reef with friends.

Even fish schools of colorful reef wrasses, which sustained the lives of those who lived on the island, would surround her while she succumbed to the quiet world.

Ahulani and her father had gone on many fishing trips together from the time she was five. The underwater realm had its own life and beauty. Manta rays and spotted eagle rays would fly through the waves—she could watch them for hours. Alika Loe was her favorite—one of the largest mantas in the reef. The ray would slide up the side of the boat to get fed chopped up fish.

"That thing only approaches my boat when you're here," her father had said. The last time she saw Alika Loe was when she was fifteen. Though she had continued to fish the waters, she had never again seen it swimming gracefully through the reef. She had hoped it had traveled out of the reef rather than having been killed by a fisherman.

It had felt as if she had lost a close friend. When her relationship with Will had come to an end, it had seemed her own life had.

The longer she was in the passageway, the more

memories came flooding back. The energy line continued to lead her forward. Ahulani decided that if she made it through, she would return to Molokai.

A pinprick of light from the ley line expanded to a bright ball. She had to stop and shield her eyes with her hand, it was so bright. She hoped the line wasn't leading her out to the deadly wasteland.

Ahulani's knees were sore from kneeling against the stone floor. Her arms and shoulders were in pain from bearing weight while crawling.

A loud, muffled yell stopped her. David?

She wanted to go back—she should go back—but the energy line zig-zagged ahead of her. It was getting impatient.

"As my spirit guides, I am asking that you let David know I'm all right. I need to see this through." A ball of light shot out from the side of the passage and headed back toward the entrance.

Was that a guide or an intelligence from the pyramid?

The shouts continued, but only for another minute. She wondered if David or Bahlam would follow her. Or if the entrance to the passageway was even visible.

The light brightened in intensity. Ahulani had to close her eyes and lean her head down.

"Come on, like I'm not dealing with enough right now!" she whispered, frustrated. Tired and hot, she wondered how long she would be squeezing her body through the tight confines.

Seconds later, she was in the center of two larger passages, both going in either direction.

The brilliant light extinguished itself, then the ley line did something she didn't expect. It split in two—one line went right and the other left. A fork in the path.

"Wait," she shouted. "Which way am I supposed to go?"

She felt drawn down the path on the right.

She turned, crawling into the wider passage. It seemed to go on forever. Twenty feet or so into the tunnel, she came across a drop—it looked bottomless. The gap was wide enough that she couldn't get across. Her heart raced and she began to panic. She wouldn't be able to turn around or back out.

She thought of the crevasse that Will had helped her over in the Hawaiian cave. This would not be so easy to overcome.

Ahulani started to back up, but something pushed her forward so fast she didn't have time to react. A strong wind greeted her as she fell straight down.

She screamed as a breeze pushed her back up before letting her drop slower.

Is this how it ends? Alone on an alien planet?

Ahulani braced herself for the final impact.

Instead, she landed on her feet. Her eyes adjusted to a large, open chamber.

A shapely female figure stood motionless not far in front of Ahulani. She wasn't surprised the medicine woman had come with her and David.

"You've come such a long way," the woman said. "You have been guided to this planet for two reasons. To rescue Eric and his parents." The long-legged, dark-haired beauty walked closer to Ahulani. "And to return home."

The chamber lit up to reveal sconces along the length of each block wall.

"What is this place?" Ahulani asked. She turned toward the phantom, who strode slowly, running her hand along the wall. "Am I in the bowels of the same sacred pyramid?"

Hearing a sound from within the recently discovered chamber, Ahulani turned to see a human figure coming toward her. Whoever it was stopped before she could make out their face.

"Lani?"

She recognized David's voice.

"Yes, I'm here," she said.

He ran to her and held her tight. Then, he pulled away and looked her over. "I was so worried."

Mentally and physically exhausted, Ahulani prayed this challenge would end so she could take back her life, and for her, that included David. "How did you find me?"

183

"We followed a strange orb of light through an opening at the bottom of the wall, near where we had been sleeping. The passage had stairs leading down, then came to an end. The only option was to go right. That's how I got here."

Ahulani shook her head and laughed, releasing a tension in her body she hadn't known was there. "That sounds much easier than the way I came." She glanced in the direction she had entered the room.

"David, the medicine woman is here. She said I was brought here for two reasons—to rescue the Torres' and to return home—whatever that means."

He walked past Ahulani and searched around the area. "Where is she?"

The covert spirit had vanished, but she was never far away. Ahulani wanted to know more about the medicine woman and the connection to her and David.

David was taken in by the same side of the wall as the medicine woman. Feeling the same pull, Ahulani noticed drawings. A hummingbird, a thunderbird, spirals, sun symbols, and Chinese symbols lined the wall.

She touched the Thunderbird symbol. "The medicine woman must have meant you returned home to a place from your past."

David pointed up at the ceiling. "Strange. Why would there be a sea creature in a pyramid located among the sand dunes?"

Ahulani looked up, too. A huge manta ray had been etched, upside down, into the solid block above. It took up half the ceiling. But it was the marking on the creature that made her drop to her knees. "No," she said. "It can't be…"

David knelt next to her. "Lani, what's wrong?"

A dark round pattern in the center of its back stunned her. She could almost visualize the ray swimming effortlessly above.

"I called it Alika Loe. That was one of my friends from Molokai when I was a child."

For a brief second, she thought she saw its pectoral wings move.

184

Chapter Twenty-four

David couldn't take his eyes off the magnificent creature. It made no sense, yet he kept getting brief visions of it flying over and through the dunes.

He and Ahulani had slept soundly after the discovery of the manta ray. They would not have made it much longer without rest, making it dangerous not only for themselves, but for the family they needed to rescue.

Had the medicine woman assured they would get such a sleep? Or was it something with the chamber itself?

Bahlam stalked into the chamber with Eric following close behind. The animal sat on the floor in front of David and Ahulani. "It is early morning and safe to leave. We need to find Eric's parents. His mother is ill, and his father is not well, either."

Ahulani glanced from Bahlam and back to the ceiling.

Could it really be the same sea creature from her youth? Or was it a coincidence? David wanted to know more about this aspect of her past but there was no time.

He took Ahulani's hand, and he and Ahulani approached the same tunnel where David had entered.

Why had she been guided to crawl through the inside of the pyramid, nearly falling to her death, when David was able to enter the same room through a passage? Was it about facing her fears?

"We do not need to return to the room above," Bahlam said. In jaguar form, he stood and stretched. "You might want to back up so I can turn into my larger life form."

"Why do you choose such a bizarre metamorphosis?" David asked.

"I didn't. It chose me. This is what I turned into when I first arrived. This structure enables my real identity. Before taking Eric to the surface, I transform to the clunky creature you see now."

What is your true self? Man or jaguar?

Bahlam had transformed from jaguar to beast within seconds. David wondered if the elephant-like creature was indigenous to the planet. He tried not to laugh as Bahlam's long ears rolled up and down.

"How are we going to get out of this place?" As soon as David asked the question, he remembered Bahlam couldn't talk in his new identity.

Eric's attention had gone from Bahlam to the manta ray. He stood in the center of the chamber, staring up at it.

David picked Eric up and placed him on Bahlam's back.

"All three of us can't fit on his back," Ahulani said.

"I know. He can return for me in a few minutes. It's going to be slow going getting to the location where Eric's parents are." He tried to help Ahulani up, but she was watching the ceiling.

"What's the matter?" he asked.

She pointed up. "It's gone."

David looked up. The manta ray had vanished. "What the heck?"

A shadow encompassed David, Ahulani, Eric, and Bahlam. It circled around them and then stopped above them. Its body could have wrapped itself around Bahlam's form.

Bahlam stepped back quickly. Did the beast want to get a better look? Or was he afraid?

The shadow started to reveal distinguishing features, including a wide body, a gaping mouth, a thin tail, and wings that flexed upward, as if flying through the ocean.

Ahulani reached up to touch its underside.

"No, don't," David said, and pulled her hand down.

The creature changed from a shadowy mass to a solid black entity. It swam around the top of the chamber several times. Then the ray dove lower, a foot above the ground, and approached Ahulani.

David could see the dark spot in the center of its back. It also had a large white spot on either side of its mouth.

She put her hand out and stroked the area behind its mouth. "It's Alika Loe. I know it."

The ray started to circle the group again—at a quicker pace.

He pulled Ahulani close and watched as it circled repeatedly. David's hair blew in every direction, and he closed his eyes. It felt like they were in the middle of a tornado.

What is happening?

Then, the wind ceased, and he felt the sun's opulence.

He opened his eyes. They were standing outside, under a sphere brighter than that of the Sun, though it didn't feel overly warm. Ahulani had remained within David's arms and Bahlam stood next to them with Eric on his back. The sand around them was darker than that of the dunes, similar to dried blood. Paths of smooth river rocks meandered over small, mountainous hills. The sand was piled up in between the hills and among the stones.

The manta ray lay on top of a sparse patch of sand. It used its wings to toss the rough red granules onto its back.

"That thing must have brought us here," David said, and glanced around. "Wherever *here* is."

The temperature felt warm, in the upper seventies and it was early morning.

Ahulani grabbed David's arm. "Maybe Eric's parents are here somewhere."

"Let's hope so." David bent over and ran his finger over the back of the ray. He was surprised at how real it felt, considering they had all witnessed its shadow form.

Eric jumped off Bahlam, knelt by the manta ray, took handfuls of sand and sprinkled it over the creature.

The ray touched the child gently with its pectoral wing, as if to say thank you. The ray then buried itself in a small pile of sand until only the center of its back showed.

Ahulani knelt by the ray and rubbed its back. "Alika Loe must have brought us here through some sort of teleportation, though I don't know how it's able to live without water."

If this giant was Ahulani's childhood friend, how had it gotten to another planet? It couldn't possibly be alive after thirty years. Could it be a spirit guide?

Eric indicated a structure buried in sand to them.

David saw a building that had been created from large blocks. "It's the temple."

Ahulani looked at him. "David, are you seeing a vision of it also? That room we were in is an ocean. I am getting visuals of Alika Loe flying through the passages and into its own private sea."

The ray explored Ahulani's arms with its mouth and fins. It flopped its body over her arms and looked up at her.

"Alika Loe has to be dead." She couldn't stop staring at the creature and her voice cracked with emotion. "Yet, here it is. I have no idea what's happening."

She stood. "Unless this planet is bringing memories to life."

He nodded. "I agree. Or, it's some sort of guide. I got a vision of it flying through the passages."

David took Ahulani's hands in his. "I think based on what we saw in that last chamber, we both have been here before in a past life. Consider the symbols on the walls and Alika Loe. Grandpa mentioned this would be a journey that would help us learn about ourselves. Perhaps being here will help us in ways we've yet to discover."

"I wonder if we were together as a couple," Ahulani said. "In a past life, associated with this place."

"I believe so."

David sensed his grandfather's presence, though he couldn't see him. "Is Grandpa still here?" He was disappointed that he could only see his grandfather with the help of a distant planet, but hoped that would change by coming to terms with his abilities.

Ahulani squeezed his hand. "Yes. He's next to you. The temple allowed you to see him, but your abilities are growing, so I believe you'll be able to see him on your own soon."

His grandfather smiled. "Let David know I returned to Shelly and revealed myself through her dreams. She is worried, but her intuition tells her you are safe."

When David dropped his hands from their grip, Ahulani put both her hands on his shoulders. "Rafael wants you to know that he went back to update Shelly. She's fine."

"That's good. It's going to be a long day." David pulled away from her hands and watched the mound of sand over the ray.

He was startled by a sudden movement from the manta ray. Sand exploded as it burst from the ground. It dove back in headfirst and disappeared.

"There's a tunnel under this spot." Ahulani first looked down, then toward the direction of the hills. "Those passages extend much farther than where we're standing."

David wondered if the sacred temple had been built for such a creature. "What do we do now?" he asked.

Bahlam looked at Eric and glanced toward his back. David lifted Eric up and placed him on the animal's back.

David turned to Ahulani. "Let me help you up."

"I can walk," Ahulani said. "Why do you think Alika Loe didn't bring us to Eric's parents?"

David walked alongside Bahlam. He didn't have an answer to her question. "I'm not sure." He heard a low, rumbling growl come from Ahulani's stomach.

She blushed. "Sorry, I'm hungry."

He'd had a fitful sleep because of his own stomach. If they were going to be here much longer, they would need food. Were there other trees bearing fruit on this part of the planet? There had to be other animals for potential meat sources.

Ten minutes later, Eric pointed to something in the distance. "It's coming back!"

They all stopped walking when the manta ray flew above the highest peak. It dove down and flew straight at them.

Ahulani observed the ray closely. "What's in its mouth?"

The ray stopped above them and dropped a bunch of fish on top of river rocks in the sand.

David did a 360-degree turn and looked up at the ray. "Where did you get this?" He didn't expect an answer, rather curiosity overcame him.

Ahulani picked up a fish. "This is Opah, also called moonfish. It's from Hawaii."

He stared at the slim, flat fish with a silvery-grey body. The fish's coloring transitioned to a rose red dotted with white spots toward the belly. The fins were crimson, and its large eyes were encircled with gold.

His mouth began to water and his stomach growled. "How are we supposed to eat this?" He laughed. "I like sushi but only when chefs prepare it for me."

Bahlam was drooling. He galloped toward the pile of fish.

David laughed ·at the animal's attempt at running. Bahlam gave David a glance that said, "Just wait until I'm in Jaguar form."

Eric had leapt off Bahlam and picked one up. "Eeewwww." He dropped it. "Slimy."

Ahulani grabbed David's arm. "This ray has been helping his parents."

"They can't be that far then," David said. "It returned within a few minutes and that included time for it to grab the fish, though who knows where it got them."

"I don't think it is able to transport others," Ahulani said. "At least not alone. The sacred magic of the temple helped. Consider how Bahlam got us all to safety."

David watched as the ray flew back in the direction from which it had come with the fish. "It was waiting for us. Your ray friend knew we were coming. It wanted to get us closer to his parents."

Ahulani picked up an Opah and handed it to David. "We should eat first. Raw might work but we should descale the fish."

David put his backpack on the ground and watched

190

Bahlam devour a couple of the fish. He didn't know if the indigenous animal form normally ate fish, but his panther side considered it a delicacy.

"I think we can manage to cook some of this before heading out." David glanced around. "I see some fire starter." He pointed at an area with twigs, grass, and bits of wood.

"Let's do this," Ahulani said.

Eric followed David and Ahulani while they gathered what they could find.

Eric tossed some grass and brush on top of the sticks and wood that David had placed on the ground.

David ruffled Eric's hair. "Thanks for your help."

Eric's stomach grumbled, then he giggled. "Don't we need a lighter to cook the fish?"

"You're right. Not sure if I have one on me."

David felt someone poke his back pocket. He felt a lighter and remembered he had brought a pocketknife.

"Are you always this well prepared?" Ahulani took the pocketknife and started to scrape the scales off a fish.

"I carry the knife, but I didn't have the lighter on me. Guess I can thank grandpa for that gift."

Ahulani descaled the fish nearly as well as a professional chef. He lit the fire and adjusted the starter material to fan the flame.

"Where did you learn such skills?" David asked.

"I used to live by the ocean. My dad and I went out on the water all the time. He taught me to clean what I caught."

"I suppose we both have some survival skills. My parents took Shelly and I camping quite a bit, which is why I enjoyed living at Kuelap while doing research. I love the outdoors. I even camp out under the stars at Petrified Forest."

Less than half hour later, they were eating the delicate Opah.

"Eric, how do you like it?" Ahulani took a bite of a smaller fish.

"Great! I was starving. This tastes like steak!"

David smiled, then wiped a small piece of fish off Eric's chin. "I bet. You've been eating mostly fruit. I am glad you had access to water. That can be a life saver."

David looked at the spot where the pile of Opah had been dropped. "Looks like Bahlam helped us finish it all."

"Is everyone ready to go?" Ahulani asked.

Eric nodded, excitement showing in his eyes. "I want to see my mom and dad."

Ahulani pointed past the highest peak. "Alika Loe went over that hill. Looks like we should be able to get over it fairly easily, or maybe we can walk through the sandy valley."

David helped Eric onto Bahlam's back, then he turned to Ahulani.

"Are you sure you don't want me to help you up on Bahlam?"

Ahulani grinned and rubbed her butt. "No, I'm good walking. Bahlam seems to know where we need to go."

David picked up his backpack and put it over his shoulder.

Bahlam's pace quickened. He made his way ahead of David and Ahulani.

Perhaps the beast sensed Eric's urgency to find his parents. The animal's pace continued to quicken and soon Bahlam was out of sight.

"He'll come back," Ahulani said."

The temperature had risen at least five degrees since the ray had brought them out into the sunlight.

David squeezed Ahulani's hand. "How are you doing? That wasn't much of a meal, and it does seem to be getting warmer."

"I'm fine. I practically lived outdoors in Molokai— scuba diving, fishing with my father, and hiking."

"You were quite the adventurer."

Ahulani bent down and picked up a smooth, oval-shaped rock. "I still am." She winked. "I wonder where this planet is among the vast expanse of the universe.

How far is it from Earth? Is it part of the Milky Way Galaxy? How long has it been a planet? How many light years would it take to get here on a spaceship?"

He noticed the peak they were heading towards had a human face. "I've heard of others who have the ability to teleport, though not sure of their method. Did we get help from the shaman? Was it Grandfather? Or was it just the two of us?"

His thoughts ran wild. What about the portal at Kuelap? Was it continuing to take more victims? How would he and Ahulani get everyone home? He knew he had been channeled by the shaman from the cavern, but would that powerful soul help them return home? Would he someday be able to find the cave from his dreams and learn more about the symbols, his past, and himself.

Ahulani wiped her brow with her hand. "Shamans and medicine people have been traveling for centuries, usually through out-of-body. Those symbols your family has been gifted with are pretty amazing. I have a feeling it's a combination of talents."

There was no sign of the manta ray or Bahlam. The sand had been replaced with a long stone path. He and Ahulani continued to walk along the stone path up the hill. The face watched them approach.

"Do you see it?" David asked, and pointed to the peak.

"Yeah. It's sort of unsettling."

"We'll have to get a closer look. Maybe we can see his parents and Bahlam from that vantage point."

They strode in silence until reddish clouds formed above the peak. David was grateful for the cool breeze that followed but wondered if they were in for a storm.

They climbed over a small, rocky outcrop, and David stopped. The face looked down at them.

Ahulani had become more nervous as they got closer. The maroon clouds darkened. One of the lower clouds drifted across the peak, blocking out the face, but still, David felt like they were being watched.

She looked down toward the pyramid and then up at

David. "My guides are saying this route is safe, but..."

David saw Bahlam's tracks in the valley below. He hoped Bahlam had found Eric's parents.

"If you want to go back down, we can come up through the valley."

"It's okay. Before the clouds rolled over the peak, I saw a path that passed by the left side of the rockface and over the hill."

He took her hand again, and they hiked the most strenuous part of the path. It was a 400-foot ascent, and though not a straight vertical cliff, it was still challenging.

David watched Ahulani as she sure-footedly climbed.

The small cloud that had covered the peak dissipated. "David, am I imagining this?" she asked.

"No. That's not the same face."

"What happened?"

David looked at her. "I noticed it when the clouds came in." He felt apprehensive yet curious. How could the peak have changed without them seeing or hearing anything? While the original face looked more serious, with deep-set eyes and a stiff jaw, this rock persona looked serene.

Ahulani held his hand tightly. "Either this is the same face with a different expression, or we're talking about two faces."

He indicated the path past the face. "The sooner we get up there, the sooner we can head down to the other side."

Ahulani hurried up the rocky path without glancing at the morphing peak.

David tried not to look, but morbid curiosity got the better of him. The kinder, more inquisitive persona watched them closely. Its eyes had shifted to the side as they continued to ascend.

He and Ahulani finally arrived at the top. Below was a landscape he didn't expect to see—dense foliage and canopy that went on for miles.

Ahulani sat on a boulder, facing the view, resting a moment. "How can we find them in such a forest?"

She grabbed David's arm. "Wait. This explains why

I saw a jungle in my dream. It's not the Amazon as my guides mentioned, but it looks just like it."

David knelt next to Ahulani. "You heard Eric and his father calling for each other. That's probably because he was trapped within the dunes and his parents were in the forest."

She put her hand on his shoulder. "I think that shaman personae *is* the reason you had the dream. He wanted to remind you of who you once were. You probably need to call on your symbols to figure out how to get us all home. Keep in mind, it's not only Eric's parents, but there could be other people trapped here."

David knew lives were at stake. He had thought Ahulani would be the critical factor in solving the mystery of Kuelap, not him. He didn't have quite as much confidence in himself. He may have managed to return the one woman home but that didn't mean he could do it again, and for several people. He was still feeling overwhelmed with the discovery of such abilities, let alone how to use them.

Markings and signs covered the side of the boulder Ahulani sat on. She followed his gaze and stood to get a better look at it.

The symbols from the cave were inscribed onto the rock, similar to petroglyphs. He ran his hand over the drawings.

"David, this is no accident," Ahulani said, and walked slowly around the rock. "Something is supposed to happen here, at this peak. I know it."

He stared up at the rock face that gazed out over the jungle. It wasn't either of the faces they had seen while climbing.

A mysterious voice whispered in his ear. "This person is someone you know well."

Chapter Twenty-five

Ahulani had never imagined this case would take her off world. She believed in many things and had many abilities, but traveling to another place in the universe without a shuttle had seemed incomprehensible, even to her. Any minute, she expected to wake up in her bed, stretch, yawn, and realize it was all a dream.

She knew better.

She touched David's arm as a third rock face appeared facing the jungle. When it did, she was shown an image of the cave.

"Lani, I think that might be the shaman who helped us get here." David never took his eyes off the formation.

This individual watched over the high canopy. He had features similar to David's with high cheekbones, a smooth face, and the same shaped mouth and nose.

"Perhaps he's here to help," Ahulani said. "This has to be a sacred place. I don't think we need to descend."

David looked away from the peak. He did his usual 360-degree turn to assess the area. "There's magic here. I can't figure out if it is the peak or the hill, but there's a familiar energy here."

She surveyed the vista of the sparse reddish terrain behind them, then viewed the glorious jungle. "Both landscapes are so different, yet so beautiful."

When she looked at David again, he was circling the peak in a quick pace.

He ran his fingers thru his hair. "I don't get it. There are no faces."

Ahulani saw a craggy boulder interspersed with indentations but no sign of human features. Movement in the thick foliage at the base of the hill below caught her attention.

"David, I saw something way below, but I can't see what it is. It's close to this hill." She indicated a thicket of bushes at the bottom. "In there. Can you see it?"

"I don't see anything." David watched but moved his focus to the petroglyph boulder after a minute. He knelt in front of it and closed his eyes, concentrating.

She sensed three overwhelming presences—spirits— nearby. She couldn't pick up on what or who they were. Could they be the faces of the peak? Chills went down her spine, and a powerful sensation came over Ahulani.

"Do you feel that?" she asked. "Something is building."

He nodded, then walked around another large boulder. "I found another boulder with symbols on it over here. Not as many, but there are some bizarre signs engraved. The weird thing is, both boulders have arrowhead petroglyphs that point to each other."

Ahulani went over to the other boulder David had discovered. A large eye had been inscribed on the center of the side facing the jungle. The iris was in the shape of a sun spiral. The end of the spiral drew her eye toward the corner of the rock where a white arrowhead, nearly a foot long, pointed to the first boulder.

David showed her the arrowhead on the smaller rock. It was at the top edge and was half the size of the other one. A perfect replica, it was like an actual arrow had been placed inside and the boulder had absorbed it.

Ahulani bent down and traced her finger over the shape. "How could we have missed this?"

She felt something behind her and quickly turned.

"We're surrounded," David said.

"This isn't bad energy, David, just strong. I'm not sure who is associated with this peak or this planet, but you need to draw upon this power."

A male spirit guide called out to her. "You both need

to work together." The voice was so loud, she thought someone was next to her.

She stood at the center of the two boulders when the tree from Oak Creek Canyon slammed into her vision. She felt the bark and could hear the stream and whispering leaves.

"David," she yelled. "This is a portal to Oak Creek Canyon."

She grabbed for his hand and pulled him next to her. "We can do this together. Your grandfather believes in you and so do I."

"How do you handle such pressure?" he asked. "I never imagined when I was brought into this, that it would be to learn so much about myself. I thought I was supposed to help you."

"You did." Ahulani kissed him full on the lips. "Repressed memories are starting to surface, and I am not fighting my feelings anymore. Will is my past." She held him as tightly as she could. "You are my future."

David put his arm around her waist and stroked her hair. "I'm glad. I want to be a part of your future." He pulled her close and kissed her forehead. "I can sense the shaman here, but I am not being channeled."

Ahulani took David's hand. "He knows you can do this. *We* can do this."

She placed her other hand on the small boulder. "David, touch the other boulder."

"The arrowheads," David said. "That's it. Make sure your hand is on the arrowhead." He squeezed his other hand in hers, creating what Ahulani hoped was an energy line.

She recalled the gifted arrowhead from the medicine woman. Did the healer know of such symbols on this planet? Could Ahulani and David still use the energy from the clear quartz arrowhead even though they didn't have it with them?

David closed his eyes, and she shut hers. She focused on Eric and his parents, envisioning them in the jungle below. She imagined the feel of the missing arrowhead tightly in her hand with its serrated edges. She focused on the spiral tip and on the last place she saw it. Maybe the clarity and ability to connect with her surroundings would work with David's talents. Hopefully.

Sense of time was mute as Ahulani focused on finding the family through remote viewing. She and David had been standing on the peak for a while before she found the Torres family by the tree of life, gazing up into the canopy. The intense, suffocating humidity created beads of sweat on her skin. She heard a river nearby, and spotted a giant shape flying above the trees. Could it be Alika Loe?

She reached out to touch Eric, who held onto his father. Her grasp went through his shirt.

Eric's mother, Linda, turned her head and looked at Ahulani. Linda pointed at her, and said, "It's the woman I saw with Eric."

At that second, James, Linda, and Eric vanished. Alika Loe swam through the forest straight at Ahulani.

Ahulani reached up to touch the ray's underside. As she did, the jungle disappeared from her view. Her body felt like it was breaking apart in minute particles.

Ahulani had never experienced anything so intense. She thought she was dying, shattering into nothingness. It was agonizing.

A cold, brisk wind overcame her, and she opened her eyes. She saw familiar trees and a full moon that lit up a forest. Someone leaned over her, calling her name repeatedly.

"Ahulani. Are you all right?"

She didn't know where she was or who it was that called her name. Blurred figures leaned over her. Finally, she recognized David by her side.

"It's David," he said, and stroked her face. "Please be okay."

She struggled to remember what had happened.

"Lani, we're home. Everyone's safe."

She dug her fingers into the moist ground for support and sat up slowly. She looked at David, and at an older male spirit next to him and remembered everything. The boulders, the forest, the transfer.

David knelt next to her.

She threw her arms around him and didn't let go.

"I was so worried about you," David said. "The arrowheads worked, along with our energy. We're home."

He escaped her hug and put his hands on either side of her face. "Are you feeling well? I felt a little queasy when I woke up."

"Yes. I had the weirdest sensation before we left the jungle. I felt like my entire body was being torn apart, molecule by molecule. I didn't have that problem when we left."

David looked at her with concern in his eyes and lowered his head. "That's strange. I didn't feel much of anything, except my feet on the ground, then collapsing next to the tree. I hope that wasn't my fault."

David helped Ahulani stand up, and she took his hands in hers. "Alika Loe passed over my head right before we transported, and I touched him. Perhaps, I was in the midst of two portals at once." She looked up at Rafael who was standing behind David and nodded at the old man. He stayed silent.

Ahulani didn't see Eric or his parents. "Where is Eric? His parents?" she asked.

"The Torres family is home. Grandpa told me they went straight home to Chachapoyas."

Ahulani looked at David in surprise, and then at Rafael. "That's wonderful! Thank God!" She was happy that they had saved Eric and his parents. Were there others who had fallen into the magician's trap at Kuelap? How could they shut down the gateway? How could they stop the magician?

"Wait, you mean you can hear and see Rafael?"

"Yes," he said.

"That's fantastic," she said, grinning. "I'm sure you two will have plenty to talk about."

He winked at her. "Yeah, I forgot how much he loves to talk."

200

Small dragonflies flew around the trees like fierce fairies. They were all different metallic colors—orange, red, and blue. Some hovered above the water. Others flitted around her and David. A large orange dragonfly landed on the top of her hand for a few seconds, darted off toward the water, then placed itself on a rock in the middle of the stream.

Another dragonfly—darker orange—joined the first. They faced each other and connected antennae. Their bodies sparkled in the sun.

"I've never seen so many dragonflies," David said. "I saw a brilliant purple one right before you returned. It floated in front of my face as I awoke."

"Your favorite color." Rafael spoke up but Ahulani couldn't see him.

She glanced at her watch. It read 11:55 P.M. Was it the correct time? "David, you should go see Shelly and Larry. They're probably worried. Let them know you're fine. I'd love to go with you, but I am exhausted. I need to go home and rest, try to absorb everything that's happened."

"Hey, we can't break this party up yet." A deep male voice came from behind her.

David's jaw dropped, but he smiled.

She turned around to see Joe, then ran and gave him a hug. "What are you doing here?"

But she already knew why he was in the middle of the forest at midnight. He had seen their return in a vision.

David shook Joe's hand. "You're a site for sore eyes."

"Thought I would check up on all of you. I knew you would be coming back about this time and wanted to make sure you had a smooth journey."

Did he know about what happened in the jungle, right before I returned?

"How long have you known?" Ahulani asked.

"A while. I saw it during David's cleansing ritual, but there are certain things a person isn't meant to know. It can change the future, and not in a good way."

Ahulani knew what he meant. As a psychic, revealing too much information could make a person change their own path—deliberately or otherwise. They might take an action that would result in a different outcome than what the universe planned. Sometimes, that could be a good thing. She suspected Joe had seen much more than he let on.

Joe stared at the moon, or perhaps he was studying the stars. Did he wonder about the planet David and Ahulani had just transported from?

"You both should get some rest." Joe looked at David. "I will make sure your girl gets home safe, and you need to see your sister. She's still up, waiting."

To Ahulani, Joe said, "He'll call you tomorrow, I'm sure."

David pulled her to him. "I'm glad you're okay. I can't wait for the future." He kissed her lightly on the lips. "We'll talk more tomorrow."

She put her arms around his neck, then gave him a deep passionate kiss, despite Joe witnessing it. The kiss made her feel as if she were floating in space.

David pulled away, breathless. "Wow, I'd do this all over again, just for that." He played with a few strands of her hair and spoke low into her ear. "I love you."

She smiled and took his hands in hers, not reciprocating his words. Instead she said, "I am overjoyed to be home, but we both know it isn't over yet."

"Come on you two lovebirds, let's go," Joe said.

She watched him walk away toward Shelly's. Ahulani hadn't expected to hear those words so soon. David had proved he could be trusted. He'd stayed close to her, ensuring her safety—off world and on Earth—and his genuine concern had made her feel adored, loved.

"You have always been worth loving," her guide said for her ears alone.

"Let's get you home," Joe said, and took her arm in his.

As they walked in silence, Ahulani's mind wandered. Would it all feel like a dream in the morning? What about Bahlam? The last time she had seen him he was heading toward the jungle with Eric. Was he stranded on the planet, or had she and David returned Bahlam to his home—wherever that was?

Ten minutes later, they arrived at her door. There were moments when she thought she'd never see her home again.

She breathed a sigh of relief as she entered. The warm earth tones of the walls, the piles of gemstones, and the Hawaiian artifacts were more beautiful than ever. Ahulani wished she could hide away in her home forever, but the mystery wasn't over. Only the case had been solved, though she should still check in with James and Linda in the morning.

Joe put his hand on her shoulder. "Get to bed. I'll spend the night on your sofa."

"I have a spare bedroom."

Joe held up his hand. "No, the couch is good. I don't want you to worry about cleaning up after me. I am fine with a blanket."

Ahulani headed down the hallway. She removed a blanket, pillow, and sheets from a hall closet and put them on the couch.

He placed the pillow against the armrest and removed the blanket.

"Are you sure you don't want a bedroom?"

Joe shook his head. "I have slept on nothing but the forest floor. I have also slept sitting up. This is great."

She went toward her room, exhausted but relieved that she had company after her terrifying excursion home.

"Oh, Lani, I almost forgot," Joe shouted.

She turned and saw Joe remove an object from his front jean pocket. "I found this near the stream before you and David returned." He opened his palm to reveal the clear quartz arrowhead.

She was ecstatic. "You found it. Thank you, Joe!" She gave him a hug., then took it from him and practically raced to her bedroom, holding it tight in her hand.

They had all thought the arrowhead was gone, that it had been stolen by the magician after Eric disappeared from her living room. Had her focus on the object during the ritual help enable its return, and their own?

She sat on her bed and flipped the arrowhead over and over in her hand several times. The medicine woman had mentioned during her brief appearance at the underground sanctum that Ahulani was meant to return there as a reminder of whom she once was in a past life. She and David both understood that they had been on the planet before as different people. How long ago? Who had they been? And what was the role they played? Ahulani couldn't be sure.

She wanted to do a meditation with the arrowhead but was too exhausted. Ahulani placed it under her pillow.

She went to the bathroom and showered. It felt good to remove the grit of the sand from her body. She dressed in a nightgown and climbed into bed—an act she had been dreaming of doing since before they'd traveled to the other world.

Rafael, two of her Native American spirit guides, and the medicine woman stood at the end of her bed, smiling. The last thing she saw was Alika Loe floating above her before she closed her eyes.

She couldn't wait to talk to David tomorrow. Her new life waited.

Chapter Twenty-six

The medicine woman, Rafael, and a bunch of her spirit guides waited next to two large boulders—somewhere deep in her subconscious. Ahulani was on top of the sacred peak of faces. In one direction, lay the red dunes and dried lakebed, and in the other, the sprawling jungle.

Not again.

She felt something against her leg and glanced down to see Bahlam in jaguar form.

Someone or something else watched. Ahulani saw a face with wide-set eyes, high cheekbones, a broad nose, and turned up lips in a half smile on the rock face.

She glanced at her guides, David's grandfather, and the medicine woman.

"What is this place?" she asked. She walked toward the stunning woman. "You gave me an arrowhead. Why?" Ahulani pointed to the boulders with the drawings.

"You told me that David and I were supposed to come to this planet to learn about our past lives. Apparently, I needed to come back through my dreams to discover more, but I am not ready to do this now."

The healer from the Painted Desert took Ahulani's hands in hers. "If you weren't ready, you wouldn't have made it here with David. You are correct. You both have had a past life here and you were a couple then. This isn't the first life you've had together. David had that disturbing dream of kidnapping you in a past life—taking you away from your lover whom he murdered before being brutally killed by a curse. There are other pasts you've had together, some as couples, some as mere acquaintances. But you've both played important roles in all of them."

One of Ahulani's Native spirit guides stepped forward.

He had straight, dark hair to his shoulders and a three-inch scar on his left cheek that did nothing to hide his good looks. "I have been promised to you as a spirit guide since you were born and have watched you grow physically, spiritually, and emotionally. Your fate has been written since birth, Ahulani."

He smiled at the face on the peak.

Ahulani noticed that the features of this spirit guide and that on the peak looked similar.

"Is David here also?" she asked.

"No. He is in another time, another place to learn more about himself."

Rafael stood near her male guide. "Not too many people can recall their dreams in detail the way you and David can. You both have the ability to see a story through, not just bits and pieces. That is huge in helping you develop your talents."

Something told Ahulani to look down. A light red arrowhead about two inches in length rested on the dirt and small rocks near her. She bent down and traced her finger over the objects.

"This is where the first arrowhead came from, isn't it?" Ahulani looked up at the medicine woman. "The one under my pillow?"

The ancient healer nodded. "Yes. This is a powerful place, more so than anyone can understand."

The healer knelt and took the red arrowhead in her hand. "Except you." She handed it to Ahulani.

Ahulani took the object and followed the medicine woman's gaze to the peak.

"I don't believe it." Ahulani stood and went toward the animate face. The eyes, nose, lips, and cheekbones now matched her own features.

"What is this place? I understand this peak is sacred, but this...this face takes it to a whole new level."

The medicine woman placed her arm on her shoulder. "This hill reflects those who have been an important part in preserving the society and culture of this planet. You are part of it, do you not see?"

Ahulani couldn't take her eyes off the likeness. She thought she saw a glint of green in the stone eyes.

The male guide bearing the scar approached her.

This spirit guide's face was the gentler of the two that she and David had seen during their climb.

"You lived here, also," Ahulani said.

He nodded. "Yes, I resided here along with you and hundreds of others, but this is a barren place now."

"That rock reflects my current looks," Ahulani said.

The medicine woman walked the circumference of the two boulders. "What's amazing is that you looked almost the same during your life here. Not Hawaiian but more similar to the Native American races on Earth."

Rafael's voice came from behind her. "I know your next question. Did David look the same?" He laughed.

She grinned. "Well, I am curious."

"His appearance was different, yet he was still rather good-looking. It took the two of you awhile to get together, but you finally succumbed to his charms."

Ahulani wondered why it had taken her so long to become one with David, considering how many past lives they had together. Amazing how much damage one life can do.

She stared down at the red arrowhead. "Too bad I can't see this place as a thriving community."

"You can," the male guide said. He swept his arm across the view of the badlands. The vast, open, desolate landscape morphed into a busy city with people milling about far below.

She saw large elephant-like creatures with those funny ears being ridden by some of the residents. A taller man walked alongside one of the creatures, stroking its side.

Smooth structures, identical to the pueblos of the southwest, were scattered on a hill. A path cut between the center of the city leading to a massive entrance of a building, which was part of a mound. She peered closer and noticed large blocks piled on top of each other. The structure alternated between granite blocks and rock.

"I almost didn't recognize it without the sand on it. That's the pyramid where we all took refuge at night, isn't it?" Ahulani glanced back at the guides, but they were gone. Except for the man with the scar.

"Yes," he said, "but it's not a pyramid."

Whether from her guides or initiated by a past life recall, she detected a series of three massive square platforms, each larger than the other. The largest block platform was on the bottom. There were five levels, at least that she could see. Her third eye revealed additional platforms underground.

A huge door slid to one side. A tall man emerged through it with long, straight hair that hung past his torso. He wore dark pants, a matching long sleeve tunic, and a long robe the same color as the red dirt. His stature was athletic and muscular. When he walked through the door, everyone stopped what they were doing and stared at him.

He wore no crown, nor did he have an entourage. Still, he had a presence that demanded attention. He strolled through the city, acknowledging everyone along his path. Those he passed bowed their heads to him. He started up a narrow trail leading to the peak.

Ahulani looked at the male guide. "Should we leave?"

"No. He cannot see us."

She watched as the man ascended with ease and surefootedness. He had a purpose.

As he drew close, she saw his defined, high cheekbones, and full lips. When he arrived at the peak, he knelt by one of the boulders. The stately gentleman pulled a tool from within his robe and began to etch a circle. Soon, the design of a stick person holding a staff emerged.

He stood, facing Ahulani and her guide. He looked directly at her before raising his arms to the sky.

Ahulani had to shield her eyes as a flash of light illuminated the peak. When it subsided, he was gone. The ancient city had disappeared as well, leaving her with more questions. Who were these people? Why did they look so much like the Native people on Earth? And what role did she play in the society?

Her guide gently touched her arm. "That was David. Or rather, the royal prince of the kingdom—before he met you."

Chapter Twenty-seven

*D*avid lay on a hard, cold surface. A large bat stared at him from a crack in the cave's ceiling, its head cocked to one side.

Yet this bat was different. It crawled purposefully, from the ceiling onto the wall, watching David the whole time.

He attempted to move, but couldn't. He thought of the 200-million-year-old logs at the Petrified Forest buried deep by massive amounts of sediment and debris from an ancient river system. His body twitched with every attempt to move.

The bat flew off the cave wall and landed within a few feet of David.

He desperately tried to turn his head to see what it was doing. He had never heard of bats eating people, but this one was too curious.

Movement came from the direction of where the bat had landed—scraping and footsteps. Then, a slight breeze as a much larger presence loomed over him.

David opened his mouth to ask who was there, but nothing came out. Tremors racked his whole body as he struggled to move. His mind and senses told him that he was in trouble, yet he was helpless.

"You've returned," a man's voice said from behind David.

David rolled his eyes up as far as he could, but the person who spoke remained out of sight.

"You traveled to these caves from your world hundreds of years ago, thinking you owned this place. You should not have come back."

He struggled to understand what the man referred to, realizing he was somehow a threat to this person.

"Now, you are defenseless in your final resting place."

David understood he must be in the upper story of the cavern, where he had found the shaman's bones—his own bones from that of his past life he understood now. What did the man mean by "your world?"

This bastard was somehow controlling him, forcing David into submission. Was he afraid of what David could do if they were one-on-one?

The stranger walked from behind David to in front of him. David could see the man wore dark pants, a long-sleeved dark sweater, and boots.

Though David still couldn't move, a chill ran down his spine. Candle glow appeared from somewhere, highlighting the man's face. He seemed familiar.

The man stared intently into David's eyes. The soft light revealed brown eyes, speckled with black spots. The enigmatic dots reminded David of a jaguar. His nose was broad and lips full, and the brown hair hung just above the shoulders with bangs dropping into the man's eyes. His skin was olive-toned.

"You don't belong here. Not now, and not back then. Unlike you, I am no longer alive. You murdered me long ago, but I swore I would haunt you forever—in all of your lives."

David glared at his enemy.

The man crawled, more like slithered, on his knees toward David. He placed his face within inches of David's. There were no hands around his throat, yet he couldn't get any air. The man's breath seemed to suffocate him. Flashes of his current life scrolled through his mind. The last image he saw was Ahulani's lovely face and striking green eyes.

That's when the symbols started to appear his mind. The thunderbird came first, followed by others he had never seen—some looked Chinese, some Egyptian, and others geometric. Finally, he was able to gasp for air.

It surprised his opponent, who backed away.

He saw two circles connected by a two-sided arrow. David lifted his right arm, punching the man in the face.

As his fist met the man's wide nose, an image of the stone house at Kuelap came clearly into focus.

This was no nightmare. He had dreamt his way into the

magician's lair. This dark enemy knew of David's love for the Andes and for the pre-Columbian ruins. The magician had followed David there five years ago while he worked at the site, perhaps planning to kill David. But why hadn't he?

Despite a bloody nose, the magician pinned David to the ground. The magician's large hands held David's arms tight—so tightly he thought his bones would break. The blood from his nose dripped onto David's face.

"Why did you do it?" David spat in the man's face. "Why did you create that portal and torture innocent people? Why not just deal with me?"

The magician increased the pressure on David's arms. "The ancients created that portal when the home was built. Why not have a little fun?"

David grimaced in pain. He kneed the man's groin with his knee.

His enemy did not budge.

"I've told you before." The magician's eyes had a life of their own. "I may bleed but I do not hurt. You can try to inflict pain, but I only internalize your anger, use it as power."

David recalled that the magician had previously revealed himself with black hair and had tattoos on his arm of vines, trees, and a parrot. The sweater probably hid the tattoos, but his hair and face were different. Who was he?

The ceiling was alive. The stalactites lengthened, shortened, and dropped to the stairs less than ten feet away.

David thought of the pyramid, the dunes, the forest, and the peak of faces. He recalled the chamber where blocks were stamped with his family symbols. And he saw himself standing between the two boulders, decorated with etchings engraved not for artistic expression—but for rituals, ceremony. And magic.

He pushed against the magician's chest with force and felt his inner animal spirit coming forward—the mighty bear.

The cave started to undulate. The ground beneath him began to shake.

The magician started to transform. His muscles bulged.

Dark empty orbs morphed into fiery devil eyes, and the man's breathing became heavier, deeper until it became more of a growl.

David let out a roar to rival that of any grizzly. He swiped the man across the face and noticed three deep gashes.

The cave sounded as if it were splitting in half. It was alive—and it felt the wrath, the pure hatred. A large chunk of the ceiling collapsed on top of the magician, but it didn't faze him.

David saw a malevolent grin creep across the man's face as he grabbed a small part of the ceiling and lifted it to strike David.

He couldn't see the symbols within the cave walls, but he could use them. They danced and merged, overpowered his subconscious, became their own entity.

The magician was thrown backward, rock in hand.

David heard him land on the pile of bones and rubble by the shaman's grave.

David awoke in bed and sat up. The clock on the nightstand read 7:10 A.M. He had only slept three hours the entire night, having fallen asleep around four in the morning, but this dream had turned into a nightmare. His body, along with the peach-colored sheets, were drenched in sweat.

He got out of bed and breathed in the air from the half-open window. His legs were shaking—though from the quaking ground of the cave or the stress of what had occurred in his dream, he wasn't sure. Whatever had happened in the past with the magician went beyond personal. It had been life or death. David had been the winner.

The man had said, "You traveled here from your world hundreds of years ago, thinking you owned this place."

What did that mean? Had he traveled to the caves from another dimension as a shaman? If so, why? And what relationship did he have with the magician?

David needed to get away. As beautiful as Oak Creek

Canyon was, he missed the Petrified Forest and Painted Desert. He considered inviting Ahulani to go with him but figured she would want some time of her own to think over their other-worldly travels.

Discarding his pajamas, he pulled on a pair of faded jeans and a long-sleeved shirt. He put on socks and tennis shoes, stopped briefly in the bathroom, and then went into the living room. It was quiet, and he didn't hear any movement in the house. The blinds were open, meaning his sister had gotten up, but he didn't see Larry or Shelly.

He grabbed a pad of paper and a pencil from the kitchen and wrote a note.

Feeling a little stressed. Went to Painted Desert, will be back around nightfall.
Love, David.

He grabbed his backpack and wallet, found Shelly's car keys on the coffee table, and went out to the driveway. He got into her vehicle and left. He headed up through Oak Creek Canyon on 89A toward Interstate 40.

David wondered if the magician had been the entity who'd nearly killed him while driving on the freeway. He sensed the man's power, the pure malevolence. Perhaps the magician had somehow encouraged David to visit the caves so he could get rid of him once and for all. Or maybe the magician *lived* in the caves.

What would happen if David accidentally ended up there again? Would the magician be waiting for him?

He drove the winding road that led through Oak Creek Canyon's spectacular cliffs and red rock formations, along the creek that led to Interstate 40. The higher in elevation he drove, the more relaxed he began to feel. He and Ahulani still didn't have the answers as to how they would be able to stop the insane spirit or how they would close the portal. But he had faith they'd find a way.

Three hours later, David arrived at the park. He felt drawn toward the Blue Mesa sun shelter trailhead, which allowed visitors to walk among badland hills of bluish bentonite clay and petrified wood.

He entered the south entrance of the park off of 180, passing the Rainbow Forest Museum, Crystal Forest trail, jasper forest, and went through an expanse of open desert beauty into mesas and gently sloping formations.

He turned off on the road leading to the Blue Mesa Member, a section of hill-like formations that consisted of thick deposits of grey, blue, purple, and green mudstones and sandstones. Created by Mother Nature approximately 220 million years ago, David considered it one of the most scenic locations in the park.

He pulled into the parking area, grabbed his backpack from the passenger seat, got out of the vehicle, and hiked the steep grade down into the Blue Mesa badlands.

He had been on the trail many times, yet something felt different. The sensation of walking among the time worn hills had always been serene and rejuvenating to his spirit. This time, there was an energy he couldn't explain.

He stopped next to one of the large, bluish mounds and the hairs on his arms stood on end. Was the magician here now?

He glanced around. He saw no other visitors.

The ambiguous hills hid a secret. David had never experienced anything like this here or anywhere else in the park. The temperature was in the low-to-mid-seventies, yet it felt much warmer.

Visions came into his mind while he continued along the trail—the dunes planet, a royal prince with a long robe and crown, the cave and upstairs platform with the shaman's bones. Was he safe here?

David picked up a small chunk of petrified wood that resonated polished rainbow tones created by earth. Made of solid quartz, the rainbow colors had been produced by impurities in the quartz., such as iron, carbon, and manganese—due to a centuries old process of minerals absorbing into porous wood over hundreds of thousands of years. Only a few inches across, it was one of the most beautiful specimens he had ever found.

David wrapped his fingers tightly around the exquisite fossil and closed his eyes. For a few seconds, the soothing blue valley he stood in switched to that of Kuelap and the stone house.

He felt an overpowering presence nearby.

"Grandpa? Is that you?"

David hoped it wasn't the magician. He started hiking again.

Intuition told him an interdimensional bond existed between the Petrified Forest and Kuelap—the alternating landscapes in his mind seemed to confirm it. Did he have past life ties at both places? What about the cavern where his bones rested? The magician had implied a connection between an ancient life on another world and the caves. Could the nefarious spirit have meant the dunes planet?

He removed his phone from his backpack and saw a text from Ahulani.

Tried calling. Hope u are doing good. Saw u in my dream. U were a prince and shaman on the planet of the dunes. Love, Lani.

David had seen snapshots of the pyramid, the peak, and the forest during the struggle with the magician. Had they both resided on the same planet?

"The planet of the dunes," David said aloud, as if it would help him recall something. It didn't.

He opened his hand and stared at the stunning fossil. It was illegal to remove petrified wood and other fossils from the park, so he knelt and put it back. As he started to walk away, a brilliant light caught his attention. The fossilized quartz he'd held exploded in mineral tones of yellow, white, and dark pink.

A shimmering door of light appeared over the fossil. Within, hazy mountains glimmered, a goat fed on moist grass, and the Pre-Columbian fortress waited.

He peered closer. The goat glanced up from its feeding frenzy and at David. Still chewing, it moved forward.

David reached out, and the animal darted away among the ruins.

Talk about doors opening.

New dimensions and portals existed in many places. Kuelap had those same possibilities—only he hadn't been open to it at the time to see them.

David didn't want to venture into the unknown again. He was still exhausted from his last journey among the universe. He had to enter to try and stop the magician, rescue any remaining victims—and determine his true purpose in life.

Were his abilities up to par? Would he survive the next encounter with the magician?

Chapter Twenty-eight

David reached his hand into the unorthodox portal. The humidity of the Andes Mountains hit hard compared to the dryness of the Arizona park.

David grabbed the petrified fossil off the ground that had opened the doorway, wondering if he would need it to return. He started to back away, fearing for his life.

"You have to do this," his grandfather said from behind him.

David wasn't so certain. "The magician might kill me. He almost did in my dream, if that's possible. Not to mention, I just got back from a godforsaken planet. I'm tired and came here to rest and recharge, not die."

"You *have* to do this. It is an important part of your healing." His grandfather leaned closer. "To know where you're going and take a step forward, you have to know where you've been."

David held the fossil tight in his hand, took a deep breath, and stepped through the doorway and into the ruins of Kuelap. The muted, layered hills of Blue Mesa wavered, shimmered, then vanished.

Would he be able to return home? He hoped so.

He heard a muffled male voice. He spun around, observing the other stone foundations. Clouds blanketed the ancient city, and he saw pale mists floating among the ruins. It was an unwelcoming environment compared to his prior tenure.

One large figure stepped through the cloud tendrils, then vanished.

David continued to watch the spot where the specter had vanished. He couldn't see any details, but its presence felt strong.

"Why do you think you're so drawn to this place?" Rafael said. "You've lived here before when these walls were being built. The ghosts here know you, David. They need your help."

Footsteps walked the circumference of a ruin next to him. David could see the imprints form in the sand. Could it be his grandfather?

David stepped into the home within the portal.

"You've gone beyond what I had hoped," said his grandfather. "You and Ahulani have been brought together to face your talents and past lives—those you've lived together, and otherwise. She needed your help. Without both of you working together, Eric and his parents would be dead now."

David didn't want to know what would have happened to the family. Eric's parents had been rescued in the nick of time. How long could they have survived without the tree of life? What life forms existed that might have found humans on the lower end of the food chain?

"Are you here to help?" David asked.

"No. You don't need me. You've accomplished so much for someone who doesn't consider himself confident."

David looked away, embarrassed, before another series of symbols got his attention. The symbols danced, circled the inside of the stone house—a black bear fetish, a solid black arrowhead tip, a rainbow symbol, a big cat, a trapezoidal figure holding a staff, and a bunch of others that scrolled by so fast, David couldn't tell what they were. Could he be doing this himself? Or was it a clue from his grandfather or his shaman self?

He knelt in front of the bear fetish. Passing his hand above the shape, he sensed warmth, peace, and familiarity. The fetish was a symbol of strength and power, and though it was not an ancient sign drawn by the pre-Columbian culture, the bear was meant to be a positive symbol.

The magician had transformed it into something sinister.

A large spirit stood a few feet away from David—a man, nearly seven feet tall, wore animal skins and a fur hood. The spirit held a spear in one hand and a leather knapsack hung crossbody over it. He stood on the opposite side of the bear and watched David, a grin splitting his face, before the spirit bent over and placed his hand on the fetish. The ancient man pointed to his chest.

The resident of the citadel looked as solid as the earth. The man stood, ran his hand along the inside of the stone house, and pointed to the fetish again. He nodded his head frantically and circled the bear with his finger. "Long time ago," he said. The man pounded on his chest with his fist. "I made this when my home was built."

David was in awe. The man was the original resident of the stone house.

He felt a new presence kneeling next to him. He had the same sensation as before he was channeled by the shaman from the cave.

"This wasn't here when I was at Kuelap five years ago," David said.

His grandfather said, "Somehow, when the magician used his powers to magnify the portal, the bear itself was brought forth. These people of the past believe it made the intent that much stronger, and it might be why some were taken to past lives."

"I am here to try and stop the man who uses this—" David gestured to the bear "—for negative reasons. I've met him. He is a bad spirit."

The ancient Kuelap inhabitant nodded his head voraciously. "He's not here."

"Probably hiding in the caves," David muttered.

The spirit stepped around the fetish and touched David's shoulder.

David didn't feel fingers, rather tenderness that emanated throughout his body from the man's touch.

"You come back to help us."

Did I know this person? He seems so familiar.

The male spirit sat on the ground in front of the bear. "Sit." He motioned with both hands for David to sit opposite him.

The symbols that circled the stone house now tumbled over each other in a haste to make some sort of order. Human shadows gathered around the perimeter of the foundation.

The man from the ancient past closed his eyes and without looking at the ground, drew signs in the dirt—a solid black arrowhead tip, a rainbow, a big cat, a trapezoidal figure holding a staff, and a few others.

"Who are you?" David whispered.

"I have waited so long." The man did not open his eyes. "Some said you would not be able to help in your current state, your new life, but I knew better."

The mysterious spirit opened his eyes. "I knew my son would come home and remember."

"Your son?" David glanced at the spectacular ruins surrounding him.

"Yes. You saved many people as a medicine man."

David struggled to understand the dreams and mysteries around his past lives. He understood that he had been a shaman in the caves, but at Kuelap as well? He supposed it made sense, considering his love for the fortress.

"I'm confused. Why am I seeing the same symbols here as on another planet? Not to mention, the same images my grandfather called upon."

"You have always been a healer, in different forms, in many of your past lives. Those symbols you and I shared have been with you since the start of your time—your first life as a hunter and gatherer during the Ice Age. You are here to prevent this intruder to our land from doing additional harm."

The spirit looked outside the walls of his small, ancient pre-Columbian home. Faint, misty figures moved around the perimeter, as if watching and waiting.

The bear fetish drawn into the ground began to radiate a white light.

"You must channel your past as a healer," his ancient father said. "Become what you once were to understand the symbols and to heal our home. Save us and the others."

Others? There must be more victims.

Startled, David jumped when hands grabbed him—one on either side of his shoulders. The grasp felt firm, but not threatening.

The spirit who claimed to have been his father merely looked up and smiled.

"Grandpa, is that you?" he asked. David attempted to see who was behind him, but he couldn't move.

The fortress, the homes, had transformed from ruins to an inhabited city. The place he sat became a home with a cone-shaped, thatched roof over his head. Chickens, goats, and children's shouts of joy combined for a whole new atmosphere.

He got up and looked outside. People in animal skins were thriving in a village with open fire areas outside the homes. Women were grinding corn, men were working on their homes, and livestock roamed freely.

David felt warm. He looked down at his body to see animal fur—what looked to be llama fur on his jacket, perhaps deerskin on his legs, and a jaguar pelt around his shoulders. An animal tooth hung around his neck. He wondered if it could be that of a bear.

A woman with long, dark hair past her waist peered at him as she placed a kettle on the fire. Her beauty drew him in.

Mesmerized, he approached her while she stirred the contents in the pot.

She took his hands in hers, and he could see himself sleeping next to her, making love to her. Had she been his wife?

A little girl about five years old ran to him and grabbed onto David's pants.

The child held onto his leg tightly and stared up at him with adoration. Eventually, she let go of his leg, and he followed her into a dimly lit, circular structure larger than that of the one with the bear fetish. A wooden bench encircled part of the inside of the home. An animal rug lay in the center. Antlers hung above the entrance, and large wooden utensils hung on the walls. It felt cozy, familiar. Had this been his home?

The little girl giggled and started to roll around on the rug. She had similar features to his own.

Turning away from her, he saw his prehistoric father in the doorway, the child's grandfather.

She ran to him, and he gave her a big bear hug. David's father motioned for him to follow, and they went outside and entered a different home—the place with the bear fetish.

His father removed a rolled up black animal skin from under the bench, placing it in the center of the home. David knelt and stroked the soft dark fur, which had spots blacker than the surrounding fur.

A jaguar pelt?

David unrolled the bundle to reveal a smudging fan made up of two large black feathers wrapped together with leather, a small clay bowl with a few bunches of copal or tree resin, a variety of stones, a medicine bag, and a small red bear fetish. He squatted and picked up the stone fetish, wrapping his fingers tight around it.

Closing his eyes, he attempted to pick up on the energy of the objects.

His father indicated the shamanic tools and sat down across from David. "You will use these."

David sat in front of them and ran his hand across the velvety texture of the fur. He felt a breeze rush through him as the thatched roof vanished, the city recalled its state of ruin, and the indigenous inhabitants returned to their ghostly state. Were his wife and child still roaming among the felled homes? Were they of the shadows now?

David placed the red bear fetish back down and grabbed the smudging fan. Whether from the tool he held, the man facing him, or the replay of his past life, David understood what he needed to do.

The smudging fan, typically used for purification ceremonies, initiated an instant visual of a large bird floating on the air currents. Turning it over in his hand to observe the feathers closer, he heard the words *Andean Condor*.

The clay bowl held clumps of white copal that emitted a pungent, earthy odor. David had learned during his Mesoamerican studies that copal resin was used by the Mayans as a food for the gods in divination and purification ceremonies. As the smoke of the copal rose, it carried their prayers to the ears of the gods.

David sprinkled chunks of the copal on top of the bear fetish. He suspected it had been carved carefully into the ground by the man before him, but he had no way to light the incense.

His phantom father waved a hand over the bear fetish; a small fist-sized flame ignited on top of the copal, and white smoke started to rise. The column of smoke represented the cosmic axis out of which the universe and all its creatures emerged and acted as the connecting thread between the worlds, and between heaven and earth.

Opaque swirls rose ever higher into the grey skies.

David took the carved bear fetish found within the jaguar skin and dropped it into the center of the drawn image on the dirt. He waved the smoke over both and thought of the evil entity who had attempted to torture him in the cave and in Shelly's house.

He started chanting in a foreign tongue while the strange symbols from his past as a healer came into focus. The signs he had seen circling the stone house hung on eye level, scrolling repeatedly in front of him. David now saw them as clearly as the environment around him—they were no longer whipping around so fast he couldn't read them. He didn't recognize the language he chanted but could feel he was working to dispel negative energy.

He continued to chant while his ancient father sat quietly across from him.

Then, the symbols vanished, along with the anonymous dialect. Drained and exhausted, David hoped his impromptu ritual had helped.

223

He looked at his father. A huge grin crossed the man's face and he nodded. Other figures stepped forward and bent their heads in prayer.

The smoke had become heavier, denser, and he could feel something else begin to happen.

A familiar figure emerged from the smoke—six-foot-tall with broad shoulders and shoulder-length hair dressed in jeans and a white shirt. The spirit of his prehistoric father watched as David's real father appeared above them.

Was David manifesting a long-lost memory? His parents had both been killed in a plane crash when he was ten, and David had forced himself to forget them…until now.

David's father circled above them in a surreal cloud form. David now understood what his grandfather had meant. He had to face his own demons from his current life before using an integral part of his past life to grow. David stood and reached for his father's ghostly hand.

The specter took David's hand and held it. Memories came flooding back—David with his father, mother, and sister playing baseball, going for hikes, and visiting historic sites and national parks. He saw lush green hills hugging a waterfall that dropped into a canyon with a sapphire blue ocean beyond—Hawaii.

A voice he hadn't heard in thirty years spoke clearly to him—his father's voice. "David, this was the last precious time we spent together."

A group of people hiked together on a tropical trail, including himself, Shelly, and his parents. There was another family with a little girl about David's age who walked beside her parents. The happy memory initiated emotions he had long buried for over thirty years—the horrifying recall of his parent's plane crash during their trip to Hawaii.

David began to cry. It started with a sudden deep sob. The tears began to flow, and greater than his fear of not being able to stop was the fear of confronting his parent's tragic death.

He felt a hand on his shoulder.

"You have pushed my memory away—and your mother's. In doing so, you have forgotten more than us. That beautiful child with the dark hair that you see hiking with us is Ahulani."

The copal invaded his mind, his senses. What were the chances that he had childhood memories with his true love? Did Shelly remember hanging out with Ahulani? How could he have forgotten her?

"We met their family the day before and had decided to plan something that day. You and Shelly liked Ahulani so much that you wanted to spend more time with her. You both stayed in Molokai with Ahulani's family, while Mom and I flew back to Oahu where we were all staying. We had planned on returning for you the next day."

His father bent his head. Even though he was a misty apparition, David could feel the man's grief, his torment.

David's father glanced at the other figure and then back at David. "The plane crashed within ten minutes of taking off. Engine failure."

Whether intended or not, David could see his father and mother holding hands tightly inside the cramped craft. He could hear the sputtering of the engine, then silence. There were no screams, no other passengers. His parents never took their eyes off each other as the small plane plunged into the ocean.

David had never dealt with the grief. Sure, he had cried on and off for a few months, but he chose to go it alone. He had been too proud to ask for help. Until he nearly died in the Amazon by hiking all day without stopping to rest or eat. There was a part of him that felt guilty. Perhaps he should have begged his parents to stay with him and Shelly.

The energy among the empty village shifted. Once again, he felt safe. With that security came remorse and regret. Tears flowed freely. He couldn't stop the pain, the hurt, the grief. Like the ruins surrounding him, David had become a shell of a man—abandoned and waiting to be made whole again.

"If you and Shelly had been on that plane, you would have died with us." His father morphed into human form, looking exactly as David remembered. He stood in front of David, holding his son's face in his hands. "Ahulani saved your lives."

Chapter Twenty-nine

An uncanny urgency overcame Ahulani. Her hands tightened on the steering wheel, and she leaned forward expectantly. She watched the side of the road for a turnoff. She felt as if her heart would beat out of her chest.

A dirt road appeared, and she made a sudden right turn. She nearly lost control of the car and barely missed a tall pine off the side of the road. Fairly smooth at first, the road became rutted with potholes.

After her vivid dream the night before, Ahulani had the need to go for a drive—guided by intuition. She had driven north of Flagstaff off 89A, past Elden Pueblo. She had tried to call David to tell him about it but hadn't been able to get through. His line wouldn't ring, and her mobile kept disconnecting.

She wanted to drive faster, but the numerous potholes prevented it. The desire to get to her destination was surreal. She had no idea where she was going, or why.

Ahulani arrived at a section of the road that crossed an arroyo. A recent thunderstorm had caused the sandy bottom to overflow onto the pavement, and she had to veer away from two large branches forming an X that had worked their way onto the road.

A female voice yelled, "Stop!"

Strangely, the voice wasn't a result of the telepathic connection with her spirit guides. This conspicuous exclamation sounded like it came from behind her.

Ahulani glanced at the back seat but couldn't see anything.

She drove uphill, around the branches and past the arroyo, before she pulled the car off onto the shoulder.

Throwing open the driver's side door, she got out and went to the arroyo. She struggled through the sandy, moist soil. Each step felt like five as her feet sank into the earth.

Ahulani noticed the remnants of walls above the arroyo off to the left. She scampered up the short hill to get a closer look and found an antiquated site. Stone block structures had fallen into disarray with individual stone lying on the ground in a pile.

Walking between the ruins, Ahulani spotted evidence of a sunken square structure about ten feet deep built from stone. She realized it could be a *kiva*, or ceremonial structure. Would the spirit inhabitants who used to dwell in this village help her understand why she'd been drawn here?

She listened intently and watched for movement while she roamed the site. A chill ran down her spine and her skin turned cold. Was she being watched?

An immense raven stared at her from atop one of the debris piles of the fallen walls. It flew up and over her, circling above her head, before landing on a tree branch near her.

This was no ordinary bird. She backed away, but it had trapped her in its steely gaze.

Finally breaking away, Ahulani turned to head back to her car, but it landed in front of her, startling her. Then raven turned to man. He had a broad nose, dark eyes, and dark hair above the shoulders with bangs dropping into his eyes. He wore dark pants, a long-sleeved black sweater, and short boots.

"It's you," she whispered. "The one who transformed the energy at Kuelap."

His gaze was threatening, dangerous. "I believe we both have something—or rather someone—in common."

Ahulani stepped back and tripped over a wall, falling on her backside.

The man took a big step forward, leaned down, and extended his hand to help her up.

She stood up on her own quickly and backed away, reaching behind her, for something, anything to defend herself.

David. He's talking about David.

The magician went from solid physical form to faded and transparent. His gaze went from Ahulani to something behind her.

She turned to see her Iroquois guide glowering at the magician. He had his hand on the sheaf of his knife.

The name, *Tall Rock*, etched itself across her inner vision.

"The magician is not human. Her Native guide stepped in front of Ahulani. "He's a bad spirit associated with David's past life as a medicine man. He's here for revenge."

A sparrow fell out of the sky and dropped to the ground, dead, in front of Ahulani.

The magician sneered—a nefarious half grin on one side of his face.

Ahulani knew how to help earthbound deceased move on, but this wasn't a typical ghost.

"I see you brought your troops with you." The magician walked around Tall Rock, sizing him up and down. "Don't you think this goes a bit beyond the role of a spirit guide?" the nefarious entity asked.

"What do you know of protection?" Tall Rock asked.

The magician stood tall, his face within inches of Tall Rock. "I was a warrior as well."

Ahulani wondered if he had abandoned the troops. Or turned against them.

"What have you done to David?"

The look on the magician's face went from an evil grin to a deathly glare. Ahulani had seen what David was capable of as a shaman. What sort of clash had the two Titans gotten into?

The magician clenched his fists and the muscles in his face tightened.

So, David was a major threat. She could see that now.

The man couldn't intimidate David, so he'd come to scare her.

Tall Rock shouted at Ahulani, but she couldn't hear his voice. What sort of danger awaited?

The Iroquois guide vanished as he continued to yell, his eyes wide with fear. Did the magician have control over the spirit guide realm?

The spiral-tipped arrowhead and the light red arrowhead from the sacred peak floated in front of her face. She reached out for them, but the mirage vanished. The ancient objects were just a clue.

The magician watched her curiously.

The clear arrowhead was under her pillow at home, and the red arrowhead from her dream had been left in her subconscious. Or so she thought. A voice whispered for her to look down.

The quartz arrowhead from the peak lay at her feet. She snatched it off the ground, holding it tight in her hand.

He stared at her strangely, his head cocked. Had he seen what she collected?

"Ahh… The arrowheads are one of your tools," the man sneered. "Just as David has his symbols for protection and guidance, you have the innate ability to call upon these."

The magician circled closer, now three feet away.

She touched the tip of the arrowhead with her index finger and a drop of blood burst through her skin.

The magician grabbed her and pulled her toward him so she faced outward. He had one arm under her neck and the other held onto her shoulder, dragging her backwards through a stand of trees.

"Let go!" Ahulani kicked her feet and attempted to stomp on his toes. She slid the arrowhead through her palm and reached back to stab him in the thigh.

The weapon met solid flesh and the magician merely winced. Undeterred, he tightened his hold on her and pulled harder.

She stomped, kicked, and bit his hand. Hard.

He pushed her away, making her fall to the ground. The arrowhead was still in his thigh.

230

He grabbed onto it, took a deep breath, and yanked it out of his leg with a deafening roar. Blood dripped from the wound.

Not stopping, the magician lunged forward with the arrowhead held high above his head, and toward Ahulani.

She searched her mind for anything that could shield herself as she ran from him.

She glanced back. His leg injury caused him to stumble and fall to his knees in the dirt.

She ran faster toward the arroyo, down the embankment, and to her car. She would not stop until she got in and locked the doors. She looked to see if he was still in pursuit.

She pressed the start engine button, but the vehicle wouldn't turn over. She must've dropped the keys in her haste. Looking out at the arroyo, she saw the keys sticking out of the sand.

With his supernatural powers, the magician would recover from the injury quickly. Did she dare get her keys or run in the other direction farther away?

Ahulani threw open the car door and ran down the dirt road the way she had come, hoping someone would be driving in her direction.

A sizeable shape flew above her, blocking the sun. It skimmed her head and landed on the road in front of her. A bald eagle faced her.

Ahulani wondered if transforming into animal form helped him heal. Or made him stronger.

She attempted to dodge the raptor, but it spread its wings wide, blocking her from the road. The magician didn't have to turn back into human form—he could easily rip her apart with his talons. But this was no ordinary eagle, rather a malevolent, spiteful spirit.

The eagle remained on the road, flapping its wings in such a ferocious manner it blew her hair back. The massive raptor leapt off the road and soared into the sky; it rose so high and so quickly that it was gone in seconds.

It, or he, would be back.

Something shifted. In the atmosphere, her soul, and her mind.

She thought of Alika Loe's chamber, the prince, and the Peak of Faces. Then, as if in a dream, her rock double peered back at her with a glint of green in the not so lifeless eyes. They weren't merely green in color—they were gemstones.

She glanced around at the mounds of maroon sands and river rocks outside the temple and looked up at the sacred hill of faces.

Ahulani heard a female voice. "You've come home. You are safe."

"How did I get back here?"

"You aren't on the planet," a male voice whispered. "Since your physical journey to the once thriving world, your connection, your ties to the sacred temple have been greatly enhanced, it enables you to visit through a private portal."

She felt drawn toward the temple and approached its giant doors. The stacked, square levels of the building were hidden by sand, but the massive elaborate door provided a clue to the culture that resided here. Solid oak with a large, etched image of the fruit-and-water-bearing tree in the center, its trunk was thick and the top of the tree bore leaves, blooms, and fruit. The trunk led to a network of roots with something attached.

Her fingers involuntarily traced the image of the Baobab tree. The gargantuan door opened, and light revealed walls decorated in symbols of all kinds. No two looked alike.

She walked slowly down the long hallway, which had wall sconces at evenly spaced intervals. As she passed each sconce, it lit up to reveal yet more symbols etched in the wall from floor to ceiling.

I wonder if David has memory of all this. There must be billions of combinations of these symbols. What are they capable of?

Ahulani looked behind her at the entrance. The door was closed.

A woman appeared in the shadows further ahead.

"He cannot follow you here. There is only one way for him to return to this world."

She recognized the silhouette of the figure. She'd seen it several times before today.

"Even in your other past lives, you would visit here."

"He's going to kill me," Ahulani said.

The medicine woman stepped out of the darkness. "You are the one meant to remove him from the Earth, to prevent him from doing any more harm."

Ahulani lifted her arm, indicating the myriad of signs on the walls. "It's David who knows all of these symbols, not me."

"His purpose is to repair the portal, to fight his own demons. David killed the one you call the magician while he was a shaman and a prince—he and David *are* one and the same. However, your crystal knowledge, your ongoing connection with the spirit world and the underworld make you a powerful force to deal with, Ahulani."

The medicine woman stepped closer and stood only inches from Ahulani. "On this planet, David obtained new talents and healed others." She enclosed Ahulani's hands in her own. "With your help."

Ahulani stared at her in surprise. She and David had a close relationship while living on the planet. By seeing her face in stone in her dream, she knew she had been an important person, but she had no idea that she had helped a prince enhance his powers.

"The magician thinks you are weaker. You have come here not just for safety, but to remember. You and David will be working together now, and in the future, to rid the universe of that which is not good. When he fixes that portal at Kuelap, he will open himself up to more abilities. The same will happen for you while you're here."

"You mean, when I send the magician to the other side?" she asked.

"Yes." The medicine woman spirit from the Painted Desert nodded, and then Ahulani saw Alika Loe glide overhead.

"But I have no idea how to do this."

The medicine woman shrugged and started to turn away. "David had no idea how to close the portal, yet he did." She looked from one wall to the opposite wall, her eyes scanning the hundreds of written symbols. "You will also find what you need in your past."

Ahulani felt overwhelmed and terrified and shocked all at the same time as she watched the healer leave the hall. She hoped David was safe. Had he had his own struggle with the magician? Were there other victims?

The medicine woman exited the temple. The light red arrowhead from Ahulani's dream had helped her stop the madman temporarily. He had removed the weapon from his leg, but Ahulani hadn't noticed what he'd done with it.

Intuition told her to continue her progress on the long hallway through the otherworldly structure. She walked slowly, taking in the drawings lining the walls. The images were drawn so masterfully, they looked like photographs. A picture at eye level showed the same image as that on the massive entrance—a baobab tree. Growing wild in 32 African countries, Ahulani had recently learned that the baobab was considered the tree of life because *every* part of it could be harvested.

Eric and his parents had survived due to the tree's water-giving bark and sweet tasting, low-hanging fruit. No wonder it was so strongly represented here.

There was something else she struggled to recall about the amazing tree—something from her past on the planet that seemed to be surfacing.

Ahulani closed her eyes, placing her hand over the image. Her third eye revealed a baobab tree much larger than any she had ever seen. The bottom of the stately tree had a space about six inches wide between two roots. A shiny object glittered inside.

A brilliant blue-green crystal with tiny, rectangular protrusions surrounded it, and grew like a bulbous growth from the thick root. It reminded her of the aquamarine waters on the Hawaiian Islands. Deeper under the roots, there was a radiant explosion. Could it be another gem?

What spiritual, metaphysical, and health-related properties could these crystals hold from a life-giving tree?

Another vision followed. She saw a side view of a young woman with long dark hair and a darker shade of skin than her own. The figure wore a headband of white flower buds, a sleeveless blue dress with gold lace at the top, and gold sandals. The girl pivoted, and Ahulani saw herself.

Her likeness held one of the baobab's gems in both hands, and resplendent rays of aquamarine exploded out of the crystal. When the light display subsided, the girl had disappeared.

Ahulani threw her hands up. "What are you trying to tell me? Could a gemstone from the tree of life be used to rid the world of the magician?"

As if by magic, her palate savored the sweetness of orange, mango, and banana—the fruit from the baobab.

The vision continued.

She saw the baobab fruit slowly drying on the branches. As it did, a thin residue leaked down and through the bark. The liquid soaked into the roots and underneath the baobab. The trees' roots could not hide the sparkles, light rays, or strength of the stones.

"I don't believe it," she whispered. "The dried fruit gives life to the crystals."

"And the crystals give life to all..." a male voice said.

Ahulani turned quickly to see a tall male figure standing at the end of the hall among the shadows. It looked like he held something shiny in his hand. "Unless you callously interfere with life."

The person stepped back and vanished into the unlit portion of the hall. Ahulani ran toward where he had been standing, her movement lighting up the remainder of the wall sconces.

In the center of the floor where the mysterious figure had stood sat a baobab crystal—a globe the circumference of a baseball. She took the stunning gem in her hand and knelt on the floor. Initially, the colors were a pale blue with emerald green undertones. As she held it, a spectacular aquamarine ocean appeared with gentle waves rolling in on each other.

Is this picking up my thoughts and memories of Hawaii?

The ocean vanished, replaced by a scene of the magician pacing the ruins—waiting for her return, most likely. She still didn't understand how she would use the gem, but she knew it would help her send him to the other side.

"I have to go back." She stood and walked down the hallway, back toward the entrance.

"No. Your battle begins and ends here."

Ahulani didn't see anyone. It had sounded like the same man who had gifted the crystal. She could still feel his presence.

She did a 360-degree turn to try and face the voice from beyond. "How am I supposed to win this fight? Help me."

The crystal provided an image of her face on the rock peak along with the petroglyph boulders.

"Of course. That's where this all ends. Thank you."

Grateful she didn't have to face the magician, she chose not to linger. She ran out of the sacred temple, down the path, and slowly up the hill. Her brief struggle with the magician had taken its toll. The peak remained faceless, lifeless as she climbed. Ahulani took a few minutes to catch her breath at the top. Her eyes scanned the petroglyphs on one of the boulders.

She sat on the ground cross-legged between the rock art boulders and held the gemstone from the tree of life. The crystal began to reflect fluctuations of deep blue and green, blending into aquamarine and then ending with a startling sapphire. "Please… Show me what I need to know."

When she placed it on the ground, the crystal showed her opponent pacing the ruins.

Ahulani closed her eyes and took a deep breath. She held it, then exhaled. "I call upon my spirit guides, angels, spirit protectors of this planet, and the entities of this sacred hill to help me with my past life recall."

The crystal reflected the growth of a gem under the roots of a baobab, which grew from the soil. Could the crystal be telling her that represented its birthplace? Did that mean it was more powerful now?

The gem showed the magician transforming between raven, eagle, and man multiple times. Why?

Chapter Thirty

Ahulani perceived energy—or perhaps more like vitality—in the crystal. Within its depths, a white glow emanated from a bunch of crystals at the roots of a baobab tree. The radiance traveled up the trunk and through the branches. Luminous green leaves and bundles of small white blooms exploded across the bare branches, providing life.

Feeling drawn to the base of the Peak of Faces Ahulani walked toward a hole approximately a foot across, and leaning over, she peered inside. A mini-baobab tree, less than half the size of the one that had helped Eric survive, stood proudly within. She still held the gemstone, her eyes level with the bottom of the tree.

Is this what is turning the stone faces to life? Small but no less powerful.

The crystal emitted a squealing noise and lit up so brightly, it blinded her for a second.

Ahulani placed the crystal into the opening as close to the base of the tree as possible, but still a foot away from the trunk. Close enough.

A rainbow of colors from the gemstone illuminated the baobab. One second, she was outside the peak—the next, she was inside the hill of faces, standing beside the baobab.

The interior of the peak was mostly hollow. The air seemed alive. She placed the round crystal ball into a concave notch against the base of the tree.

The magician's face appeared within the crystal.

He looked terrified. Did he realize what was happening? Perhaps, the malevolent spirit had picked up on who Ahulani had been.

The word *banned* popped into her mind, along with an image of the magician with darker, longer hair. She placed one hand on the tree and the other on the crystal, then a scene played out in her mind.

His hands were tied, and he was being dragged by two men. They wore maroon dress robes draped over black pants. The guards took the magician up the hill and forced him to his knees at the top between two boulders.

A vehement face turned from the direction overlooking the jungle, stopping to look at the magician. A deep voice echoed throughout the land. The face on the rock started to speak. "You were one of us. You grew up learning our ways, our history. You used that knowledge *against* us for your own gain with an opposing race. Lives have been lost, and now you must pay the price."

The prince she had seen in her dream stepped forward and stood in front of the magician, staring down at him. He held a wooden staff in one hand that had elaborate swirls etched onto it. "You were on the path to becoming a true warrior, yet you wasted your abilities. Thanks to you, my brothers have perished, and other innocents have been killed."

The magician watched the stately figure with contempt. "You are weak, Sohonam. Rather than fight me, you bring me here."

Sohonam pulled the magician off his feet. "Fine. We will travel to the place of our training—to the underworld."

Sohonam held the magician's arm, and with his other hand stamped his cane onto the ground. There was a small poof along with a blinding light, and they were gone.

The crystal went from light blue-green to black. Did the sudden darkness within the crystal represent the darkness of the cavern?

She opened her palms and noticed spots of his blood. She wrapped her hands around the beautiful ball, then

Ahulani closed her eyes. She used her energy, the memories of Sohonam, and the magician's DNA to trap him through the powerful life-giving crystal.

The gemstones and their source were designed to give but they would also take away.

Chills crawled up her spine. The hair on her arms stood on end and a tingling sensation ran across the back of her neck. "He's here," she whispered. "Mikiele is here."

Ahulani didn't know where the name had come from, only that Mikiele and the magician were one and the same.

He had made it into Ahulani's world of her own doing. Even in spirit form, he had been able to punish others. Now, it was *his* time.

Yet there would be no battle. There didn't need to be. The hours of twilight had always taken care of the enemy.

"Please show me where Mikiele is."

The gem exposed Mikiele gazing upon the temple door. His hand floated over the wooden baobob then he leaned his head against the door. She knew he had to be reliving memories—good, bad, or otherwise. *What had happened to make him become a traitor against his people?*

After a minute, Mikiele turned away from the temple and began to walk toward the path that led up to the peak. She thought of David stuck out in the deadly evening atmosphere.

An angry, swirling mass of dark red sand took over the inside of the crystal. The dunes transformed into miniature tornados that looked like the sea as they rose high and dove back into the ground, melting into the soft, unforgiving landscape they were created from.

The gemstone showed Mikiele somewhere among the tarnished sands of time. Could he have been transported from the pyramid to the dunes through the reminder of what David had experienced?

Mikiele attempted to start walking again, but his feet sank into the dunes. He struggled repeatedly to go forward. Exhausted, Mikiele collapsed to his knees, shielding his face from the dangerous twilight air.

Part of her had trouble watching him suffer. Yet he would have killed her in a heartbeat if she hadn't found the arrowhead.

She looked away to avoid watching the inevitable.

When Ahulani checked again, he lay face down on the gritty surface, the sands blowing over his body. Would it really be possible to *kill* a person that was already deceased?

"Forgive me," she whispered.

The crystal retained an image of the lifeless magician. Ahulani felt drawn. She bent down and placed her hand on the largest, strongest root of the tree.

She stared at the mystical globe resting in its birth spot. The crystal ball showed Mikiele's form being absorbed by the sands of a once thriving planet whose people relied on the trees of life for spiritual, emotional, and physical sustenance.

A sapling sprung out of the maroon particles making up the dunes. It grew to about five feet tall, then four branches reached in each direction: north, south, east, and west.

"Another Native heart has sprouted."

"David." Ahulani looked around. The voice sounded like his, yet how could that be?

Ahulani bowed her head and cried. She was happy that it was over, yet emotional from both learning about her past on the planet and her fear of perishing at the hands of Mikiele, then performing a ritual to end a sad life.

A single tear dropped onto the root she held. The tear initiated the growth of a tiny, shiny violet globule—an amethyst with square columns and other protrusions sprouting from the core. As a tool for psychic development, spiritual protection, and purification, amethyst was responsible for helping Ahulani develop her own abilities as a child.

This was the most beautiful gem she had ever seen. Did it represent a whole new level of spiritual growth?

Chapter Thirty-one

Ahulani stood with David at the Puerco Pueblo within the Petrified Forest National Park. The pueblo was a 100-plus room pueblo site located near the Puerco River, a major drainage bisecting the park. At its height, archaeologists had estimated 200 inhabitants.

She and David had wandered among the room blocks off the main trail. A large raven flew overhead and landed on the ground near them.

For a second, Ahulani's heart stopped.

Fortunately, this one paid them no mind. It pecked at the dirt, cocked its head at another bird that flew overhead, and then took off. There was no one else around.

David squeezed her hands in his. "We've been through a heck of a lot in the past few weeks, few days, and hours even. Before I return to work, I wanted to spend quality time with you here, the place we met, to tell you something else I found out at Kuelap."

Glad he was with her, she asked, "What? Did we have a past life here?"

"Who knows, we might have." He stared out at the main road. "Lani, I told you I saw my father after the ceremony to close the portal."

Ahulani nodded. She was happy for David. He had never talked about his parents, and she had been surprised to find out they had both died when he was young. "Of course."

"I didn't tell you everything." He led her to a bench, and they sat down. "I didn't tell you how they passed.

My parents died in a plane crash when I was ten, traveling from Hawaii to Oahu."

She put her arms around him. "I'm so sorry, David. I can't imagine going through such a thing."

He pulled away from her but held her hands. "Lani, we've met before…a long time ago in Hawaii. My family and yours hung out together on the big Island."

"I…I don't think so. I'd remember something like that."

"Maybe, maybe not. It was thirty years ago. I didn't remember…" David looked in the direction of the river. "Well, because of what happened, I'd blocked it out. My father reminded me. He mentioned our two families met and hung out together. My sister and I really got along well with you, and apparently, we decided to travel back to Molokai with you and your parents while my parents flew back to Oahu."

She couldn't believe what she was hearing. She and David both knew they had *past lives* together, but she had no idea they had met as children in this life. Why couldn't she recall meeting him?

He stroked her face as tears started to roll down his own. "You saved my sister and me. If we had gone to Oahu, we'd have died on that plane with my parents."

She inhaled a breath and let it out. "Oh, wow. David, that's about the time when my medium abilities began to surface. I was so overwhelmed with the daily, nightly visits from spirits, the constant vivid dreams and ghosts vying for my attention. After so much time passed, I must have forgotten."

He kissed her lightly on the lips. "It's okay. We didn't keep in touch because of the grief I was going through, but my father visited you soon after that. Grandpa told me that a negative entity had attached itself to you, so my father kept you safe. He knew the two of us would find each other again, and he felt the need to protect you. He knew you were special."

Ahulani placed her hand over his. "Wait, what about your sister? Does Shelly know that we hung out so long ago?"

He nodded, then slowly smiled. "Yes. She and Larry were surprised. She cried a bit when I told her. She was more surprised that neither of us remembered you."

David's eyes followed a raven as it circled the sky prior to landing in the middle of the path. "She considered it a miracle that we found each other—twice. Can't say we didn't have help, though, between Grandpa and our spirit guides."

"David, did your father have the same abilities as you and your grandfather?"

He shrugged. "I think so. I asked him, but he never answered. I wonder if he's helping me adjust to all this. It's been such a change."

He kissed her again, longer this time, and held her close.

"Lani, Mikiele meant to finish the job. I could've lost you. We had a fight in that cavern in my past life as a shaman, and I managed to finish him off. Unfortunately, he found a way back from the dead. I'm sorry he came after you." David shook his head. "I should've been there."

"No, David, I needed to do that alone. We're both safe now."

Looking out at the landscape, he changed the subject. "I wish I knew the real name of the planet. I'm sure we will figure it out someday. I wonder if Grandpa or any of our guides know. I have a feeling the medicine woman knows, but she is probably waiting for us to recall the name."

Ahulani ran her fingers along the side of an ancient room block. "Yeah. I believe as we continue to develop those talents and connect with our past lives, it will hit us. Our guides can't provide all the answers."

She heard soft chatter nearby—whispers and voices among the wind. Chanting accompanied the voices, though it sounded farther away.

She looked at David. "Do you hear that?"

"Yeah, I do." He stood and looked around at the myriad of prehistoric room blocks.

Then, David put his hand gently on Ahulani's arm to get her attention. "Speaking of…" He pointed to the medicine woman, who was gathering something from the ground. A young girl, about eight-years-old, with two long braids on either side of her head stood next to the woman. The girl wore an outfit made of animal skins with matching moccasins and a medicine bag around her neck. She skipped off toward the dry riverbed.

The beautiful Native woman stood alone and looked as vibrant as Ahulani had ever seen her. She wore a simple, long white dress with no adornment, small white flowers intricately woven into her single long braid and had bare feet. She extended her arm, as if to beckon Ahulani.

"Go ahead," David said.

Ahulani approached the healer, put her hand in hers, and immediately heard the word *Princess* whispered quietly on the breeze.

"Does Princess refer to you?" she asked.

The healer nodded her head and smiled. "My father hardly ever called me by my true name, which was Mariana. Like many little girls throughout the ages, he preferred to call me Princess. It made me believe I could achieve anything."

Ahulani watched the young child skip around and through the walls of the ruins. "Who is she?"

"*She* is you—my younger sister."

"*What?* I knew you were here to help both David and me, but…"

"I have been with you since you were ten years old, before you met David in Hawaii. I was there to watch over you, guide you, and protect you."

The little girl jumped over a wall and vanished into thin air before her feet landed on the opposite side.

Mariana went on. "We were very close as sisters and have many memories together. You were on the path to becoming a healer—like you have been in most of your past lives."

Mariana side glanced at David, who listened intently.

"Until someone else came along and stole your heart. He became your healer."

"Destiny," David said.

"You and Ahulani have been together in many lives, which you'll discover over time. I kept close to both of you during this mystery because you are my family."

Ahulani ran her hand along one of the ancient stone walls. "So, we lived here at Puerco Pueblo?"

"Yes, a long time ago. David inhabited a site near the Blue Mesa, which is why he feels so drawn to that part of the park. You met after he had finished a successful hunt. There were a couple of different tribes joining together for a feast."

She couldn't believe the ties between her and David. She wondered why she couldn't have met David instead of Will to avoid the heartache, but life wasn't always accommodating. Ahulani continued to find out things about herself and her past lives on a daily basis. She supposed it would be a lifelong learning experience.

"What about the Marble Caves? David and I have past life ties to that place as well."

The princess gazed out upon the spot where the child had vanished. "David had traveled to the caverns as a prince, though I'm not sure if it was the Marble Caves. I believe you did roam to other dimensions and worlds through your innate abilities, but never to his place of warrior training."

She pondered if Bahlam was an actual spirit guide due to her relationship with him in a past life in the Marble Caves or a god, as he had said. Ahulani hadn't seen Bahlam since the shapeshifter left with Eric on his back. Perhaps his main mission had been to help her and David with the rescue. She wondered if she'd ever see him again.

David stepped toward the princess. "So, I trained there as a warrior? Not to mention drawing upon the energy of the symbols. But those creatures that matched the environment of the cavern—there was something odd about them."

"That cavern is a pre-eminent place, a sacred sanctum among the people of that planet, coveted by the race of the people you protected. You knew it and so did the magician. He followed you there once without your knowledge and decided on his first visit that it would be his. Fitting that the cavern is where he died, and by your hand. You never knew he found it—not when you brought him there for that final battle, and not after he died."

"I do now," David said. He bent down and picked up an unusual multi-colored stone off the ground. "Did the magician know about those creatures?"

"I doubt it. They hid from him, knowing his true self. Those creatures are the keepers of the symbols."

"I should have known," Ahulani said. "In my dream, one of them had a symbol on its body, and I thought I saw signs etched onto the cave walls."

Mariana watched a magnificent collared lizard, its blue-green body adorned with yellow dots and a black collar around its neck, basking on the stone wall of the ruins. "David, the symbols originated in those caves. The creatures gifted your planet with their knowledge."

"Wait," Ahulani said, and glanced from David to Mariana. "The gem gifted to me revealed a scene between David, or Sohonam, and Mikiele. The magician was being punished because he had given away knowledge of the planet's culture. I wonder if it had something to do with the symbols."

"I have a feeling the symbols were a significant part of his demise," David said. "My ancient father from Kuelap mentioned those signs that appeared to me have been with me since my life in the Ice Age." David closed the distance between them and put his arm around Ahulani. "I suppose those creatures could have been around during that time period."

Mariana took the lizard gently in her hand, petting its back. "You're right. They have been around since long before the Ice Age. That is when you originally received the signs. You connected with their underworld while on a mammoth hunt—probably due to your powerful warrior abilities. They sensed how special you were and provided you some of their knowledge through intuition and dreams."

She bent over and removed an object from the ground. Rather than pick it up off the surface, Mariana seemed to pull it from within the earth. Then, she was gone.

Ahulani picked it up, and peeked inside the undecorated, round clay pot at the edge of the ruins. She saw an object made of fabric. She tipped the ceramic pot over, and a leather medicine bag slid out. With the small bag in one hand and the pot in the other, she saw a brief vision of the little girl who had appeared with Mariana. She could also see the child placing the medicine bag in the pot.

David gently took the fragile ceramic pot from her.

Ahulani pulled the drawstring that opened the medicine bag.

"What's in there?" he asked.

She looked up at him. "Nothing. I think it used to be her sister's—or rather mine. I got a vision of the little girl we saw holding the pot and placing this medicine bag inside."

David searched the series of rooms that formed part of the pueblo. His jaw slack, he touched her on the arm and pointed to where he was staring.

The ground collapsed less than ten feet away, taking a few of the ancient rooms with it.

"The medicine bag," David said. "The earth opened up after you looked into it."

She and David waited until the earth settled.

Then, she approached the hole and glanced down. Piles of pottery similar to the small pot Ahulani had found, as well as other debris, littered the ground below.

David put his arm around her waist. "Do you think it's trying to show us something? I wonder if there could be more pueblos down there."

As she observed sherds of reddish pottery scattered on the bottom of the pit, it started to fill with water. It rose so fast that she stood and backed away from the hole, thinking she would get wet.

"Lani, what's wrong?" David asked. He hadn't noticed.

She cautiously approached the rim and gasped. Her manta ray friend swam gracefully through the once empty room.

"Alika Loe."

As soon as she said its name, the manta ray stopped, turning its eyes upward to look at her.

The ancient potsherds now rested on top of yellowish brain coral, white porkchop coral, brilliant orange cup coral gathered together with their stems floating freely, and branching fire coral in a subtle tone of yellow.

A variety of fish swam among the reef, including a yellow, blue-lined butterflyfish, a few red ruby cardinal fish peeking out from the brain coral, and a Moray eel with dark brown markings. It watched her from its cozy hiding place in the sand among the cup coral. Other fish that she couldn't identify, small and large, swam inside the collapsed portion of earth.

"Lani!"

She jumped when David touched stroked her neck. "I've been trying to get your attention. What's going on? What are you seeing?"

Ahulani couldn't take her eyes off the surreal scene. "This pit transformed from a prehistoric place of mystery to a Hawaiian reef. I'm seeing all sorts of fish and coral, and Alika Loe is here. Do you not see it?"

The stark ocean beauty of the mock reef contrasted harshly against the dry, wide expanse of the Painted Desert. The ground she stood on was hard and unforgiving, the sand below rife with life hidden among the soft particles. Only surrealist painter Salvador Dali might have imagined such a scene.

A collared lizard, possibly the same one Mariana had held, moseyed up to the hole cautiously, a few feet from Ahulani. As soon as it peeked in, Alika Loe swam up and splashed the desert creature.

It scampered backwards, held its head sideways, then turned and raced off past the ruins. Had it really seen the water and manta ray, or did the lizard sense something else?

Ahulani laughed, watching the startled lizard disappear. She knelt and stroked the manta ray's back before it dove back under the water's surface.

She placed her hand in the water. All of the fish frantically scattered before the scene faded—along with the opening to the buried secrets of the prehistoric past. Ahulani was in the center of one of the ruins. It was as if they had never collapsed into the ground.

"Wow," David said and placed his hands on her shoulders. "I didn't see what you did, but the earth closed up again."

She nodded. "Yeah, it all vanished when I put my hand into the water." She stood, staring at the ground as if the buried secrets or reef would reappear.

David looked out toward the road running through the park. "It's weird how no one has stopped by this place. Puerco Pueblo usually has a steady stream of people, especially this time of day."

Movement from the beginning of the trail caught her attention. A large man with legs the size of small tree trunks walked toward her and David. He wore a short-sleeved polo shirt and khaki shorts. Two jaguars appeared on either side of him—one spotted and one as black as night.

"David," Ahulani whispered.

He took her hand in his. "I see him, I mean them."

"I saw this same man near my home while out walking weeks ago. Only, I remember one jaguar."

"I wonder if he has a tie to Bahlam, or to you in a past life." The jaguar man continued coming toward them purposefully. He didn't take his eyes off them.

"Anything is possible, but I didn't pick up on it when I first saw him. He died fairly recently and had some major power struggle issues."

David stepped in front of Ahulani as the man got closer. "It's okay, David."

He moved aside so she could see.

The jaguars placed themselves in front of their human, then laid down. The man placed one hand on the spotted jaguar's head and his other on the black jaguar. As he did, his attire changed from everyday men's attire to that of a Mayan priest. He was bare chested except for an elaborate clay necklace. His headdress displayed various resplendent bird feathers pointed toward the heavens with a figure of a jaguar in the center. He wore a blue kilt with an apron in front and sandals on his feet.

Ahulani tried to pick up on the man's name, but her spirit guides told her nothing.

He looked at David. "There is no one here because it is not meant to be." His voice was deep, powerful, and resonated throughout the area.

He stared at Ahulani. "At least not while your past has caught up with you."

The pueblo and its ruins had been hidden from view during the supposed cave-in. Could the man in front of her be responsible?

"I know your death is fairly recent. So why are you revealing yourself as a high priest to us?" Ahulani asked.

"I never felt as if I belonged in the modern age. I had vivid dreams of my life as a Mayan leader since I was born."

"I first saw you while on a walk in Oak Creek. Did you used to live in Sedona?"

The jaguar man smiled. "I am not from Arizona or the Southwest."

David nudged her. "Lani, this could be a spirit guide. After all, you and Bahlam had some sort of connection."

She shook her head. "No, he's not. This is different. He is different."

Ahulani didn't think of it before, but something was vaguely familiar about the man.

The jaguar man squeezed himself between his two sleek pets and stood face to face with Ahulani. "It took me awhile, but I finally found you."

"Wait, you were a friend of my father's, weren't you?" She glanced at David, then back at the massive man before her. "I met you as a child—a few weeks before I met David, Shelly, and their parents. You came to my house and had dinner with my family."

"That's correct. I lived in Brazil then. I had to reside in the jungle, as I did during my life as a priest in Mesoamerica so long ago."

The spotted jaguar stood up and circled David, Ahulani, and its master. It was non-threatening.

"When I first met you, I could see your life in an instant—your childhood, your marriage to Will, your divorce, the move to Arizona—I saw it all. Just as your father did."

David put his arm around her shoulder. "What are you telling us?"

Though David asked the question, the man watched Ahulani as he answered. "Her father was a medicine man, though he didn't want her to know. He didn't advertise it, but I'm sure she will remember certain points of time in her life where she wondered."

It sounded as if he would continue the sentence. She waited, but he merely stared at her.

She recalled certain evenings where her father didn't come home from fishing until late. Or, he would tell Ahulani and her mother that he needed to visit a friend in the community. Then, he would remove a mysterious, ornate silver box high from the closet in her parent's bedroom and take it with him.

Her mother would merely smile and tell Ahulani that someone needed her father's support.

Ahulani side glanced at David, then looked at the strong Mayan personae before her. "Why didn't I pick up on such a thing?"

The enigmatic man stroked the black cat as it sat next to him. It closed its eyes and purred in contentment. "Your father ceased his healing activities soon after. He never provided a reason why."

"How did you know him?"

He didn't respond, rather faded before her, along with the two large felines.

She couldn't take her eyes off the spot where they vanished.

David pulled her to him. "Lani, I believe you need to reconnect with your father. Everything that's happened here, at this location, leads back to your roots in Hawaii."

Perhaps she had brought the reef to her, like she had called upon the dunes planet. It could be that her spiritual talents were growing, bringing her reminders of her past in Molokai and of her culture. She wondered if there could be some sort of tie between the jaguar man from her childhood past and her past life with Bahlam.

She and David had their own distinct abilities—some were ancient talents brought forth from past lives—including her love of gemstones and David's use of signs and symbols. They both still had so much to learn.

She and David would be working together, using their combined abilities to help others, as they had done in other past lives.

Ahulani glanced down to see a perfect heart-shaped stone. Soft whispers echoed around her as she picked it up—indistinct words that floated on the currents.

David stared at the rock, incredulous. "Where did that come from?" He searched the dry, mysterious landscape that held so many secrets set in stone among the ancient logs and in the earth itself.

Ahulani ran her finger around the edge of the stone. The words, "Native heart," escaped her lips.

"Native heart," David repeated. He took the smooth stone from Ahulani, sandwiching it between his palms.

She placed her hand on his shoulder. "David, I heard you speak those words after the ritual to end the magician's reign of terror. You must have somehow been tuned into me or the planet. Native heart is what they called the trees of life." She looked in the direction of the dry Puerco riverbed. "Only, I don't think they considered it a tree, rather an animate living soul, a tenacious life source, and the heart of their indigenous, otherworldly home."

Ahulani clearly understood that those two words represented the past, the present, and the future for her and David. To her, Native heart meant staying true to who she was while maintaining a strong connection to her past—her more youthful past, as well as her past lives.

The sun temporarily blocked out an immense shadow. Ahulani looked up to see Alika Loe glide gracefully above her—a creature foreign to the colorful high desert near Winslow, Arizona. Yet the proud manta ray acted as if it owned the Southwestern sun and sky.

She knew she needed to return to Molokai—to reconnect with her parents, her culture, and find more about herself—and learn what *Native heart* meant to her.

Stardust, Soul Travel, and Beyond...

The stately star held me in his arms while we slow danced next to my queen-sized bed. I gazed up yet didn't see a mouth, eyes, nose, or other familiar features. I recall straining my neck, my eyes running up its light tan and cream-colored trunk, struggling to find the top of its form.

We moved in gentle motion for a minute. Without music. I felt no hands around my waist. Only the sensation of peace, pure love.

"Are you one of my star visitor guides?" I asked.

A narrow mouth came into focus among the dark brown swirls. It whispered, "Yes."

"What is your name?"

A pronounced sigh came from the endlessly tall form. "Konde."

Determined to learn more about the enigmatic being, I inquired, "Is that spelled K-O-N-D-E?"

This time, the response was a simple nod.

Glancing down, my feet were a foot off the carpet.

Merely a dream? Not quite. This chance encounter is the result of years of communication with my spirit guides and angels. Some are born with the ability to connect with the deceased at birth. For many, such intuition blossoms during childhood or adulthood. My own spiritual sojourn started with the writing of my first paranormal murder mystery, *The Ancient Ones.*

It started with pendulum beginnings, and worked its way toward clear hearing, seeing, and sensing. Past life readings and spiritual counseling transitioned to other talents, such as animal communication, and passing the deceased on in dreams. Becoming a psychic medium is not always a choice. It is an alternate reality—a path I've been committed to from a past life as a medicine woman. I have been strongly guided to help others gain closure, provide encouraging words and spiritual guidance, or help the deceased cross over.

Our guides, our angels with us, are around us at all times—as muses, protection, and guidance. Deceased relatives and friends, past life connections, other-worldly beings, and elementals such as fairies and sprites, are not beyond imagination. They are in our own backyard.

This book is fiction, yet it reflects the magic and mystery that surrounds us. It was inspired by my spirit guides— some of whom are characters in the book.

Keep your heart and mind open.

Aspire to live a timeless journey of painted memories and crystal dreams.

For a past life reading, to connect with loved ones, or for information on Lori's works or upcoming events, visit facebook.com/LoriHinesParanormalAuthor or http://lhauthor.wordpress.com.